Playing Days

Playing Days
a novel

BENJAMIN MARKOVITS

faber and faber

First published in 2010
by Faber and Faber Ltd
Bloomsbury House
74–77 Great Russell Street
London WC1B 3DA

Typeset by RefineCatch Limited, Bungay, Suffolk
Printed in England by Mackays of Chatham, plc

A CIP record for this book
is available from the British Library

ISBN 978–0–571–25181–0

2 4 6 8 10 9 7 5 3 1

To my Father

'But I hate things *all fiction* – there should always be some foundation of fact for the most airy fabric – and pure invention is but the talent of a liar.'

BYRON

I

My first recognizably sexual experience took place in the weight room of my junior high school, after class, during basketball practice. I say 'recognizably'; I'm not sure I recognized it at the time. We were working our way through various exercise stations, one of which required you to suspend yourself, with lifted legs, from two raised armrests; and I remember, as I closed my eyes with effort, the slow spread of strange sensations beginning to crowd the area between my thighs. It was basically a chemical reaction, nothing more, though I felt a little weak-kneed afterwards, and it may have been the same afternoon or another one that a few of my teammates decided to make fun of the hair on my legs.

'Look at those man-legs,' somebody said, and I looked down at them and tried to work out if they were too hairy or not hairy enough. Then the other boys joined in. They might have been mocking me for their smoothness, and it seems typical of the age that I couldn't be sure and was simultaneously ashamed of being girlish and overdeveloped.

Sex talk, of course, was one of the things you had to learn to deal with in the locker room. On the basketball court, too. Practice is the only time in school a coach gets a class full of boys to himself, without any girls around to inhibit him.

'Been playin' with yourself last night?' one of our coaches would ask, whenever someone let a ball slip through his fingers.

General snickering. Coach Britten, we called him, though he was also the assistant principal and probably the first black man I had known in a position of authority. I was slightly terrified of him, of the shameful things he might accuse me of. Tall, straight-backed, he patrolled the baselines and sidelines in dark suits and well-shined shoes. Sometimes, when we had disappointed him, he would line us up against the wall of the gym and stand at center court with a basketball in his hand.

'Stand still,' he called out. 'Keep still.'

Then he would take aim at one of our heads and we had to scatter out of the way. I don't remember anyone ever getting hit or hurt, though ball struck brick with terrific force. But he got his point across. Two points, really: sometimes you got to listen to me, and sometimes you got to trust your instincts. He considered it an important part of his job that he should teach us, among other things, to be men – in ways that teachers and parents couldn't or wouldn't. I've always assumed that one of the reasons I struggled in high school sports is that I didn't learn.

My father likes to claim that it was his Uncle Joe, and not Kenny Sailors or Bud Palmer or Belus van Smawley, who invented the jumpshot in 1931. My great-grandfather, Ari Markovits, was six foot ten inches tall and weighed over two hundred and fifty pounds when he died at the age of ninety-nine, two weeks before my father's bar mitzvah. 'I used to be tall' was one of his jokes in old age. He must have been a giant in his youth, and Uncle Joe spent his childhood trying to shoot over him.

Our family came to the States from Bavaria just before the First World War. Basketball has always been a ghetto game but in its early days the ghettos were Jewish and many of the stars were Jews.

The Markovitses worked their way up in the usual fashion. My grandfather was conceived in Munich and born on the Lower East Side in New York. As a young man, he entered into his cousins' grocery business and helped to expand it into a franchise. He moved to Middletown with his family to set up the new head office and commuted two hours each way to Manhattan three nights a week to get his law degree from Columbia. The house my father grew up in was prosperous, middle-class, but he used to boast that he had never read a book out of school till he got to college: he spent his after-noons at the ballpark.

'Markovits,' his high school coach once told him. 'You may be slow, but you sure are weak.'

But he had a sharp eye and quick hands. These seemed to me, when I was a boy, just two of the instruments of his general authority. I was the son who had inherited his passion for sport, but I had also inherited something of my great-grandfather's height and a little of Uncle Joe's athleticism. We used to play every kind of game together, basketball, tennis, pool – and spent much of my rather friendless freshman year hunched over a miniature ping pong table, no bigger than one foot by two foot, every day after school. My father has a great deal of patience, but he doesn't play games to relax. By the time I was twelve or thirteen, we could test ourselves against each other without holding back.

The family fortunes followed the usual trajectory. The grandson of an immigrant, the son of a lawyer, my father had become an academic. His own son wanted to be a writer. The house I grew up in was full of books. We trav-eled to Germany every summer, where my mother was born and raised, and he brought back with him antiques and rugs that filled our sunny house in Texas. There was a big backyard, and in a far corner of it, he built a court for his kids to play on.

I don't suppose I've ever been happier anywhere than on that court. But something had happened between my childhood and his, and the difference wasn't only the money we grew up with. Basketball had been his excuse for getting out of the house; it was mine for staying put. The game had changed, too. There were no Jewish stars anymore, and blacks had taken their place in the neighborhoods and the ballparks where they lived and played. Half of the kids I went to school with were black, fewer in the honors classes, more on the basketball team. The court was one of the rare places we hung out together, but even there the diffidence of what you might call my class sense got in the way. For example, it had never occurred to me to dunk a basketball.

It hurts, that's the first thing you learn, until the inside joints of your fingers grow calluses, preserving under the skin a few pixels of blood. My mother, an old socialist, remarked when she noticed them, 'With hands like that you'll survive the revolution.'

Not that it helped much on court. On Friday nights, during my high school years, my father followed the team bus around Texas to watch me. To places with names like Del Valle and Copperas Cove, that flew Confederate flags outside the school gym. He sat in the stands with the other fathers, while I sat on the bench on top of my hands (to warm them up). I was scared the coach might put me in the game. I suppose a lot of parents have a sense of what their children are capable of in the confidence of solitude. We measure up one way in the world and another way in their love, and the difference must be painful for them to observe.

'Do you want me to talk to the coach?' he asked me

once on the car-ride home. Sometimes I traveled back with him rather than on the team bus.

'Please don't talk to the coach,' I said.

But he persisted. 'They could have used you out there. I've seen what you can do.'

'Please don't talk to the coach.'

My shyness proved just how far he had come up in life since his childhood on the streets of Middletown.

But by senior year in college I had also traveled a certain distance. And somewhere among the four drifting years of undergraduate life, it occurred to me that I might be able to support myself playing basketball – nobody I knew had ever made a living writing.

A friend filmed me in the varsity gym, shooting and dunking by myself. That was the résumé I sent out, along with a small but crucial piece of information: that my mother was German, allowing me to slip under European quotas for foreigners. My classmates were busy applying to grad school and law school and med school, and waiting for their admissions notices. I walked out of the dean's office one windy March day, carrying in my hands the four thin pages of a contract an agent had just faxed over, on the strength of that video. Showing whoever came near me our signatures at the bottom. It seemed so wonderfully implausible. I hadn't put on a uniform since I was seventeen, but there was someone in Ober-Ramstadt willing to represent me.

I wanted to return to something, to my father's childhood as much as my own. A steady jumpshot and a good left hand were the things he used to strive for, instead of an education, a salary, tenure and a mortgage. Ordinary adulthood struck me as one of those weird formal occasions you have to go to as a kid – wearing a jacket and tie that don't fit, saying things you don't mean. Basketball was my excuse for not going. Also, I wanted a chance to do the things I hadn't done in high school.

Two days after graduation, I flew to Hamburg and spent the summer going from train to train and hotel to gym. In those days I traveled light, just a duffel with a spare of everything, including sneakers, and the bulge of a ball in the middle. I washed my laundry by hand in the bathroom sinks. Most of the big cities were taken up by soccer, it was only in the countryside, in the villages and market towns, that basketball had room to breathe. By the end of July I had landed a job in Landshut, just north of Munich, for a second division team known locally as the 'Yoghurts.' So I flew home for a month and spent the summer as I always had, wandering between the cool of the air conditioning and the bright reflected heat of my father's court. At the end of August, I got on the plane to Munich to begin my new life.

My father drove me to the airport and sat in the car for a minute with the motor running. He touched a hand to my shoulder; I could tell he had prepared some advice. 'Do me a favor, will you,' he said at last. 'Don't mess around with these guys, these ballplayers.'

'What do you mean, mess around?'

'You know what I mean,' he said, 'gambling, that kind of thing. These aren't the kids you grew up with. And while you're at it, watch out for the women who hang around them, too.'

On my way through security, and check-in, and the long windowless corridor to the gate, I noticed something odd. For the first time in my life I was scared of flying.

3

The club sent someone to meet me at the airport, an American by the name of Bo Hadnot; his accent was southern. He was about six one or two; probably an ex-player, I thought. With strong teeth, that forced open his lips a little and gave him a thirsty look. And strong hands – he took my duffel from me out of mine. It seemed a sad kind of job for an ex-pat to sink to.

I was often 'met' that summer, at airports, train stations, bus depots, by various team managers and club lackeys. Fat, badly dressed men, whose last claim to youth was that they still lived with their parents. Some friend in the front office would give them a job, arranging beds and time-tables, hauling prospects from hotel to gym, cleaning up in the locker rooms afterwards, washing the jerseys, etc. Still, they got to lord it at first over the nervous recruits, over guys like me. Most of them didn't know my name, and Hadnot was no exception. It was enough for them that I was a basketball player, they figured on spotting my head above the crowds.

Sweating from the flight, stinking and shy, I fell asleep a few minutes into the ride. Hadnot got lost on the way from the airport. He had to wake me outside a

11

gas-station to ask directions, gently, repeating 'Son, son,' a little louder each time – he had seen me speaking German to one of the customs men. Back in the car, on the road again, I asked him how long he'd lived in these parts, and without much irony or embarrassment he told me, five years. What have you been doing with yourself, I said.

'Playing basketball.'

Eventually we made it out of the fretwork of highways surrounding the airport, and into the real countryside, which was pleasant and modestly farmed. Country lanes, bordered on either side by tall grain. And villages that ran the gamut of names from Upper to Middle to Lower (Ober to Mitte to Unter), none of them larger than a bend in the road with a few farmhouses. The town itself, as we descended into it, turned out to be pretty and old. We bumped along the cobbled high street for several minutes, past a church with a tall brick spire as clean cut as a factory tower, before pulling over just in front of the river at a little Italian restaurant named Sahadi's. There were woven carafes hanging in the window under a striped red awning. Most of the cars parked outside were blue two-door Fiats with new license plates: a sign that the basketball team had congregated. But Hadnot said he had to pick up his daughter from her grandma's and pulled away as soon as I shut the car door.

Sahadi's was named after its owner, a Turk who had come north over the Alps from Turin when the Germans relaxed their immigration laws in the late 80s. He was the kind of man my father loves, a rootless polyglot salesman type – the kind I spent my childhood watching my father 'chat up.' He guessed by my height I was another player and led me under several low brick arches, strung with vines. Bavarians, he told me (I was plying him, as my father would have, with questions) had little interest in Turkish food, which is why he cooked Italian, but sometimes he managed to suggest a few eastern influences. Mr. Sahadi seemed genuinely excited to meet the new basketball players and detained me briefly under an arch with his hand on my elbow, to have his say – my first little touch of celebrity.

The last room was hardly more than a cave; it contained a low table and a half-dozen men lounging and trying to get their knees underneath it.

'Where's Hadnot?' someone shouted, as I ducked my head under a potted vine and looked for an empty seat. He had to pick up his daughter, I said. 'Are you the American?' called the voice. 'Sit thee down, brother, sit thee down, for I would have a chat with thou.'

The man talking to me was one of two black men in the room. He made space for me beside him at the head of the table and reached over to get a clean plate, which he heaped with spaghetti from one of the serving bowls set among the bottles of fizzy water. Most of the others had eaten. There wasn't much left, but he gathered to himself what he could and offered it to me: breadsticks and hummus, cold calamari, Parmesan, lemon, a little Frascati. Charlie, he said his name was, Charlie Gold, and introduced me to the rest of the team: Olaf Schmidt, Axel Plotzke, Willi Darmstadt, Milo Moritz, and Karl.

Charlie kept most of the conversation to himself. He was small-featured, low-browed, balding – impish without being youthful. For example, he hadn't bothered, as many athletes do, to shave off the straggle of curls around his ears and neck and towards the back of his head. The skin of his cheeks was as rough as acne. You could strike a match off it, an image that probably occurred to me because so many players at the table were smoking.

Their cigarettes were stubbed out among the leftovers, in the olive bowls, in empty cups of coffee. Charlie hadn't joined them, I could smell that at once. I could hear it, too, in the tone of his voice, which suggested, when he passed one of the candles for a light, both amusement and disapproval. He was glad to disapprove; it put him in the right position. He said to me, 'You don't smoke, do you?' and when I shook my head, he added, loud enough for anyone to hear, 'These Europeans, they think they artists; they think they rock stars. When the game starts, they talk about how many drinks they had the night before. They want you to play nice. Let me give you a word of advice, young man. Don't play nice.'

Then, laughing, one of them answered, 'Yes, but we're happy.'

'Na, you ain't happy, Milo, you won't be happy when I'm done with you.'

Milo had a boxer's face, thick-fleshed, with a broken-backed nose. Smiles tended to stick on it. As I was eating, a middle-aged man with a flourishing moustache made his way between the chairs to our end of the table. I must have been in his seat, for he looked at me queerly for a moment, until Charlie spoke up, 'That's all right, Coach. Our boy was hungry, so I told him to sit with me.'

I recognized Herr Henkel from the try-out and rose to shake his hand.

'Where's Hadnot?' he asked me.

'He had to pick up his daughter.'

'He never picks up his daughter,' Henkel replied and looked around briefly at the rest of the team.

There was something fatherly in his cursory glance, and something filial and homesick in me responded to it. 'Do you want your seat back, Coach?' I said to him, making my appeal in German, but he replied in his abrupt English, 'Don't give up your ground, isn't that right, Charlie?' And then, to one of the boys at the table, 'Move over Darmstadt.'

Darmstadt was a high school kid with an uncut blonde bob. He pushed back his chair and stood up, and for the rest of the afternoon remained leaning with his shoulders against the wall; nobody said anything. In the silence, Charlie decided to pick on some people – his own phrase. He had a restless manner, which seemed to me even at that first meeting not particularly happy. You sensed that he wanted bigger fish to fry and was making do with what he had. But he amused himself along the way. The man he'd introduced to me as Plotzke was a fat, long-armed German with the slightly exaggerated features of a pituitary disorder: a hanging, oval face; large cow eyes. 'How much weight was you gonna lose this summer, Axel? Or was you working on gaining?' This kind of thing.

'Ja ja,' Axel said. An educated voice, peevish, too. But nearly everybody at that table came in for his share of attention. Darmstadt he left alone, until provoked; but there was another high school kid Charlie planned on 'claiming as his best friend.'

Let's just call him Karl. There's the legal question, for one thing, but quite apart from that his present fame would obscure the charm he had then, in his first professional season, when he was still more or less undiscovered. 'You and me got a lot to talk about,' Charlie said. Karl smiled at his banter and didn't much listen and didn't much seem to care. He had the kind of flat large face that isn't particularly pliable to emotions. There was something very German about him, especially about his taste in clothes, which seemed almost officially casual: brown denim trousers, leather sandals and a bright yellow t-shirt with the words HIGH ANXIETY printed across it in smoky letters.

Later, when he ducked into the bathroom, I recognized the most remarkable thing about Karl: he was seven feet tall and looked normal. It was the rest of us who seemed shrunken or out of proportion.

Since Charlie couldn't get to him, he shifted his attention to Olaf, the other dark-skinned player at the table. 'You still eating?' he said. 'Want a little more time?' Then, in an undertone: 'Man's too lazy even to *feed* himself.'

Teams are full of toadies – people began laughing. I had to cover my own lips with a fist. Olaf continued to pick at his food. He had the muscular patient air of a Greek sculpture, a six foot seven, black, two-hundred-and-fifty pound Greek sculpture. Patience wasn't Charlie's word for him. Lazy lazy lazy; he sang it out like a church hymn. Holy holy holy. Olaf lifted his hand and lowered his head, a characteristic gesture.

'I know what you're saying,' Charlie added. 'Leave me alone. Well, I won't.'

The voices of Germans often sound sweet in English as weak tea. 'No, I tell you what I say,' Olaf said. 'Du kannst mich am Arsch lecken, Kleiner.'

This caused a small sensation, of quiet, and Charlie asked, looking around, 'What's that, what's that?'

Darmstadt, still shifting on his feet against the wall, started giggling. 'That boy'll laugh at anything,' Charlie said. 'That boy'll laugh if you throw him off a bridge.'

Olaf continued in German, 'It is a shameful thing, I think, to come here and beat up on little kids.'

Smiling, Charlie turned to me. 'What'd that lazy son of a bitch say? What'd he say?'

For a second, I met his stare. Milo called out, clapping his hands, 'Wir haben einen Dolmetscher! Einen Dolmetscher.' An ugly humble German word for translator. Olaf looked over, too, and I could tell from something sheepish in his glance that he was a little afraid of what he'd said, a little afraid of Charlie.

I looked at Charlie, I looked at Olaf, and I looked at Herr Henkel, who said with a forced laugh, 'Take it easy, Charlie.' He had a kind, ordinary, Bavarian face: brown and dignified and rough. The face of a prosperous farmer. Only when he joked or smiled, something cruder broke out in it, a humor he had picked up in the locker room. He was smiling very slightly now.

'I thought this was what you paid me for. My pre-season pep talk.'

But Henkel put his hand on the black man's head. 'No, we don't pay you for this. You give us this extra.'

'I'm a generous man,' Charlie said.

A few minutes later, Henkel called the meeting to order and launched into his own 'pre-season pep talk.' He outlined what he expected of us, his ambitions for the year, and also described the way the next few weeks would play out. In spite of the bad temper and awkward-ness of the meal, I was touched to see how many of the men were sentimentally affected. Partly because they were a little drunk. Olaf rested his cheek on his large palm. Milo, as Henkel stood up to propose a toast, quickly stubbed out a cigarette and re-filled his glass. You can't imagine such an odd collection of human kind –

18

like mismatched chairs in a junk shop. Almost every-body there was some combination of too tall or too fat or too skinny. 'To winning,' Henkel said, 'because it is better than losing.' We all cheered hopefully.

It was Charlie who drove me home after lunch – I mean, to my new apartment. His car was a little bigger than the others, a VW Golf with a pair of miniature Nike high-tops dangling from the rear view mirror. I wondered if he was staking some kind of claim to me. We drove back through town and up into the hills again, the hills that opened out into farmland, and passed under the red brick arch of an abandoned railroad bridge. Only trees used the tracks now.

On the right a horse farm perched on a narrow strip of level land; beyond it, the ground fell away into a wooded valley. Charlie turned left, up a short concrete drive and parked behind a row of shuttered garage doors, which ran along the back of a big purple 60s apartment complex. He didn't get out to help me with my bag, but the way he sat there suggested that he wanted to say something, and I waited a moment before opening the door. As I had with my father, twelve hours before.

'I have high hopes, young man,' he said, 'that we can make it out of the minor leagues this year. Karl won't be sticking around, so we better make good use. But every-body got they role to play. You too.' After a pause, he repeated, 'High hopes' – and those are what I left him with, as I grabbed my duffel from the backseat and stepped out.

Mine was one of the apartments overlooking the road. Most of my teammates had lived in that block, at one time or another, but there were also civilians, as you might say. Evidence of families, too: small bicycles cluttering the walkways, watering cans, rubber boots. The bright variety of life displayed on washing lines, strung between bathroom window and balcony railing. Herr Henkel had given me the keys, and I struggled with one of them to enter the windowless stairwell. Jetlag had begun to set in. A day before I was in another world. Alone at last, I thought, almost grateful for the darkness as I walked up a short flight to the front door numbered on the keychain.

The room it opened onto had a big bed in the middle, which looked luridly comfortable in the dusky light coming through the curtains drawn over the window opposite. These were thick and ugly, and the first thing I did was tear them down with a violence that suggested to me, for the only time that day, the carelessness of a young man's joy. The waxy patterned cloth filled my fists; I pushed and kicked the curtains onto the floor. It was five o'clock on a summer's afternoon, and the day had more or less cleared up – the sunlight had brightened as it leveled. The window overlooked a dirty walled-up balcony, which drained poorly; standing water had discolored the tiles. Beyond that was the road, and beyond the road were the farm and the valley and the woods. The transparent western light thickened to bronze before it faded altogether. That was the light I fell asleep in.

It was dark when I woke up, partly from cold. I was hungry too, but not hungry enough to go looking for something to eat at that hour (it had just gone ten), so I decided to get cleaned up and changed and to head back to bed. We had an early start in the morning. Practice began at nine, and we opened the doors to the press from eleven o'clock. My duffel was lying where I had dropped it, on the pillow beside me, and I took out the basketball and began to unpack my clothes.

When I was in college, I never had much interest in fashion, but I did develop a strange sort of ambition, regarding my wardrobe, to pare it down to a useful minimum. When I bought pants, I looked for a pair I could take inter-railing through Europe, or wear to a funeral, or to a job interview – that would suit me in hot weather or cold; in rain; on long journeys; at grassy and dirty picnics. Even the sneakers I wore, all-black Air Jordans, once did service, under dark trousers, at a college ball. I liked to consider myself, not handsome or fashionable, but unattached, light-footed, always ready to leave. Folding my few things away, into the heavy antique wardrobe that loomed over the bed, I had the sense that one of my vanities had been put to use at last, had justified itself. That I was living as I had dreamed of living.

The apartment had three rooms: a bedroom, a

kitchen, a bathroom. Only the bathroom overlooked the inner courtyard. There was a high window, designed no doubt to let a little air in, but I was tall enough to see out of it. Lights from the apartment complex glimmered in irregular squares. In the morning, I could give a shape to the pattern they made. The buildings were identical, but brightly and diversely colored; they'd also been set at odd angles to each other. But all I could see that night were a few lit windows, and I stared out at these for a minute, enjoying the sense of having arrived at a place where other people were already (inscrutably) at home.

After a while, the glow in the nearest window resolved itself into a few dim shapes, and those shapes resolved themselves into a head, an arm, a loose dress. I realized that I was looking at a young woman with long hair. She was brushing it out in a way that suggested to me – I have three sisters – one of the last quiet rituals a girl performs before going to sleep. I was almost homesick for her; I certainly found it hard to look away. But someone or something called her into another room, and I continued to stare with a racing heart at the bright empty space she left behind her (nothing but a wall framed by curtains) until, with a sudden feeling of renewed loneliness, I turned off the bathroom light and went to bed.

4

The guy who met me at the airport had asked me, in the car, why I'd 'come so far to play basketball.' As if he'd been wrestling with the question himself. 'On a lark,' I told him, and this is really what it seemed on the breezy sunshiny morning I woke up to. The weather was just warm enough for me to walk up a sweat on my way to the gym. I passed under the abandoned bridge and noticed, on the far side of it, a row of shops that included a newsagent, a baker, and a little *Kneipe* or bar called the Unicorn. A man in overalls was rolling kegs of beer down the basement hatch. The darkness inside the bar was spotted with green dust; an aproned woman inverted the upturned chairs. Real work, I thought, and continued towards the river.

It flowed, if you followed it far enough, south and east to Munich, the city my ancestors had fled almost a century before. The sports hall stood on the far side of it, a low sprawling municipal-style complex. Two large pillars framed the front entrance. They were the only nods to grandeur, to the contests that had taken place inside. Part of what excited me (this is the thought I've been leading up to) is the idea that I was about to find out if I was any good. Basketball, of course, is a team sport, but a big part of its tradition is the solitude in which you learn to play it: by myself, on my father's court, through the heavy rains and the heavier heat of a thousand Texan afternoons. I felt that I was about to test my imagination against the facts of life.

A fat young man with fat wide-open nostrils pointed the way to the locker room. To anyone who has played on a team, such scenes are familiar enough: the peculiar smell, the gray pervasive shadowless light, the sound of dripping showers, the slick rubber matting on the floor-tiles and the rotting wooden benches. The atmosphere of wet nylon and athlete's foot, the feeling of trench camaraderie.

The kid Darmstadt was already dressed when I got there, buzzing around and looking for basketballs; he wanted somebody to play with him. An open bag of training uniforms spilled onto the ground. I picked out a pair of shorts and a jersey and quietly put them on: for the first time stepping into the part of professional athlete. Olaf was there too and told Darmstadt to go chase his tail, or something like that – to get out of his hair. Some of us, he said, are still trying to wake up, and he gave me a sympathetic look.

I wandered out, looking for the gym, and had to turn back on myself several times, among the unlit corridors, before finding it. The court itself was vast and dusky and looked like an airport hangar. The floors were made of some green material. Light reflected dully off it, giving the space a kind of subterranean gloom. Somebody had found the basketballs and the sound of them echoed irregularly against the high aluminum rafters. Milo was practicing jumpshots: shooting, chasing down each miss, stopping dead, shooting again. He was already breathing audibly.

'Young man,' a voice called out to me, 'young man.' Charlie wanted a game; he passed me a ball outside the three-point line and crouched into a defensive stance. 'Let's see what you're made of,' he said.

I began idly to dribble, presenting my side. I wasn't sure how seriously to take this, but he ducked and reached, slapping his palms against the floor.

Charlie played me to the right hand, which I favor. Most right-handed players are left-footed – it helps them to balance in mid-air. It's one of my idiosyncrasies that I'm not. I used to spend hours after school dribbling and driving against imaginary opponents. An inner critic judged me: had I been quick enough, etc. but the real point is, that I picked up the quirks and irregularities of an autodidact. Also, a few mispronunciations, or their sporting equivalent. Anyway, I like to drive left and crossed over in front of Charlie, paused at the top of the bounce and pushed past him.

'Do that again,' he said, after I laid the ball in. 'And again,' he said, when I repeated the move. The next time, though, I spun out of the dribble and knocked down a fifteen-footer as he scrambled to make up the ground.

Breathless already, I closed my eyes to keep the sweat out and heard the thin, almost painful drum-roll of a heartbeat in my ears. It was the rhythm to a quiet refrain of self-congratulation: maybe you're good enough, maybe you're good enough. 'Young man,' Charlie said, rubbing his hands, 'we're about to get to it' – but Herr Henkel blew his whistle and summoned us to the middle of the court.

What followed was about an hour and a half of repetitions. Henkel was a technical-minded coach. The session had been plotted to the minute on a clipboard he propped up between his wrist and waist. Not that he was above the odd ad-lib. Halfway through, he let us catch our breath with a round of free throws, got pissed off at a few tired airballs, and gave the whole team a suicide for every subsequent miss. A suicide is like a hundred-yard dash in a prison yard: you have to keep switching back, and the court rang with the squeaks of stretched sneakers and the slap of hands on the ground.

I missed both of mine. The blood in my head had begun to color my vision like a changing bruise. Charlie missed one of his, too. He had a strange little stroke, like a corkscrew trying to discharge a cork, that began somewhere behind his head. He wasn't the quickest between the baselines, either (that honor belonged to Milo, who took it very seriously), and I began to wonder whether Charlie really was the boss of the team. At a quarter to eleven, Henkel opened the doors, and a few smiling portly gentlemen, in ties and casual trousers, holding cameras or notebooks, strolled in. By this stage I could hardly stand.

Coach split us into fives. Olaf and I played with Plotzke and Darmstadt. Plotzke was a great ogre of a man, big-bellied, with the hitched-up shoulders of a hunchback; his voice, though, was soft and complaining. He was taking a year off from his MBA, he explained to me during a breather. This was just a vacation, he said, and smiled, purple-faced. Charlie had Karl on his side, Milo, and a tall stick of a clean-cut young man named Michel Krahm, who moved like an insect and hadn't said a word all day. Most of us had found something to gripe about.

I wish I could say we held our own against them. That was when I realized what Charlie had been proving at lunch; why everyone let him talk. He had a high angry dribble (in spite of being the smallest player on the floor) and pounded the ball like a judge's gavel as he made his way up court, gabbing all the time, shouting, telling the rest of us what to do. 'Backdoor, backdoor,' he cried at one point. Milo stared at him helplessly, and Charlie threw a pass that caught him full in the nose, cut to the basket, picked up the ball off the bounce and laid it in. 'Nice pass,' he said afterwards, sprinting back up court.

Later, after a long rebound, Olaf released me on the break. Only Charlie had tracked back. I had him to myself at the top of the key and shifted through the gears of the crossover that had beaten him before. He jumped on the dribble so quickly that I was still leaning into the move as he began to push the ball the other way. 'Fool me twice,' he called over his shoulder, 'shame on me . . .'

But the real revelation of that training session was Karl. I don't know if he was faster or stronger than the rest of us, or what. He seemed to be moving according to a different scale. Once I tried to step in the lane in front of him, and after a second, wondering where he'd gone, found him hanging from the rim behind my head. 'Look at the Kid!' Charlie shouted. 'Look at the Kid!'

Charlie had a way of praising his teammates that sounded like bragging, but he made the nickname stick. Even the local papers began to adopt it. (Germans have a strange passion for English words.) Somehow the name covered up the fact that Karl really was a kid, a seventeen-year-old young man, nervously stepping into the role that his talents had thrust upon him. He had a habit of fading on his jumpshot, ridiculous in a seven-footer; took too many threes and front-rimmed a lot of them; loafed on defense, trusting his long arms to make up the ground that his feet had failed to.

In fact, that's how we almost beat them. Karl gave me the three-point line, and I managed to find my eye and knock down a couple before he reacted. The next time down, Charlie pulled him off me (by force, with two hands) and bodied me up as soon as I crossed midcourt. I pushed my way to the blocks, then cut back up. Olaf set me a screen at the elbow, and I curled off it, catching the pass, and straightened up to shoot. I've got seven inches on Charlie and knew he couldn't reach my shooting-hand. What he did instead was give me a little nudge with the butt of his palm against my stomach. The ball fell short and I cried foul at the same time. Coach sucked on his whistle but didn't blow, and Charlie shouted, 'I thought this was a man's game,' and winked at me. By this point, Karl was flying up the wing and Charlie had picked up the outlet. He cradled the ball against his wrist, like a roll of carpet, and sent a long looping pass down court that reached Karl in his stride. He dunked in stride, too, and let the weight of his run carry him back again the other way.

Game over. Cameras flashed, and I could see in the morning paper what the look on his face had been. A barbaric yawp, I want to say – except that his eyes, which were stretched wide open, seemed anxious rather than joyful. I stared at this photo (there was another beside it, which I'll come to) for several minutes in the course of my tired and almost hungerless breakfast the next day. *Giant Steps*, the caption read, but another came to mind that captured much better my sense of his odd look: Pretending to Roar. He was imitating the stars he had seen on TV, most of them black, and hadn't yet learned to feel the anger or joy they felt at their own gifts, and which the game allowed them to express. Karl was whooping because it seemed expected of him.

The newspaper was called the *Bayrisches Bauernblatt*, the Bavarian Farmers' Page. Circulation: twenty thousand. I got up early the next morning to buy a pint of milk and picked it up from the shop at the bottom of the hill. Most of the stories had to do with the weather, the price of feed, the agriculture ministry, etc. It was printed in town at an old-fashioned press in the office itself, which was on the third floor of a 19th century townhouse, just across the river from the theater. The floor below was occupied by the local radio station, which shared many of its employees with the newspaper. These pictures made the front page. After breakfast, I cut out the second photograph to send home to my parents. They kept it and framed it and gave it back to me, when I asked for it, a few years later. I'm looking at the photograph now.

My younger self looks back at me, faded to nothing more than an outline on the cheap thin paper. A drop of spilled milk over somebody's shoes has turned pale purple with the passage of time. It's a team portrait, arranged in two rows. The front row is kneeling, and includes Charlie Gold, Willi Darmstadt (grinning like the schoolboy he is), Milo Moritz and Herr Henkel. The back row, made up of the taller players, are standing arm in arm; Karl has his hand on my shoulder. With a burst of affectionate presumption, I've rested my palm on Charlie's head, on what's left of his curly hair. 'Playing Days,' the caption says.

The cameras made for happiness, that's what I remember. I don't just mean the photo itself, but the presence of the photographers. (The press never showed up to any other practice.) They turned the gloomy hangar-like court, at the edge of a small market town in rural Bavaria, into a scene of importance; they turned us into basketball players. Just a few lines of the article have survived the picture's framing. Herr Henkel, it reads, has brought in several young talents to make a push for the first division. He says that Charlie Gold, last year's star, is just the man to bring them into shape. The only question mark is Hadnot's knee; whether he can recover from surgery in time for the season. In the event of the worst, they've signed a young American to replace him . . .

5

The Yoghurts was a division of the local sports club, and far from the most important one. Some of the ice hockey players, it was rumored, made six-figure salaries. We shared gym time with a dozen other sports and exercise classes. On Wednesday nights, for example, aerobics for the over fifties met before us. A dozen grey-haired ladies in their leotards stood aside to let us in when the bell rang. We often had to stack their floor mats before beginning play.

Herr Henkel had big ambitions and thought that hard work was the way to realize them. He pushed for two two-hour slots a day and got them: from ten to twelve in the morning, and from eight to ten at night. There was a lot of grumbling about these night sessions. It was hard to know when to eat, and by the time we got home, aching and sweating, we were mostly too wired to sleep. I had to wait till eleven to shower or the sweat would break through again. After that, a meal, if I could face it – usually something cold left over from the afternoon.

Breakfast and morning brought the same set of problems. I forced down some toast and a bowl of cereal around seven o'clock, then tried to catch a few more winks before heading to the gym. Strangest of all were the long dead afternoons, stretching from noon to eight, in which the only thing to do was muster up an appetite for lunch. I lost ten pounds in the first month. All I could do, all I wanted to do, morning, noon and when I woke dry-throated in the middle of the night, was drink.

Some of the other clubs practiced only three times a week. They had a few full-time professionals; the rest of the guys squeezed in training around their other jobs. Henkel, it was Olaf who told me, one night at my apartment over cold leftover chicken, hadn't paid much for his roster of players. He had negotiated a high salary for himself by persuading the boss that he could win with mediocre talent. Olaf gave me a look to say, no hard feelings. It was only then I realized what he meant: that I was one of the guys brought in on the cheap.

We were sitting in my kitchen, which had no curtains. The dark country night outside made the lone lamp glare in the windows. Flies, big horse flies from the stables on the other side of the road, settled and resettled on the cooking tray; from time to time both of us waved our hands at them. Olaf was a grumbler – the fact charmed me a little. In spite of his great placid beauty; in spite of his obvious abundant physical gifts. What was charming was just his air of unhurried dissatisfaction with life. He could always find more to complain about, he was never in a rush.

'I don't mind if they're tight,' he said, 'but Henkel shouldn't brag about it.' He had asked the owner, an old lady known to us all as Frau Kolwitz, what she wanted:

33

an expensive coach or expensive players. 'She doesn't answer. He tells her, "There is only one coach, but there are twelve players. In your shoes, I would buy expensive coach."'

'How do you know this?' I said. It was almost midnight, and Olaf had pulled out another chair to rest his feet on.

'Because he tells me himself! That's what I mean: he brags. He can't help it. Twice he tells me this story. I don't mind, it's none of my business, but who has to pay for their meanness? In the end? We do: two-a-days in August. In the second division of the Deutscher Basketball Bund. I've never heard of such things. I tell you now, all the other players in the league are laughing at us. They are on the beach somewhere, with their girl-friends: that's how other teams get ready. Hadnot is the one I admire. He is too smart for these games. At the end of every season, he hurts himself and has to spend the summer resting. Henkel is furious, but there's nothing he can do. He thinks this year he will drop him, because of Karl, but it is a mistake. Karl is too young; a great talent, yes, but too young. And no matter how much we run in August, no matter how fit we get, we are still just OK cheap-ass basketball players. And he is not such great coach.'

Olaf was enjoying himself. Such talk, in spite of itself, has a way of flattering. Even if you're no good, he was saying, and they work us like dogs, at least you can say this much: you're in the know.

But I didn't mind the running. It tired out the loneliness that might otherwise have filled my days. I was either resting, or eating, or drinking, or showering, or playing basketball. I didn't have time for anything else, and though we had each afternoon to ourselves, it wasn't just the rate of my pulse that slowed down. I expected a little less from each day than I used to. By the end of the month I could chase down a bus and pay for my ticket as if I'd been waiting at the stop. I began to *walk* differently. I have never been so fit in my life, I said to Herr Henkel one morning before practice, but I can hardly get out of bed, I can hardly walk to the gym. Yes, he answered (he had understood me), but you could run to the gym in a minute, is that what you mean? It is a wonderful thing to know what your body can do. Especially when you are young, before everything turns to fat.

In spite of what Olaf had said, I was beginning to fall under Henkel's spell. He was about my father's height, that is, a head shorter than me, and his thick moustache reminded me of the men of my childhood – of my father's friends at the beginning of their family lives. I used to see them at faculty picnics, throwing a Frisbee, or on the soccer field in the spring during the law school's Sunday league. They smelt of aftershave and sweat.

Theirs was a different generation. A colleague of my father's, who happened also to be a fraternity mate, had gone on an athletic scholarship to Cornell, where he helped them make a run at the NIT semifinals in his

35

junior year, 1958. I used to play basketball against him: a quick-handed, quick-witted, middle-class Jewish guy. Such a kid these days might not make it onto his high school varsity, but his was the success I measured my failure against, as my father followed the team bus around Texas to watch me sit on the bench. I wanted him to watch me now. He couldn't, of course, but Herr Henkel could and did, and had the advantages besides of professional expertise and personal indifference. What I hoped to find out from him was an answer to the old question: what do you think? Am I any good?

After a week of practice, Henkel split us into two teams – for the purpose of drills and scrimmages. Team 1 and team A, he called us, to cover up his preference, but his preference was easy to spot. Team 1 had Karl, Charlie, Olaf, Plotzke and Milo and wore the blue jerseys that matched our game uniforms.

Milo, the thick-lipped Croat, was the choice that hurt. For a few days in that first week, I ran with Charlie and Karl, and Milo played the three spot for the second stringers. We sometimes guarded each other. One evening, Henkel was walking us through our offensive sets, and Milo had the basketball on the wing. I bellied up to him and propped my forearm against his chest. He held the ball at his hip with both hands, which he suddenly lifted up; then he swung his elbows round and caught me in the jaw.

'Easy,' he said, as I staggered blindly back. He spoke

always with the quiet watchful assurance of a thug on a street corner. 'The coach was only showing us position. Give me a little room.'

After that, we ran through the play and Milo got the ball a few feet inside the arc and went straight up for a shot, which he made. Henkel rounded on me. 'This is fucking walk-through,' he shouted, 'and you are too stupid or slow to put hand in his face?'

Milo said nothing, and the next day, Henkel switched him to the first team. After a while we settled into our jobs; mine was guarding Karl. Henkel thought of himself as an eccentric, an innovator. He wanted to teach the Kid, who was seven feet tall and weighed roughly two hundred and forty pounds, to play in the backcourt, which made him my responsibility. Karl owes him a great deal. If he has played his part in changing the role of big men in the modern game, it was Henkel, his first professional coach, who helped him to define it.

Karl was a problem, though, and not just for me. Henkel wanted his first-team players to scrimmage together, to get a feel for each other, but they were so much better than the rest of us that practice became uncompetitive. Occasionally he'd give us Karl or Charlie for an afternoon and swap Darmstadt or me to the first team. But Darmstadt was just a kid, a real kid, a high school student with a milky moustache and arms as skinny as fresh pasta. He couldn't run the offense, which defeated the point of the exercise; and Karl, when he switched sides, used to take us all on single-handed, which made for some close games, but not much progress. The truth was, and Henkel was beginning to admit it, that he had spent too little on his players. It's up to the benchwarmers, guys seven, eight and nine on the roster, to keep the play sharp in practice even if they never make it on court in games. This was supposed to be my job and I wasn't doing it.

Not my first taste of failure, but something about that month left a deep print. I still feel its mark on me. OK, so we all guessed that Karl was something special, that he might become famous in time. But he wasn't famous yet, and whenever he beat me to a rebound, or took me off the dribble, or casually lifted a jumpshot over my outstretched hand, he seemed to stand for all the other seventeen-year-old kids in the world who could whip me too. I just happened to end up in Karl's hometown. There were probably a hundred other towns in Germany, I figured, where the local high school hero would give me the same treatment.

Relativity is one of the miseries of the minor leagues. When you lose, it isn't just your opponent who beats you, but everybody else in the leagues ahead of you.

One day, after the morning session, Henkel led us outside to the soccer pitch, which was surrounded by a sandy track. It had rained overnight, and the red sand stuck to our shoes. Henkel divided us into groups, and we began to run intervals, starting at twenty meters and building up to the full hundred before winding down again. After we'd warmed up a little, he offered to make a competition of it and stood at the end of the track with the whistle in his hand.

A hundred meters is a long way; it only feels like a sprint if you're winning. I came in fifth: Karl, Charlie, Milo and Krahm, our skinny back-up power forward, outpaced me by at least ten yards. Olaf would probably have beaten me, too, if he hadn't pulled up lame after twenty paces, holding his hamstring, and trotted the rest of the way with a great show of pain. Afterwards he explained to me that they didn't pay him enough to make him run horse races. A horse race is just what it felt like. Basketball is a team sport and the nuances of the game leave you room to blame what happens on other people. But that sprint left no such room. I felt afterwards that my flesh had been weighed and valued. If I hoped to make a name for myself in that league I would have to make do with inferior qualities.

But I had good days, too, when my shots fell and Karl was too lazy to come out and challenge them. And other things on my mind. Sometimes I skipped the banter of the locker room and got cleaned up at home. Then I'd shower in the dark, bowing my head beneath the flow of water. The darkness kept out, from my own thoughts, the stares of other people. I felt the day drain from me; I closed my eyes against the rising heat. Afterwards, drying off, I liked to look out the little bathroom window above the sink, at the lights of the complex – which dotted the night air according to one of those intricate changing patterns that seem both human and mathematical. But the truth is, I spent most of that time looking out for one window in particular. The window where the long-haired girl had stood.

Around half past ten at night, she tended to show her face. Probably it was her bedroom window, and she liked to look at the view a minute before turning in: the horse farm across the road and the land falling away behind me into the darkness of the countryside. She might have seen a few stars. Landshut grew very dark at night. The luminous hum of Munich did not reach it.

When her hair was down, her silhouette seemed simpler and whiter. I guessed that she wore it up in the day and loosened in the evening, that she slept in a nightdress. Sometimes, though the light was behind her, I could see the details of her day clothes: black cardigans with bright buttons, square-cut blouses in strong primary colors. She was very thin. Her waist seemed no broader than my thumb. The fact that she stood there with the curtains wide open at the same time each night struck me almost as an act of communicated intimacy: we shared a ritual.

Not that she always looked out. Sometimes I watched her going about the slow quiet business of putting herself to bed. Folding clothes away, applying night creams, combing out her hair. I worked out the faint top edge of a standing mirror against the wall, above the line of the window sill. Beside it, a low skyline of bottles and jars and boxes. Her dressing table. Once in a while something or someone called her out of the room: a telephone? a boyfriend? Though she always re-entered the stage framed by her bedroom window, after a few minutes, alone again and without a phone in her hand.

Even at the time the racing of my heart gave away the fact that my interest was not quite wholesome. On the other hand, the desire I felt for the world within those rooms, warmed by her presence, seemed to me also a decent and natural desire – for a normal and less lonely life. And on those few occasions when I saw her unbuttoning her cardigan or throwing her hair over her head to pull up a blouse, I rarely lingered for more than a few seconds before turning away to get dressed for bed myself.

6

Two weeks before the season began, Bo Hadnot showed up to practice. I can't say I recognized him. Henkel, for once, was late, and most of the guys had gathered at the far end of the gym to watch Darmstadt fooling around. About ten o'clock in the morning. It seemed a sign, and I muttered this to Olaf as we sat on a bench lacing up our hightops, of what being professionals had done to us. After a month of training, we lay around waiting for Coach before picking up a basketball.

Only Darmstadt, a schoolboy, was out on court, grinning the broad uncontrollable grin of a kid being looked at, and trying to prove to us that he could dunk. For him, practice was just a small part of an ordinary life, maybe even an escape from it. He was sixteen years old and about to begin his final year at the Fachschule. His father was a pharmacist; his mother grew up on one of the smallholdings outside Landshut and still spent most of her days at the family farm, helping out. Darmstadt was a real local; he didn't expect to make it out of town. Henkel had drafted him as a part of his economy drive, after somebody from the club spotted him in the youth league and figured he could fill out the practice squad. The team paid him a few hundred marks a month for showing up: a windfall, from Darmstadt's point of view. Every day after the morning session, two of his high school friends met him at the bike racks outside the sports hall, and he took them out to lunch at McDonald's. Later it would probably seem to him the best summer of his life.

Not that he couldn't play. He was skinny and pimply, with long arms whose elbows almost knocked against his hips. Size fifteen shoes don't suit many people; they look especially awkward on a teenage boy still growing into his length. But he had a quick first step and a cheerful indifference to every aspect of the game that didn't involve getting off his own shot. With a decent run-up and a lucky grip on the ball he could just about squeeze a dunk over the front rim. Whenever he did, we cheered him, with a loud irony that made him blush – out of pleasure and embarrassment. In any case, it gave him an incentive to try again, and again.

'It makes me tired to look at him,' Olaf said.

Meanwhile, somebody had begun to warm up at the other end of the court. He wore a t-shirt and tracksuit pants and what looked like a pair of loafers (by the way he shuffled around in them) over white socks. Loafers are what old ballplayers turn to when their backs and knees go, but I didn't know that at the time. I assumed some guy off the street had seen the open door and wanted to try his hand. He bounced the ball a couple times and lined himself up just outside the three-point arc. Then he put up a shot, not hard enough it seemed to me, but the ball went in. The spin drew it back and he waited for it to come to him, then shuffled a few more steps along the three-point line.

Something looked wrong about the next shot, awkward or sidelong, but it also went in, and not till he had reached the top of the key did I realize he had shifted to his left hand. When he missed, he chased the ball with heavy steps and returned to the spot he'd missed from and knocked down three straight slowly, with great deliberation, before moving on. I watched him for a few minutes, drawn to the sight as we are to any private act in a public place: a man tying his shoelaces or crying; a boy and a girl holding hands. Then Henkel called us to order at the center of the court, and the stranger reluctantly collected his ball and walked over.

I recognized him then – he had picked me up from the airport. Only Olaf came over to greet him and slapped him teasingly on his off-season belly. Hadnot made a fist. Then Henkel introduced him to the new guys and the fat young man from the front office took him inside to get his ankles taped.

Bo had changed out of his loafers and sweats by the time he came out again, but he didn't look much better. Whether or not his knees still bothered him, a summer on the couch hadn't done the rest of him any good. He untucked his shirt to give his belly room and moved with the slow persistence of a man trying to find something he might have dropped earlier. Then we ran drills; for the first time all week Henkel took it easy on us. A lot of jumpshots, half court traps, free throws. Nobody talked much, and I had the strong impression of an imminent shift in the weather.

Olaf told me during a water break that Charlie and Hadnot didn't get along. The court had no fountain. Most players brought their own bottle, but if it ran out you had to wander through the bowels of the arena to fill up at the locker room sink. Olaf always added a tab of magnesium, which fizzed whitely and tasted of chalk, and made full use of these breaks, sometimes drawing me into his little truancies. Basketball players are ass-kissers, he said. They like to suck up to the big stars (this was his phrase), and Charlie had had the whole show to himself for about a month. Now Hadnot was back every-one had to work out who was boss. Don't be surprised, he said, if Charlie makes a move on you. Olaf was very funny on the subject; he had no respect for the team mentality. He was also boasting about his own sullen independence, but I liked him for it, even if his account put our relations in an awkward light.

Henkel spent most of the second hour walking us through our offensive sets. Practice was light enough, in fact, that I skipped the showers and made straight for the open air. It was a clear late summer's day, as clear as autumn but a few degrees warmer, and I sometimes felt about the gym the way I used to feel about school: it was the window I leaned out of. Which was why my heart sank a little when Charlie caught up to me at the bike racks. 'Young man,' he said, 'young man, let me take you to lunch; you look like you need it.' I saw Darmstadt walking off with his two friends – six hands in six pockets, three heads bent – and envied them briefly.

7

Charlie led the way to his apartment. The Sports Halle stood in the new section of town: lots of chunky 60s architecture, the sorts of buildings a child would design who had just been given his first ruler. Square and brightly painted. But the new cobbled streets gave way to old cobbled streets as we approached the river. The courthouse and the theater, overlooking the water, were equally simple but much more elegant; they showed to its best advantage the virtue of German order.

Landshut had its heyday in the 1500s when some Prince of Bavaria settled there. It was the market town into which all the hills surrounding poured their harvests. The Isar connected it to Munich and the rest of Germany, and the place still had an air of commercial pride and prosperity, which only partly depended on tourists. Trains ran every hour from Munich. We got some of the spillover from Oktoberfest and even out of season attracted just enough Americans and Brits to support a few kitsch Biergartens on the High Street. Charlie, in fact, lived next to one of them, on the top floor of a sagging medieval townhouse, whose stairs were so short and narrow that I had to bend double and climb them with my hands on the steps in front.

'How long have you lived here?' I asked, when he showed me in. The apartment was lighter, more spacious than I had expected, but practically unfurnished. A chair in one corner of the room faced one of those cheap wooden rolling units on which you can stack a TV and VCR. Other than that, there was nowhere to sit, apart from the two bar stools pushed up to the bar that separated the kitchen from the living room. A row of cookbooks from the same Learn to Cook series (Italian, Thai, French, etc.) leaned against the counter wall. French windows at the far side of the living room gave on to a deep narrow balcony all but overgrown with flowerpots.

'I don't live here, I work here,' he said. It was the tone he would have taken on the basketball court, where his motto was: always correct. And then, a little embarrassed, he added, 'About four years.'

We ate lunch on the balcony. Charlie had prepared it before practice: a cold pasta dish with chili and soy and fish. He offered me a beer, a local Pilsener, which I accepted but hardly touched; he nursed his bottle for most of the afternoon. Over lunch he showed me photographs of the house he was building outside Chicago, towards the Michigan border. That's where he 'lived,' he said. He spent every off-season with a few buddies adding to it. His father had worked in construction, Charlie practically grew up on building sites, and his dad was doing a little job for him now, digging the foundations for a tennis court at the back of his yard.

'Somewhere to retire to,' I said, 'at the age of thirty-five.'

He thought he'd have to wait longer than that. His face seemed almost hidden beneath the rough scars of acne; it was capable of keeping a great deal back. He said, 'I don't suppose you're in it for more than a year or two. You got other plans.'

'What are those?' I asked, smiling.

But it seemed the wrong note, and he didn't respond. I told him eventually that I wanted to be a writer, that I thought basketball might be an interesting way to pay a few bills. Besides, I could always write something about the experience.

That's right, Charlie nodded. 'I guessed you had something else on your mind.'

'What do you mean, something else?'

'Something other than basketball.'

In the course of the afternoon, he had quietly attended to his flowerpots, deadheading the late roses, looking for slugs, etc. and he stood up now to fill the watering can from a tap in the outside wall. 'I've played with guys like you before,' he said, 'stuck inside they own head. So you let all these bullies push you around. I know, I'm one of them. You got to stand up for yourself.' He lowered his voice a note or two and put on his angry face, his 'black' voice. 'I'm talking about Milo,' he said. 'Don't let him be teaching you nothing. You ain't his A student. He ain't your teacher. Next time he tells you what to do, I don't care what it is, just cold cock him.'

He slapped a fist against his hand. After a minute, he added, 'You're giving me that look again. Like you're taking it all in.'

The watering can was empty, so he returned to fill it. And began to explain himself, as he made his parade among the flowers. He had been in this country ten years now. The first job he took was in Gelsenkirchen, which reminded him of parts of Ohio, prosperous, industrial. At that time, the club was in the fourth division. They didn't have the money to pay him a full wage. Part of his job was looking after handicapped kids. He was twenty-two years old and had rarely been out of the Midwest. The homesickness was as bad as pneumonia; it all but put him to bed. He had never dealt with disability before, and the experience came at a difficult time: he was young and healthy and full of himself. And beginning to doubt himself, too – a bad combination.

'I hated those kids,' he said, 'didn't want to look at them. But I took them swimming, got them changed again. Cleaned up they poopy diapers. Some of them four, five years old. Most of them happier than me.'

He had expected, if nothing else, that the basketball would be OK – he could put up with a lot so long as the basketball was OK. He figured on teaching the Germans how to play. Instead he discovered that there were a lot of guys who could shoot better than he could shoot, jump higher than he could jump, run faster than he could run. If someone had asked him back then, would he last till Christmas, he'd have said, hell no.

'I'm hoping to make it to Hanukkah,' I said.

He looked up at me then. 'Oh, you're not that bad,' he said. 'That just shows how much *you* know.'

There was a garden attached to the clinic, and he used to help out the nurse responsible for keeping it up. Gardening was supposed to be very therapeutic. That was one of their theories, and it's true, the kids loved it. He had been raised in Chicago in a tenth-floor apartment with a balcony just big enough for his mother to hang up the washing. It was always full of washing; there wasn't room for anything else. What he meant was, he didn't know anything about gardening until he got to Gelsenkirchen; but he was having a bad year, and among the best things to come out of it were some strawberries, which he had planted himself and was allowed to take home and eat. At the end of the season, Gelsenkirchen moved up to the third division – he had played his part in that, too. Later, he got a job in Hamburg for a second division club; then Freiburg and Nürnberg and Landshut. Everywhere he went he took his pots and his big TV.

'I guess you're waiting for the point of this story,' he said.

'You mean, if I don't watch out I might be stuck here for another ten years.'

But he shook his head. The point of the story was to tell me that he had won the league his first year. 'Basketball is just like anything else. You can make out of yourself what you want to make out of yourself.'

There was a moment of awkwardness as I left. 'What are you doing,' he said. 'We got all afternoon.' He planned to watch a video and then maybe have a nap, but I was welcome to join him for the movie.

'You only got one chair,' I pointed out, making my way to the door, and he stood in the doorway watching me back down his narrow stairs.

8

I arrived at the evening session early only to find that most of the guys were already warming up. There was a second court in the sports hall, on the third floor, which was much pokier than the first. It had wooden backboards, not glass; there was no room for a bench along the sidelines. On Wednesday nights, we were forced to make do with it: a ballet class had been oversubscribed and they needed the space downstairs.

In fact, I preferred the second court, which was small enough that you could smell the heat of play after a few minutes. Everyone seemed happier there. Basketball felt more like a game and less like a profession, which isn't to say that we took it easy. Walking in that night, I sensed something restless, fractious, playful in the air, and wondered how much of it had to do with the American's return. He was quietly shooting free throws at a side basket.

After a light warm-up, Henkel dragged the practice jerseys onto the floor. The first team had Plotzke, Olaf, Milo, Karl and Charlie. The second team was made up of me, Darmstadt, Krahm, Hadnot and another late addition, a big man brought in by Henkel at the last minute with a very English-sounding name – Thomas Arnold.

Arnold was a large, pale-faced, fair-haired, amiable kid, who had just passed his music exams and was hoping to study choral singing. His basketball experience stretched no further than a useful role on his high school team in Berlin. To escape the army, he had enlisted for civic duty and been assigned to a children's hospital in town. He got in touch with the Yoghurts mostly because he didn't know anybody in Bavaria, which struck him as a barbarous place, full of backward people who spoke incomprehensible German.

It should be clear by now how unfairly matched we were. Plotzke was the only weak link on the first team, but even he had been playing club basketball for the best part of a decade. He was physically ugly, a great complainer and dangerously clumsy, but also, and partly because of that fact, surprisingly effective. Milo had started in the second division, Olaf in the first. Charlie had done time in the NBA, even if he had never made it past the pre-season camps. And Karl was already being publicized as the most exciting young talent in the league. On the other side, Arnold and Krahm were both, essentially, university students, who had taken up the sport as a hobby. Darmstadt was a school kid, and I hadn't started for an organized team since junior high. That left Hadnot to pick up the slack, and he was fat, hurt and out of shape. Even so, as Krahm said to me, pulling the mesh jersey over his t-shirt, 'It can't be worse than before.'

The second unit, in the course of a month of beatings, had become demoralized; the whole team had suffered.

We were going through the motions, of losing, on the one hand, and winning, on the other. Everyone was flat. Failure gets to be good and comfortable, like any other habit. But Hadnot took us aside for a minute before tipoff and said without any sort of introduction, 'You and you [pointing to Arnold and Krahm], keep your shoulders wide on the block. And look out for me; I like to come hard off screens.'

Then, to Darmstadt: 'What's your name, kid?'

'Willi,' he said.

'All right, Willi. I want the ball to my right hip. The pass should get there same time I do. Every second counts; I'm old and slow. Who's got Karl?'

I raised my hand. 'I'll take him,' he said. And then, with an air of practical kindness: 'He's lazy on defense and I want to get a few shots in. You guard Milo. I don't care if you have to knee him, keep him out of the baseline and off the boards.'

Hadnot had rearranged us all around him. Not that I minded. He had conveyed nothing so forcefully as the fact that *this* game mattered, a Wednesday night pre-season scrimmage on a half-sized court, in a small town forty-five miles outside Munich, where the only sports that anyone really cared about were ice hockey and soccer. 'Let's beat these sons of bitches,' he said. 'I hate losing.'

They say you get one good game, coming back, before your legs give way and you have to build them back up. Maybe that was the game Hadnot had. Nobody benefited from the smaller court more than he did. It was easy to get up and down or track back on the break; the hard part was finding a wrinkle of space in the half-court to maneuver in. The weight he carried on him served a purpose, too; it demanded room. He warned us that he liked to come hard off the pick. I could barely move my right arm the next day: that was the shoulder he curled off, coming up from the block. Didn't matter how many screens it took to set him free, after a while that's all we looked for. He hit from the baseline, from the elbow, from the top of the key. He knocked down little ten-foot floaters that may be the toughest shot in basketball: letting the high slow arc of the ball take back the force of the drive. When the angle was there, he went glass; otherwise, his shots dropped through like he'd been standing over the rim.

To an unfamiliar eye, there must have been something very gracious and gentle about the way he scored. He seemed to preach self-restraint, the shots floated so quietly in. But boy was he pissed off. Not that he talked much. Charlie liked to keep up a flow of conversation with everybody on court. Hadnot said something only if he wanted something. 'Ball!' he shouted, 'ball!' every time he snapped off a screen. Karl spent about a half hour trying to fight his way through, until Charlie instituted a switching defense. After that, Hadnot was everybody's business. They ran double-teams at him whenever the switch was made, they had him covered both over and under, but Hadnot found a way to work through them. He used headfakes to get the help defenders in the air, then planted a shoulder or elbow in their jaws to force the foul. 'Foul!' was the other thing he used to shout, clapping his hands for the ball. After a few of his elbows, even Charlie tended to switch a little slower off the high screens, and Hadnot had his inch of space.

We took the first game with something to spare – the first game we had won all year.

Why he was angry, I don't know. But anger had something to do with the show he put on. It wasn't just the fact that he singled out Karl to score his points on – although he did that, too. It was the way he played the other side of the ball. Hadnot was giving away more than ten years, six inches, and fifty-odd pounds to Karl. The Kid also had the quickest first step on the team and I didn't see any way that Hadnot could keep in front of him. Keeping in front of him, in fact, was all he did. As soon as Karl crossed half-court, Hadnot bellied up to him, and Karl never got the chance to stretch his long legs. A certain amount of grabbing, shirt-clutching, knee-banging were all part of the American's plans, and a strict-constructionist referee might have fouled him out of the game inside ten minutes. But there was no referee, and Henkel didn't trust himself to whistle any of Hadnot's tricks. You had to call everything or nothing, and everything is usually too much.

Charlie tried to find other means of getting his own back. Once, on a break, he saw Hadnot back-pedaling and led Karl with a lofted pass just shy of the rim.

Hadnot took Karl's legs out – he ended up on his rear five feet behind the baseline – then walked straight over to pick him up. The Kid was too dazed by the violence of the foul to retaliate. He had become used to my defensive tactics, which operated more or less on the principle of appeasement. I'll let you score if you don't hurt me. Maybe it pleased Henkel to see Karl's mettle tested. As it happens, he gave into bullying as quickly as I did, though Hadnot's example inspired in all of us a few stubborn and rebellious gestures.

He had told me to stick my knee into Milo if he tried to go baseline and that's what I did. 'Junge, Junge,' Milo complained each time, with a great theatrical frown on his face, as if he smelled something rotten. Until I caught him just above his own knee where the muscles of the thigh begin to tighten. He collapsed in a heap and came up limping with his arms stretched out for my throat. 'Cold cock' him Charlie had advised me. What I did was close my eyes and stick out my hands defensively, but these found his sweaty face, so I pushed. It was over in a second. We flailed at each other; one of my fingers might have got stuck in his eye. But Charlie, to my great relief, stepped in to separate us, though Milo made a show of resistance and had to be held back in the end by Olaf and Plotzke. He spent the rest of the night hobbling and taking bad shots.

We won three out of the first four, though Hadnot began to tire in the second hour and Charlie took on himself the burden of their scoring. Darmstadt couldn't keep him out of the lane. Krahm, who was stubborn and sharp-elbowed, and Arnold, who was merely clumsy, fouled him as much as they could, but it wasn't enough. He had a wonderful way of disappearing inside a forest of legs and arms. Speed wasn't the secret of it. He simply moved between the rhythms of other people and caught the defense perpetually out of step. The basketball itself makes up the beat of the game; it's easy to become enslaved to it. Like an actor who can turn a line of blank verse into ordinary speech, Charlie had mastered the art of being natural.

Even his jumper, that awkward irregular invention, began to fall. 'One at a time,' he said, as the shots dropped. 'That's all I need to make: one at a time.'

When he wasn't scoring, he set up Olaf and Plotzke for lay-ins and dunks. 'Unselfish' – that was the other thing he called out, at every successful pass. A strange sort of immodesty, another little dig. We finished the night all square. Hadnot, bent double, pulling his shorts over his knees.

Afterwards, in the showers, Arnold began to sing. Something Italian, an aria familiar from an ice-cream commercial that was running on German TV. He looked very pink and plump in his altogether, very large and very young at the same time. We mocked him for singing, though it more or less expressed what we all felt. A return of high spirits. Hadnot, with his feet still taped, stood perfectly straight and closed his eyes against the fall of water. I could see he was going bald; his hair fell thinly across his forehead. Krahm began to clap his hands in time to the music. He had long arms and long fingers and looked like a string-puppet; the bones of his face and figure had a wooden mechanical correctness. Most of the first team had gone home by this point. Only Olaf had stayed behind to shower – to protect me, he joked, in case Milo was hanging around. Later, as we were drying off, he asked me if I wanted to go for a drink. He could never sleep after practice but stayed up too late with the television on, lying in bed, watching the two o'clock reruns of the twelve o'clock talk shows.

'Are you trying to recruit me, too?' I asked, and we set off together into the cool clear night, amid the glow of streetlamps.

9

A week before the season began, Henkel gave us Friday night off. He sometimes let us out early for the weekend, if (as he said) we had been 'good.' The truth was, Olaf once told me, that his family lived in Regensburg, two hours away by car, and he was desperate to get home himself. He had only recently retired from playing. Regensburg belonged to the third division, whose clubs, as a general rule, can afford only one or two full-time professionals. Henkel, in his day, had starred in the first; but he recognized at the age of forty the need for new ambitions and took the Regensburg job as a player/coach because it would allow him to get into management. Landshut was the next step up, and his first year out of uniform, as it were. His wife and two young daughters had stayed behind in case things didn't work out. The team gave him an apartment near the gym, in the Neustadt, as it was called, and for five nights a week he batched it alone. Which partly explained his insistence on evening practice: he had nothing else to do with himself.

I sometimes used those free afternoons for going into Munich. It was a ten-minute cycle ride to the train station, across the river and through the flat lands outside town, where the battle between farms and suburbs and industrial estates was still being played out. Eventually I found a route that took me, in that late summer, through fields of high grain; these excursions into the big city offered me really nothing sweeter than that short journey on two wheels. The road was mostly downhill, and I could exercise as I liked the play of new muscles in my legs or let them rest. I have little enough nostalgia for that year of my life, but what I have is aroused most often by trains. Not by the smell of them or the sight of them – just by the waiting involved. I remember very clearly my outlook on the world as I bought my ticket and stood at the platform: lonely, unexpectant, cheerful.

Nothing, I supposed, would ever happen to me in Munich to change the steady slow course of my days, though it was in the hope that it *might* that I continued to make my way into the city.

That Friday Olaf had invited me to dinner at his parents' house. He had gone up after the morning practice, and I followed a few hours later, after lunch and a nap. It had been raining all week, hot summer rains that left everything sticky to the touch, but the afternoon was dry enough and a little cooler. A low white density of air hung over the trees and looked more like the sky itself than a cloud. The bike shed had flooded and reflected the pale day back at us; I locked my bicycle among a bright multiplicity of spokes. A man in a moustache and tie stood at the cobbled entrance to the train station and applied a long hose to the driveway, spraying the water back into the road. He just paused as I passed him.

The train was fuller than usual but I managed to find a seat at one of the dining tables, facing the wrong way. I didn't expect to stay the night and had brought nothing along but my book, a taped-over copy of *Three Men on the Bummel* from the local library. Also, folded in the pocket of my jeans, a leather yarmulke.

On my first trip to Munich, I looked up the neighborhood where the Jewish side of my family once lived: Schwabing, an area that has now become fashionable. It may always have been, though I doubt very much whether my great-grandparents were among those progressive Jews whose spiritual and intellectual experiments gave to the culture of turn-of-the-century Germany its radical and modern tone. No, I suspect, from what I know of that side of my family, that they had always been argumentative, curious and entrepreneurial, but essentially conservative people. The tall streets of stuccoed apartment blocks, as I wandered among them for the first time, conveyed a sense of pleasant cosmopolitan comforts: wrought-iron balconies adorned by flowers and bicycles; and behind them, tall French windows, which always suggest to me breakfast and newspapers and dressing gowns, and idle rainy days. There were still bakers among the shops that occupied the wide ground floors of the apartment buildings, not to mention newsagents, tobacconists and restaurants dark with potted plants.

My father had told me the street number of the block his grandparents lived in, and I spent a very happy Friday afternoon trying to track it down. It was a long street, leafy, curving, cobbled. But the numbers must have changed; at least, I couldn't find theirs.

What I did find, or rather, stumble across, was a fat young man with a machine gun at his hip, standing guard outside an otherwise unremarkable doorway on one of the quieter side streets. I had spent two years of my childhood in Berlin and knew what he signified: there was a synagogue inside.

My own relationship to Jewishness has never been straightforward. My mother is not only German, but Christian. Though I was raised as a Jew and bar mitz-vahed (by a rabbi who snuck to his car during the party afterwards to check the radio for updates of the Texas/Oklahoma football match), my knowledge of German and the war stories I listened to at bedtime, of depriva-tions and narrow escapes, belong to the Christian half of my family history. When I got to college, something ambiguous about my claim to Jewishness prevented me from stopping by Hillel on a Friday night, or showing up to high holiday services. Lots of college students drift away from their religions, just as many turn towards them again. I suppose I was always likely to be one of the drifters, too much of a mongrel to take comfort from a sense of community. But there was a time, around my fifteenth birthday, when I remember wanting just such comfort – when I encouraged my father to light a candle on Friday nights and say a few words in a language that has remained to me incomprehensible.

Shabbas, I guessed, is what they were celebrating inside. A man at the door in a black suit and tie asked me for some kind of identification. I took out my driver's license. The irony, of course, is that the name of a Jew, if not Jewishness itself, is passed down from father to son. I had inherited both his name and his face: narrow, angular, a little hungry-looking. *Markovits* and a strong nose were enough to get me in. Another young man, this time in a tallis, which he wrapped around himself in a cozy, almost feminine manner, offered me a choice of yarmulkes from a wicker basket. I picked out the leather one for its heaviness, since I didn't have a clip, and ducked under a low doorway into the red dusk of the synagogue itself.

All I could see by the light of a stained glass skylight was old men and not very many of them either. Rows of wooden benches, with an aisle down the middle, had been set up under the simple ark, which stood open. The men were *davening* in front of it, tirelessly, and the comfortable repeated motions of their backs and heads reminded me strangely of one of the warm-ups Charlie used to make us do before practice: rolling from toe to heel and back again, in order to stretch the Achilles tendon and strengthen our calves. In fact, my knees and ankles began to throb a little as I joined them, with a bent head and my hands clasped in some embarrassment across my stomach. I had hoped to sit down.

It was their voices that kept me going, the low continuous echoing voices of their prayers, which afflicted my own throat with aching sympathies. Their prayers were different from the ones I'd grown up with, softer, more sibilant, and the cadence of their chanting seemed older and less musical. Even so, something about the blind urgency of their singing, which wasn't quite singing, seemed familiar. The Sunday school I used to go to, until the class times interfered with football season, treated Hebrew as a language to be repeated rather than understood. I had no doubt that the men rocking on their feet in front of me could speak Hebrew, but the words they chanted had broken down into something more basic than meaning: into tones and beats.

By this point in the pre-season everything ached, not least my heart, with homesickness and the sense of failure. Exhaustion had on me the effect of sentimentality – I began to cry.

Nobody noticed. In any case, such a congregation probably had enough to grieve about; they wouldn't wonder too much at a few tears. The Holocaust had always struck me, in my American childhood, as a symbol of something terrible: both of the evil people were capable of committing and of the suffering they were capable of enduring. It seemed so powerful as a symbol. For the first time it struck me as a fact, which made it much worse.

Most of the men before me were survivors; they must have been roughly my age at the end of the Second World War. Their parents might have known my grandfather's parents – might have tried to dissuade them, a generation before, from emigrating to New York. Munich had once had a prominent and lively Jewish community, but most of the synagogues were destroyed in the war along with the Jews who had prayed in them. This makeshift temple had been carved out of a postwar apartment block, hastily erected in the gap a bomb had made between the taller, older and grander buildings on either side. The first and second floors had been removed. All that was left of them was a narrow gallery running along three of the walls. It was there the women prayed. I spotted them for the first time, leaning over and looking down, when I finally had a chance to sit.

I suppose the men there were as various as any other set of old men, but to my eyes they seemed mostly short and a little fat. It was something of a relief, after a week devoted to the perfection of the body, to spend an hour or two among people who had long ago accepted the eccentricities of their own. Besides, I didn't want to understand the prayers; incomprehensibility was a part of their charm. We bowed and ducked and shouted and mumbled. Sport is the art of repeating meaningless and tiny acts: I liked the idea of a God who required a similar duty in his people.

In fact, it was the idea of that God, presiding over his dying congregation, which I developed in the hour or two of each service, and which kept me coming back. Success didn't matter to him. (It was hard not to imagine a *him* with the women sequestered above.) Bad luck and losers were also among his creations. He did not intervene. The business I was in depended on percentages and probabilities, but I had never seen so vividly demonstrated, by the men who had survived to reach that *shabbas*, the terrible operation of chance.

Of course, this is just loneliness talking. Loneliness theorizes. The truth is, it was a place to go and sometimes sit down in a strange city on Friday evenings among people who seemed familiar, and who accepted me. I kept (or stole) the yarmulke they had given me and remembered to bring it along whenever I got the train into Munich, just in case.

Olaf's parents lived in Schwabing, too, and I wondered whether I had time, before dinner, to stop in on the service. What surprised me is the mild rush of disappointment I felt at the thought of missing it. I had taken the soft leather cap from my pocket and begun to twine it in my fingers.

The train was making local stops: young farmers from Bruckberg, from Langenbach, got on. A Friday night crowd was heading into the city, in clean jeans and buttoned shirts; a few of them had already opened tall cans of beer. I began to feel a little self-conscious and stubbornly resisted the urge to put the yarmulke back in my pocket. It might misrepresent me, as the kind of Jew who ordinarily wore one, but that wasn't the thought that made me a little uncomfortable.

Not that I had ever experienced anti-Semitism in Germany. The Germans of my acquaintance were much too afflicted by their parents' history to acknowledge even that Jews existed – I mean, as a group with distinguishing features. 'We're all the same' was the lesson they had too faithfully learned. But the Germans of my acquaintance were mostly northern and middle-class. I wondered if Bavarian farmers might show a different curiosity. At the same time it struck me as a measure of my loneliness that I could waste any headspace on such fantasies. Not only headspace: I glanced around to see if anyone was staring at me.

Nobody was, of course; but then, a girl in one of the backing seats across the aisle gave me a sympathetic smile. My first thought was to hide the yarmulke again. My second, that she looked familiar. She carried her small head with great assurance on a long neck; she had freckles and sandy hair, and blue, slightly unblinking eyes.

Just as I recognized her, with a hot blush of shame, she leaned over and said, 'Do we know each other? I have been trying to catch your eye since Gündkofen.'

She was the girl from the window, and I wondered for a second if she had seen me spying on her. 'I don't think we've met,' I said. 'At least, in person.'

In fact, that doubt stayed with me for the rest of our conversation: that she knew I sometimes watched her preparing for bed. There are girls who might be flattered by such attention, who might think they deserved it. It's not entirely to her credit that she gave me the impression of being one of them. She seemed very sure of herself, of her looks, for one thing, and treated me with a kind ironic condescension that suggested she knew my secret. But then, pretty girls often have that air. The secret they can be sure of guessing is that young men, however shyly, are attracted to them.

'Are you very famous, then?' she said, smiling. There was a seat free next to her, and she began to pat it, nervously enough. 'Is that what you're saying? Would I have seen your picture on TV?'

She was teasing me, I thought, so I said, 'Not yet, but maybe in the newspaper.'

At which she clapped her hands together. 'You don't mean the *Bauernblatt*? I work for the *Bauernblatt*.'

'Yes, that's probably what I do mean.'

'No, but I have seen you more – personally than that.' After a pause: 'Do you live on Kardinger Weg, in one of the apartment blocks?' It was cruel to tease me this way, if she knew, but she went on. 'That must be it then. You see, I live there, too. We're neighbors.' And she held out her hand, stiffly, across the aisle. 'I'm Anke.'

To reach it, I had to stand up, and afterwards, it seemed as easy to sit down beside her as return to my seat. She had noticed the yarmulke in my other hand and took it from me, a gesture that annoyed me only when she put it on her head. One can grow tired of the presumptions of pretty girls.

'It will be simpler for me to wear it on the way home,' she said, 'after I get my hair cut. That's why I'm going into Munich, to get it cut. Nobody in Landshut understands my hair.'

Such talk came easily to her, self-mocking and boastful at once. After a silence, which I did nothing to break, she took a fistful of her own hair in hand and asked, 'What do you think? Should I cut it all off?'

'Why do you want to cut it at all?'

'Are you very Jewish?' She had grown bored already of her own self-absorption.

'I don't know that it's something you can be less or more of . . . No, not very.'

'Otherwise you would wear this all the time on your head and not give it to girls?'

'I didn't – '

There was more in this line; it looks even worse on the page than it sounds in life. Aside from the shame I felt – at having stumbled in broad daylight, as it were, over a guilty secret – which never left me till the train reached Munich and we separated, I was conscious of a slight but affecting disappointment. So this is she, I thought. Hers is the life I had imagined stepping into.

She picked up my book and pretended to read it for a minute. 'Are you English?' she asked. 'I thought you were only a little stupid.'

So I made a show of interest in her own book, which bulked out of her bright red handbag: a copy of *Sophie's World*. It was the summer that everyone seemed to be reading *Sophie's World*. The novel had begun to irritate me, as an example of popular literature that had been packaged to appeal to our pretensions of higher taste. I had the sense, though, to hold my tongue. The fact was that I *did* find her attractive, in spite of or perhaps because of her little presumptions. A bead of sweat trickled along my ribs. My heart had already increased its speed, as if I had run a lap or two, warming up. She was the first woman I had talked to in over two months.

After her haircut, she planned to meet a girlfriend for a drink; she gave me the name of the club. I should come along: her girlfriend was very nice, and pretty. And loved basketball. I had told her by this point what brought me to Landshut. Anke had made a face; the line about her friend was a kind of apology for it.

Munich had begun to appear, the flat white faces of its suburbs. In the distance, the jumble of low red roofs promised an older and lovelier city. As we entered the slow descent, she turned to me suddenly with her hand on my sleeve and said, she was getting her hair cut because – she had a daughter – and she was cutting her hair because – her daughter was two years old – and she was tired of letting her pull it. She supposed I would find out in any case. 'I hope you can join us,' she repeated. 'This is my big night off.'

10

I walked past the synagogue on the way to Olaf's apartment. The fat young man with the machine gun had a way of standing and shifting on his feet that kept the foot traffic moving; he seemed to direct you with the tip of his gun. For once, I let him turn me away.

Many of the avenues were bordered by tall lindens. Their leaves, sticky with summer, left a green film over the parked cars. Olaf's parents lived on a road with lindens. The bark of these trees I always find very attractive: plain and brown, but yellow underneath. Their flakes look like the dappling of water. Some of the trees reached the tops of the apartment blocks; their branches entangled themselves against the iron balconies.

When I rang the bell, nothing happened for a minute, then I heard Olaf's voice drifting down from one of these balconies. The buzzer was broken, but he was sending his sister to let me in. I waited another minute or two, and then Olaf himself appeared at the front door in what I recognized immediately as his city clothes: a pair of fashionably torn jeans and a thin white linen shirt half unbuttoned. He had the sheepish, almost resentful air of a boy introducing you to his parents.

There was no elevator, which meant we had to walk

the five flights to their apartment. Basketball players hate walking. By this point in the season everything hurt, my knees, my back, the balls of my feet; running at least provided a drug to ease the pain of motion. Steps were particularly painful, and my breathing echoed upwards in the broad, tiled stairwell. To hide the noise of it, I told him that I might want to go to a club later on and mentioned the name Anke had given me.

'Nobody goes there,' he said, 'only middle-aged women.'

We climbed the rest of the stairs in silence. The door at the top was open; Olaf's sister was lying on a pale leather sofa watching television. She shifted, resting her arm over the sofa back, and leaned out inquiringly when we came in. 'Lazy sack,' Olaf said, by way of introduction. And then: 'This is Brigitte.' She was about half his size, with short brown curly hair and a wide mouth, which she twisted into a forced smile. She was also white.

Olaf had never mentioned that he was adopted. His mother came home shortly after with a bag of groceries under one arm. She was a doctor and had the kindly neutral worn-out air of a woman who has spent the day dealing gently with strangers. Katrin, she asked me to call her, taking my hand somewhat limply before unpacking the food and beginning to cook. She looked like her daughter, only thinner and flat-haired. Brigitte, in fact, was in the midst of applying for a residency and had come home to await results. Her house-share had broken up over the summer; she seemed embarrassed about living with her parents. *Wohngemeinschaft* was the word she used, which means a commune, though it sounded more conventional than that.

'I'm the big sister,' she explained at one point, reaching up to pat Olaf's shoulder. 'He's my little brother.' The pleasure she took in his size was touching. Their relations seemed to me collegiate, almost flirtatious.

A large purple painting above one sofa was the only splash of color in the room, aside from the windows. These took up most of a wall and looked out on tall trees, whose branches, heavy and green in that late summer, seemed almost ornate with silence. The gardens below it included a children's playground and a stone ping pong table. A group of teenagers were sitting and smoking on it.

'We used to smoke there, too,' Brigitte said to me, looking down. 'Or rather, I smoked and Olaf tried to play ping pong.'

When the food was ready, his father emerged from his study; he had been at home all along. Herr Schmidt was tall and slender and carried himself well – upright without stiffness. His curly hair was receding and he had let it recede. From time to time he brushed the stray locks behind his ears. 'Olaf gets his height from me,' he joked, 'and his hairline, too.'

'Have you been working?' I asked, after Olaf introduced me as a friend from the team.

'I used to be a lawyer,' he said, 'but I have given up the law. Perhaps I could most pompously describe myself as a radio personality, which means that I work two hours a week and spend the rest of the time reading newspapers and keeping *up to date*. At my age, that is work.'

Over dinner he presided very naturally. I had not talked so much since graduation and had to resist the urge to mention my writing; he was pleased, among other things, to hear where I had gone to university. I didn't want Olaf to think our friendship depended on my curiosity. With Charlie, it didn't matter, but Olaf and I had made a joke of drifting together. We played basketball because it seemed a pleasant way of not doing anything else. In fact, I could tell his career was a source of anxiety to his mother. It didn't seem to her the kind of thing that could 'go anywhere.' Besides, you can't keep it up much beyond thirty. She asked me how long I expected to play basketball, someone with my education.

'I'm afraid that someone with my education,' I said, 'isn't really fit for any kind of profession at all. Apart from teaching, and I don't really want to teach.'

But Katrin couldn't help herself. 'At least you have an education,' she said. 'That's something.'

It was Herr Schmidt who introduced the subject of Olaf's adoption. They were children of the 60s, he confessed, and had all of the wonderful illusions and ideals of their generation. Katrin had very much wanted a child, to give birth to a child, but it seemed to both of them, given the state of the world – well, he supposed I could guess the conclusions they had come to. Now, of course, Germany had a very different problem. Middle-class couples weren't reproducing nearly enough to sustain the economy, which depended more and more on the supply of skilled workers from the former Soviet satellites. The culture was beginning to – he didn't want to say suffer, but perhaps it was kindest to put it this way, to dilute. But Germans, German Germans that is, if he might be forgiven a simplification, were too attached to their lifestyles to give up so many years of it (*twenty* was a conservative estimate, for two children) to a family. 'In this respect, they differ entirely from your countrymen,' he said, 'who consider their children to be a necessary part of the all-American lifestyle.'

When Brigitte was born, they moved to Schwabing – to this same block, as it happens, though to a different apartment. The neighborhood was very mixed at the time: Africans, Turks, and, of course, poor Italians. The building itself was in a terrible state. All of this more or less suited their 'ideals.' But then something began to happen, both to the neighborhood and to their own lives. Most of their friends, it seemed, and not only their friends, but the kinds of people who might have been their friends, the kinds of people, in fact, who became their friends, had had similar ideals. Together, they moved up in the world.

Katrin began earning as a consultant; his law practice found its feet. The wonderful cooperatives, which they had set up to foster a sense of community, did their jobs too well. They became exclusive. Property values climbed and the poor moved out. Katrin and he had feared that Brigitte would grow up in the ignorance of privilege. She wanted another child, but they really couldn't justify such an addition. To have one may be a right, but two seemed an indulgent luxury. That's how they thought at the time.

Olaf was a happy compromise. Katrin had been volunteering in a community center for African immigrants, and one of the case workers put her in touch with an adoption agency connected to the Ivory Coast. That's where Olaf was born; they had been encouraging him lately to seek out his birth-father.

'You have been encouraging him,' Katrin said.

I asked Brigitte if her parents' plan had worked, if she had grown up in the 'ignorance of privilege.'

'As far as that goes,' she said, 'privilege in the 80s mattered much less than being cool. And there was nothing cooler than having a black kid brother.'

'That's not true.' Olaf had looked up at last. 'Being black was only cool in gym class. The rest of the time they called me names. And before I got too big for them, they did worse; I was always getting into fights.'

Brigitte put her hand on his wrist, in careless sympathy. 'You're right,' she said, 'I had forgotten. They called me names, too, though mostly they told dirty jokes about Katrin. In fact, that's how I learned about sex: from the jokes that nasty boys made up about my mother.'

'Oh oh,' Herr Schmidt broke in, from sheer good humor. This sort of talk amused and pleased him.

'When did you get to be too big?' I asked.

'By my fourteenth birthday,' Olaf said, 'I was almost two meters long and weighed a hundred kilo. I could buy beer from a supermarket. When you can buy beer, everybody wants to be your friend.'

Katrin cleared our plates away and Herr Schmidt sat back in his chair. 'What people never understand,' he said, 'is that prejudice is practical. People become tolerant when it's no longer in their interest to be racist. The trouble with immigration is that it produces a society in which a number of minority groups have an interest in scoring off each other: it's really nothing more than the guild system brought up to date. The middle classes are always tolerant because it's always in their interest to be so. Immigration brings them cheap labor and good food. Of course, all of these discussions in Germany are complicated by the question nobody asks: what did your father do in the war?'

'That's not true,' Olaf said again. 'It's complicated by sports, too. In sports, being black is like a style, but in the rest of life, it's just a fact.'

His father stood up to prepare himself an espresso from one of those bright monotone Italian coffee makers that look like a child's toy. Like a toy, too, it made a burst of ugly noise. I guessed this was his particular role in the kitchen, the maker of coffee, and he offered each of us a shot. Only Brigitte accepted. When he was finished he continued standing, enjoying the freedom of thinking on his feet with a cup in his hand. 'That's because in sports,' he said, 'it's to the advantage of white children to play with their black friends – if they want to . . .' But he had seen where his own argument was going and hesitated for the first time.

Olaf completed his thought. 'If they want to win?'

'That's just fascism,' Brigitte broke in – one of her favorite words. 'Whites always say blacks are better at sports, so that they can claim to be better at other things. *That's* where their self-interest lies.'

'No,' Olaf said. 'It's not in their self-interest, at least as far as basketball goes. Being black is just a style in sports, a very popular style. If you have two players, one white and one black, the black one will always have an advantage with the coach, because of his style, even if the white player is just as good or even better.'

'Are you thinking of Hadnot?' I asked. 'Hadnot and Charlie.'

'I wasn't thinking of them, but they're a good example.'

What he was thinking of involved him in a longer story, in which Katrin took a particular interest. She was one of those women in whom tiredness brings out, like opening buds, her worries; and she was tired that night and struggling to hide it. For whatever reason, Olaf had remained a source of guilt and concern to her. The conversation about race had been making her uncomfortable, but she was glad when her son took the floor.

A few years ago, he told me, he had accepted a scholarship at a college in San Francisco. To play basketball.

He was beginning to get bored of club sports and had half a mind to study medicine, like his sister. The family had once made a holiday to Yellowstone, his only visit to the United States. San Francisco seemed a little like Munich. Not too big or too small; very hip, but quite rich, too, and safe and pleasant.

When he got there, his coach arranged for a tutor to help him. The assistant manager gave him a list of professors who were known to be sympathetic to the basketball team. Few of the players had any kind of academic ambitions. One of the big men, a white guy, as it happens, was majoring in pre-med, and Olaf became friendly with him, which was actively discouraged.

'By the coach?' I asked.

'Not just by the coach, even if he was behind it. By the other players, by the black players. It wasn't what they said; it was what they made me feel. That we should stick together. But in America, I didn't feel very black. It was just one fact about me, not the whole story. I don't know what the coach had to do with it, but he didn't like the idea of me studying medicine. It would take up too much time. He said it as if he thought I should be pleased, that he had such ambitions for me, that he wanted me to play from the start. I told him I had even bigger ambitions – that I wanted to become a doctor. He decided pretty soon I was a problem character. For the rest of the guys, it was the most important thing in the world to play college basketball. But I showed him some things were more important to me.'

He paused for a minute to eat, as if that were the end of the story. So I pressed him; for some reason the job was left to me.

By the time the season started, his friend, whose name was Wally Thrupp, was in the doghouse with him – that was Coach Hatton's word. Wally hardly ever got off the bench. It was his senior year; he hoped to play for a club in France, where his family spent their summer holidays. He asked Olaf lots of questions about European basketball. Wally took his benching quietly for a few games, then on Monday morning he went up to Coach Hatton before practice and told him he was going to sue him for racial discrimination if he didn't play the next week. Hatton left him on the bench, and Wally sued. His father was a big-shot lawyer in Berkeley. The story made it into all the papers: it was the first time a white player had accused a white coach of discrimination. Hatton, it turned out, had said a few stupid things in the heat of the moment, and there were fans in the front rows (all of them white) who were willing to give evidence for Wally.

Olaf was asked to testify, not only on the subject of these remarks but about the overall atmosphere of Hatton's locker room. This put him in a tough spot. Most of the team had rallied around their coach, who was well-liked across campus and admired in the media as an old-school disciplinarian with a talent for getting his players to graduate. The *San Francisco Chronicle* ran a big feature on Wally Thrupp, which painted him as the spoilt child of privilege, trying to win in a court of law the recognition he had failed to earn on the basketball court. Olaf was caught in the middle. If he refused to testify, he had a chance to salvage his relations with the coach and the rest of the team; he might be able to start over. Wally, on the other hand, was his only friend in the locker room, and one of the few he had made on campus since arriving in September.

His girlfriend, to whom he was engaged, had taken a shine to Olaf. The three of them used to have a regular pasta date before game days, to load up on carbs. She had promised to set him up with one of her sorority sisters.

Olaf, though he never admitted as much, must have been terribly lonely – for female company as much as anything else. What he said was this: that the white girls on campus were scared of him for being big and black, and the black girls thought of him simply as a foreigner. In Germany, he had always been the black son of a white family – there never seemed to be a contradiction in that. But in America, he was neither white nor black; he was nothing. The Hatton case gave him a chance to take sides, but the fact was, the coach *had* said what Wally claimed he had said. It was a simple question of telling the truth.

'Most of the coaches I know,' I said, 'shout things like *Get that white boy on the bench*, but they would play him, too, if he deserved it.'

'If he deserved it, maybe. But sometimes it is hard to deserve something in the wrong situation.'

'So what did you do? What did you say to the lawyers?'

He hesitated a moment, and I wondered if he was leaving something out. 'It was an impossible situation (*unmöglich*). I did the only thing I could do. I went home at Christmas and didn't come back.'

'I think you were homesick, darling,' Katrin said.

'No.' And then, surprisingly: 'Sometimes you have to stand up for what you think is right.'

'It was hard for you; your English wasn't very good.'

But Olaf ignored her. 'When Charlie came, he made a few comments, about the brothers, all of that, which I think he considered a great compliment, as if every black man secretly wants to be American. But I put a stop to it, and he hasn't forgiven me.'

'That doesn't sound like Charlie to me,' I said. 'He's come a long way in life, too.'

The phrase gave Katrin another excuse to mother her son. 'You were very young; it was a long way to go for someone so young. I think you might find it easier now.'

'You have to be black to understand.'

There wasn't much we could say to this, so I tried joking: 'I suppose Henkel thinks you're a problem character, too.'

'No, you're the problem character,' he said. 'Everyone can see that you're in it for yourself.'

He never got the chance to say what he meant by that. The oven bell rang, and Katrin stood up to retrieve dessert, a sort of casserole made of applesauce, jam and breadcrumbs, which we ate with cream.

* * *

It was only later, in the long months ahead, that I learned what Olaf had been keeping back – for the sake of his parents, perhaps, or simply out of shame. We spent so much time together, empty time, on buses and bleachers, between games. There was nothing to fill it but conversation: boasts, mostly, and a few confessions.

Something had happened between Wally and him. As the season wore on and the tensions in the locker room mounted, something unpleasant had happened, though Olaf refused to tell me exactly what. I guessed that it had to do with the fiancée, that there had been either an improper approach or a jealous accusation, or a little of both. Maybe one of the sorority sisters was involved. In any case, Wally had accused him in terms he must later have regretted himself. There's nothing that brings out, in your average respectable white American male, the racial feeling quicker than sexual jealousy. Afterwards, Olaf's situation really had become 'impossible.' There was no side he could decently take. Thrupp and the university eventually settled out of court, but by that point Olaf was long gone.

The whole episode, which took up from start to finish no more than a half-year of his life, had become a sort of bruise in his memory, which he couldn't leave alone. But the real source of his regret surprised me. Olaf kept coming back to the fact that Hatton had promised him, before the season went sour, a significant role. He had passed up the chance to test himself against America's best. What he wanted to learn from me was whether, at

85

the age of twenty-five, he was too old to play college basketball; whether the incident might still count against him, even after all this time; whether I had any connections among American college coaches. Olaf had read about an Israeli player who came to the States after doing a stint in the army, by which point he was already in his late twenties. Even so, he had a wonderful college career. Perhaps, Olaf wondered, Jewish coaches were more accustomed to taking mature players because of the military service requirements in Israel.

Meanwhile, he was looking for a way out of small-time club basketball; maybe he could still go to med school. He didn't suppose Landshut would ever make it to the first division, which entailed a very different lifestyle: more money and travel, the European super league, etc. Once, when he was nineteen, Olaf had played for a first division club. Coach Hatton discovered him by watching a game on TV while on holiday in Spain. A blind piece of good luck. At the time he thought, that's it. Everything is beginning. But here he was, back again where he had started. Nothing had changed, except that he had gotten older, and his store of useful years (there are about ten of them for a basketball player) was reduced by half.

None of this came out at dinner. Brigitte rose first. She was meeting a friend on the other side of town and promised to do the washing up when she got home. She gave Olaf a look; he had been invited along, too. Katrin offered me the spare room in case I wanted to stay over.

86

She was sure Olaf wouldn't mind sleeping on the couch. I thanked her but said I had already made plans to see someone and couldn't be sure where the evening would end up. A line that provoked, unintentionally, a ripple of polite amusement. But by the time I made it down the five flights of stairs and into the street, I felt much too tired and sleepy with food to do anything more than catch the last train home – I never made it to Anke's club for middle-aged ladies.

11

Monday morning I showed my face early at the gym and found Bo Hadnot and Willi Darmstadt warming up. And felt a little jealous – that he had recruited the unshaved high school kid to work out with him. Also, I figured Hadnot could teach me something about how to shoot.

Darmstadt was feeding him baseline jumpers, just inside the three-point line. They always had two balls on the go, but even so Hadnot knocked them down faster than Willi could fetch them. There was the sound of him catching the ball; then the sound of his feet touching ground; and the sound of the ball going in. Darmstadt scrambling around to keep up. It was like watching a kid trying to keep dry in the rain. The rest of our shots seemed to be governed by luck or chance: we were two out of four, three out of five shooters. Hadnot on his own was nine out of ten.

The real surprise was when he *did* miss. It happened so rarely that you couldn't help but read into it to some strange and tiny flaw in the machine. After each miss, a few more misses, while the machine reset itself; and then the steady return of his natural rhythm. Boom boom boom. There's something about the alignment of eye, hand, elbow and foot that resists being bent into a straight line. Hadnot had it bent pretty good. For the rest of the year, he spent about a half hour before practice and a half hour after it working on his jumper, and some of the guys used to show up early just to watch him.

Karl was one of them. He had got his first taste of what might be expected of him in his great career, the work-rate necessary – and didn't shy from it. By Wednesday he had asked me to stay back fifteen minutes before hitting the showers. He wanted to improve his mid-range game and needed someone to set him up. 'We can take it in turns,' he said. So I agreed.

Not that I liked Karl. Many years after all this was over, I was eating ice cream at a pavement café with my wife and baby daughter. A girl in a red summer dress was eating ice cream at the next table and being chatted up by a young man in a thin striped woolen shirt and fashionable sandals, and I suddenly thought of Karl. The girl had been upset by something, and the young man commiserated, with great sweetness, while eating up spoonfuls of her ice cream. His sympathy seemed only a piece in the general arrangement of his hair and the expensive disfigurement of his jeans and the casual untidiness of his footwear. I don't mean to say that he seemed insincere – he certainly seemed in earnest about his clothes. It's just that he didn't make any distinction between his sympathies and his looks.

Karl, during one of these sessions, told me that he played basketball because he was good at it. 'This is why

I do most things,' he said. A perfectly sensible reason for playing basketball, but it's not why Hadnot played, and it's not why I played. I wanted to see him doubt himself. He was one of those guys whose self-confidence is as natural and obtrusive as a big chin.

Hadnot, at least, made him worry a little. Once, while the American was shooting, Karl wandered over to Darmstadt to help him feed the balls back out. After a while, he pushed the kid aside and took over, with a broad smile on his face and a kind of showy humility: he bent his full weight into the chest pass back. Hadnot kept shooting. I don't think he even looked down. After a minute or two, Karl got bored and (it might have been on a whim) jumped up and caught the ball over the mouth of the basket. Hadnot waited for him to pass it back, patiently, but without any expression of amusement. On his next shot, Karl did the same: lifted a long arm skywards and plucked the ball from the air one-handed. He was laughing by this point, he wanted everyone to share in the joke. Most of us couldn't help smiling with him. Hadnot walked off to the showers.

In the evening scrimmage, after a hard screen, Karl switched out on Hadnot at the top of the key, and the older man, without skipping a beat, launched the ball two-handed into his face. They were standing about three feet apart. The ball caught Karl in the nose, and he bent down at once to catch his breath. When he stood back up he had a handful of blood beginning to drip through his fingers. Hadnot, by this point, had retrieved the basketball and offered to open play.

It was our ball, he said; Karl had touched it last.

Coach Henkel sent Karl to the showers to get cleaned up and, being a man down, stepped in himself to take his place. For the rest of the afternoon, Henkel and Hadnot went at it like cats, and nobody else dared to say a word till it was over. Even Karl kept quiet. He sat on the bench holding an icepack to his empurpled cheek. His eye had the white, glazed look of an afternoon headache.

Henkel astonished everyone. Sweating, pot-bellied, two years into retirement, he controlled the flow of play and snatched rebounds over the heads of men a foot taller and half his age. Over me as well. When he sat down again it was because he was too tired to stand up. His moustache hung dripping over the rim of his mouth. Furious during the game, he remained for several minutes afterwards almost too angry to speak, red in the face, which gave him an air of disgust, as if he thought, you bums. Even Olaf was impressed. Only Hadnot stood up to him; they almost came to blows.

Afterwards, in the shower, I could still see Karl's blood darkening the grouting in the floor; some of it washed over the tiles. 'When something isn't fair,' Olaf said to me, 'you get anger on all sides. Even you were angry. What happens when the coach loses control of his team. A bad business. Bo wants to prove he deserves to start, which he does. Henkel wants to save face. I'm glad you won.'

In the morning we learned that Hadnot had broken Karl's cheekbone. He spent the rest of the month wearing one of those see-through plastic masks whenever he stepped on court. But I'll give Karl credit: all he did by way of revenge was play hard.

The truth is, Hadnot was out of shape. Ballplayers get one good game after a layoff, and Bo had had his game; but for the rest of the month, he struggled to find his wind. It's one thing to make nine out of ten in the cool of the morning with fresh legs and a willing lackey feeding you the ball. It's another thing to do it with sweat in your eyes and your legs shot and a kid with a seven-foot wingspan crowding your release. It pissed Hadnot off, I'm sure, that Karl had made a joke of his warm-up routine, but mostly he was mad that Karl was beating him to the ball, beating him off the dribble, putting him off his shot, and scoring at will. Karl's real sin was being better, and Hadnot may have been embarrassed by the fact that most of us knew it.

We weren't a close-knit locker room and didn't have the makings of one, but if there was a subject we could gossip about, Hadnot and Karl was it. Somehow it had become a question of taking sides. Charlie liked to argue that you can't teach what Karl had, and if you didn't have it, none of the other things you *could* teach counted for shit. He lumped himself, with Hadnot, among the mass of mediocrity whose abilities were of the acquired kind. Plotzke wouldn't hear it. His antipathy to Karl was partly and mysteriously German, class-related, and inexplicable to outsiders, but the sum of it was simple and obvious enough. Karl was the golden boy; Plotzke was the smart, oversized butt of children's jokes. Hadnot, though shorter and better-looking, bore a kind of fraternal resemblance to the man Charlie called 'Frankenstein.' They both seemed to be badly, almost painfully put together. Plotzke was getting old, too, in basketball terms; they had begun the rapid and long decline that sets in at thirty.

Most of us had a stake in believing that Hadnot's brand of perfected and bloody-minded mediocrity would trump Karl's talent in the end. Milo, for example, used to watch Hadnot warm up with an almost religious attention: if he had any hope of making it up the basketball foodchain, it was because *that* kind of dedication paid off. Yet people don't always believe what their self-interest tells them to. Olaf had more raw ability than anybody on the team barring Karl. But he didn't like Karl, and he did like Hadnot, and when their names came up in the pockets of gossip that develop in any community of rivals, he used to promise, with a mocking appropriation of Charlie's slang, 'That Karl would get *his*.' Others are charmed by talent as people are charmed by money. They just like to see it being used. Thomas Arnold was one of these. If Karl had a friend on the team, it was the pale-faced, fair-haired music student, who was always offering, to anyone who would talk to him, one of his selection of cream-biscuits that he carried in his sports kit. Both of them, in an odd way, cared less about basketball than the rest of us. One, because he wasn't much good at it; and the other, because he was too good.

Henkel was harder to read. Professionally, he had backed Karl. I liked him and trusted that his conscience, in the final analysis, would override his obvious ambition, but he must have realized the chance Karl offered him – to make it out of the bush-leagues on the young man's coat-tails. I didn't know this at the time, but the scouts were about to swarm over us like ants at a picnic. Anybody who wanted to talk to Karl would have to talk to his coach first. The kid was just an oversized visiting-card with Henkel's name on it. I have no doubt that he planned to slip it into the Rolodexes of a dozen NBA general managers. If Karl liked him well enough (and why not?), he might insist, if only for comfort's sake, on taking his old coach with him. Stranger things had happened.

As Olaf pointed out to me, Henkel thought of himself as a coach's coach. He had big ideas but needed big-time players to work them out. 'Not you or me, little one.'

'But he is right,' I said. 'Karl is already a more dangerous player.'

Whether I believed that or not, I don't know. Conversation for us was also a form of competition. It hadn't taken me long to learn that every time you open your mouth on a basketball team, you should have something to argue or prove. Which was just what I admired about Hadnot: the way he insisted on his superiority. All week long, game after game, he talked Karl down. 'This kid is nothing but a bully, nothing but a photo-opportunity.' Etc. In spite of the fact that he was almost a foot shorter; could only shamble along in loafers after playing, because of stiffness; was ten years older. And whenever the plain facts of what was happening on court contradicted him, he repeated, 'That's all right, that's all right. We're just getting started here.'

On the Friday before our season opener, I ran into Hadnot for the first time outside the confines of the Sports Halle. More than a few of my free afternoons I spent fixing up my apartment, buying pots and pans from the High Street, bookshelves, a rug, and it often surprised me how rarely I bumped into my 'colleagues.' It's not a big town; we were easy to spot.

I think most of them spent their days resting, lying back on the job-lot two-seater couches provided by management, watching videos, playing video games. Twisting the blinds until the sun went away. Microwaving frozen food. But that Friday I saw Hadnot with his arms full outside the Spar near the bottom of my hill – our local market. Spar leaves used fruit-boxes by the cart-rack and customers can take them instead of plastic bags. He was carrying one of these, with a bag of Kinderschokolade and a German brand of ice cream sandwiches resting on top. I made a joke about fueling up for the big game, but he had been staring at some long-haired skinny kid, who was horsing around on a skateboard against the curb. Hadnot said something like, 'I had my day with that,' and I wondered if he meant the skateboard or the kid's t-shirt, which advertised the Nine Inch Nails.

'You look more like someone who used to be the kid who beat that kid up.'

Then the boy came up to me and requested my auto-graph. It surprised me and I laughed, and pointed at Hadnot and said, 'His, his' – my German sometimes comes slowly when I'm surprised. 'You should get his autograph. Have you seen him shoot?'

But the boy didn't move. He was holding out one of the little grey notebooks that are standard issue in the schools, and a pen. I saw pages of messy numbers in it that looked like algebra homework and signed the first page underneath his own name, which he had dutifully inscribed. 'You don't want me,' I kept repeating, worried that Hadnot might be offended when the boy pushed off on his skateboard – down the hill, with a happy air, as if released from supervision.

In fact, Hadnot said to me, 'When they ask for your autograph, just sign. They don't care who you are. They want you to be the big man.'

His apartment took him closer into town, away from mine, but I followed him anyway. I liked being seen with him and mentioned the farms that lay just the other side of the hill: a string of hamlets descending into the valley. I had got in the habit, I said, of bicycling through them on my free days, knocking on the farmers' doors and buying whatever they had to sell that would fit into the basket on my bike. I added, trying my luck, 'You should come along some time.'

At first, he didn't answer me, but just before we passed under the arch of the abandoned tracks (at which point I had really decided to turn back), he asked if I meant to go Sunday afternoon. He had his daughter for the day – the day after our first game, that is – and she might like to see some of those farms. The truth was, he added, he didn't speak much German; she was almost three years old and didn't speak much English. They got along fine but ran out of things to say to each other. We had stopped before the shadow of the railway bridge. 'I guess you could help me out,' he said.

12

I could tell that Henkel didn't think we were ready. He had promised us the night off, to let us rest, but changed his mind after the morning session. So we spent the early evening walking through our sets in street clothes. This was followed by a compulsory appearance at what Henkel called the team *sauna* – a low dank room carved out of the steam tunnels, with rubber flooring and an atmosphere that smelt oppressively of peeling paint.

The sauna itself was nothing more than a kind of broad porcelain urinal set into the floor. A trickle of lukewarm water ran along the basin of it, which could be augmented by a single black hose. Olaf refused to undress. He stooped under the low underground ceiling with his gym bag strapped across his back and watched us disdainfully.

'Markovits, Markovits,' he said, as I dipped a skinny foot into the water, 'Du bist auch so einer.' *You're as bad as they are.*

The rest of us settled back more or less uncomfortably – the porcelain ribs dug into our rear-ends, already sore from running. Henkel himself undressed in short quick movements. His little pot-belly, tight as a drum, emerged from his training-top. He was anxious to sit between

Karl and Charlie, who had claimed the one hose for himself. From time to time he draped its loop of tepid water over Henkel and Karl, and I noticed with interest a strange little moment when the water rested on the younger man's private parts.

Nobody said anything, but Hadnot used the brief awkwardness to take the hose away. Closing his eyes, he ducked his wet head under its gentle pressure, and I remembered something that Olaf had once said to me: that Charlie was gay. Needless to say, I never got a turn with the hose.

I slept very badly that night. Around eleven o'clock, I dropped off briefly with the television on. NBC Europe used to broadcast the *Tonight Show with Jay Leno* at two-hour intervals throughout the night, and when I woke up, shortly after one, I found myself in the middle of the same show. A disconcerting experience; I was suddenly, unhappily awake. By morning I felt almost ghostly with insomnia – pale enough for the sun to shine through me. Walking down to the gym, at two on a bright afternoon, I pressed my fingers to squeeze the cold out of them.

The Sports Halle showed already the little agitations of a match-day. A travel coach had parked at an angle in the drive; two catering vans waited in the loading bay. A few fans, even, had begun to trickle in. Mostly young boys in oversized NBA jerseys, ball in hand, who hoped to sneak a few shots on court before the players came out. Their fathers, with newspapers. I jogged up the steps to work off a sudden anxious rush of blood.

That first hour, before a game, is like the hour before take off – a non-hour, it rests in the shade of the event. You might as well not exist. In fact, the passage of time seems to involve a kind of coming to life: you emerge only at the end with your wits about you.

I discovered Hadnot in the locker room, flat on his belly, lying on a towel on one of the central benches. The fat man from the front office was winding a roll of tape around his ankles. Almost tenderly, with great concentration. I had noticed him vaguely before, a slightly pathetic figure we all called Russell. Officious, stubborn, useful: he wore a sharp fist of keys on a belt loop and guarded tightly the supply of energy drinks in the medicine cupboard. His face had the soft asymmetries of mental illness.

Olaf had told me the secret of his nickname. A few years before a sales rep from a sporting goods store had left the team a bagful of goodies to distribute amongst themselves. XXX jerseys, sweatpants, windcheaters, designed to fit obese young men and not the tall narrow frames of athletes. None of the players wanted them, so they gave them to the overweight assistant from custodial, whom they named, in fact, after the logo on the sportswear: Russell Athletics.

We watched him now, slowly rolling the strips of white adhesive around the arch of Hadnot's bruised feet, across the knob of bone above the ankle, leaving bare only his heel and toes. There was something soothing about the little variations required, the gradual advance of tape on flesh; something disturbing, too. Russell had babyish pink hands and cheeks and a large head of gingery hair, combed back. It was beginning to thin on top; he looked like a child, preserved. Even the red bristle of moustache above his lip, carefully trimmed, suggested somehow a mother's anxiety to make her son presentable. He sat straddling the bench at Hadnot's feet, as if he had taken possession of them. Bo lay with his head turned aside and his eyes closed.

I caught a look of something like disgust in Olaf's face and felt ashamed. Yet we continued to sit there with our feet in unlaced hightops – Olaf Schmidt, Axel Plotzke, Michel Krahm, Thomas Arnold and I – until Henkel came in pushing a rack of balls.

Some of the boys who had made it on court were shooting desultory five-footers as we filed in. Quick anxious shots; they were waiting to be told, sit down. The irregular sound of basketballs: a noise like a workman's hammer on a bright suburban morning, beginning and beginning again, suggesting at the same time idleness and preoccupation. Plotzke shooed them away, but the boys returned, bearing pens and programs, and from time to time we stood aside to sign the small black-and-white photos of ourselves inside them. They didn't want to talk, they just wanted us to sign, but even so I felt powerfully for a second the distance I had come since childhood and saw myself through their eyes: a tall silent stranger.

Nobody could find Milo (Darmstadt had seen him arrive almost an hour before), so Henkel sent me out to look for him. I discovered him in one of the bathroom stalls, sitting on the pot with the lid down, already in uniform. He was rocking back and forth with his hands over a pair of earphones and his elbows on his knees, as if he were praying. The bass-line had led me to him; I could hear it in my ribs.

I knew Milo wanted to win more than I did, but I didn't know that wanting to win looked like this: angry, almost crazy. His eyes were closed and he didn't look up when I pushed open the stall door. Twice I called his name, to let him know we were warming up, then I tapped against one of the earpieces. At first, he didn't recognize me – his eyes had the muddy, unreflective quality of an addict's. Then he nodded and lowered the headset again and I left him.

The stands had filled by the time I came back on court and a few men in overalls were preparing something under one of the baskets. Our opponents had arrived from Nürnberg; they looked more or less like us. Too tall, a little awkward, mostly pale. They loped through their lay-up lines and let the ball, its odd bounces and lazy getaways, force them to stretch their legs.

I recognized one of the guys from an earlier try-out, a stocky two-guard named Torsten – technically sound, hardworking, a step slow. He saw me, too, and we drifted together at center court.

'I'm glad you found a job,' he said.

We had shared a bed one night in Paderborn, a first division club we passed through in early summer. The management had been too tight to give the players their own rooms. Torsten slept on his back with his mouth wide open, noiselessly, and I spent much of the night watching him.

'I thought they would make you an offer on the spot,' he continued. 'There was a rumor that you wanted a lot of money.'

'I played badly the next day in Odenthal. I think the word got back to them. One of those days I couldn't find the end of my leg.'

'The main thing is to have a job, to play. It's terrible, isn't it, all this waiting around. We have been fighting like cats in practice.'

'Are you any good?'

'One or two of us. The fat one can't be moved from under the basket, not with a truck. And the little Russian is very clever. But most of us are just part-timers. We play when our wives let us. Not so hard: the wives don't much want us around.'

His answer put me in mind of something else he once said. After my sleepless night, I showered early and came down before him to breakfast, then decided to wait. It was lonely enough just sitting amidst the bright indifferent glitter of the hotel tables. I wondered whether anything like intimacy would grow out of the close quarters in which we had spent the night. Perhaps it had. What he told me, over the cheese and sliced meats, probably seemed to him embarrassingly confessional. At least, it did the work of his life's story. He listed all the clubs he had played for, including a high school team in New Mexico, where he had done a year's exchange.

After breakfast we waited outside the hotel, among the flowerbeds and parked cars, for the team van to bring us to the station. A hot cloudy July morning that smelt of gas fumes and sprinkler systems. I asked him where he hoped to end up.

'It doesn't matter to me,' he said. 'I will never be very good, but if I work hard, if I don't get hurt, if I eat well, in the off-season, too, and train very hard all summer, I can be a useful addition to a second division club with not much money.' He never mentioned anything about a wife.

'What are those men doing?' I said at last, pointing to the crew in overalls.

'Getting the fireworks ready.'

The season was launched in a burst of soft flares that rose against the metal rafters and blew up in a shower of sparks that settled and turned grey and disappeared. Everyone stood up to cheer – about two hundred locals, bunched irregularly on the pine bleachers rolled out from one of the walls. I turned to count them, the pink thumbprints of a crowd in rows. The face that kept appearing before me was my father's. He had watched from the stands at dozens of my high school games, waiting for the coach to send me in. I wanted him to see me now: standing in uniform with my hands clasped behind my back, as if a photographer had lined us up to take our picture.

Anke had not come; it was almost a relief. After the show, two boys pushed wide brooms between the lines to collect the scattered shells. Then the brief, almost ceremonial gathering at mid-court. Ten men waiting, a sharp whistle. Karl jumped center for us. His heart must have been racing like mine: the inaugural act of his professional career was to tip the ball six rows into the crowd. Torsten put it in play, and the first five minutes of the game passed in a drift of smoke. I sat on the bench next to Hadnot, who was quietly, intensely angry.

By the time the smoke cleared, we were down ten points. Henkel had also warned us about the 'little Russian,' a guard named Jurkovich, with a quick, flat-footed, left-handed release. Balding, with a drinker's vague beard just curling over his lips. He must have been thirty-five: Nürnberg was one of his stops on the way down.

Our league was full of guys like Jurkovich, trading on the difference between talent and youth. They played out their careers in small market towns a medium-haul plane flight from their wives and kids – until their knees finally gave way, and they moved into management or went home and entered whatever business their brothers-in-law had built up while they were shooting hoops. Jurkovich had made it to the C squad of the Russian under-18 world championship team in 1986, the one that didn't get to travel. That was the kind of story people told about him – that was the level he might once have aspired to. He spent a few years in the 90s playing for Livorno in Serie A, and when they dropped down, he began to bounce around second-tier teams in Europe till he ended up here. Nürnberg probably paid him ten thousand marks a month during the season, most of which he sent home; and Olaf didn't suppose he practiced with the team more than twice a week.

Still, whatever he had left was too good for us. Milo was guarding him, and maybe this is the time to say a short word about him. He had beaten me to the two spot, which was enough to make me dislike him. I had other reasons: there was something ugly and thick-skinned about him, in a physical sense, too. Bruised lips, a crooked nose. He smoked twenty a day, ostentatiously, and made a point of winning every drill, no matter how meaningless. He had the fastest hundred-meter time on the team. I know, Henkel measured us. After his sprint was over, he trotted to the side of the sandy track and pulled a pack of Marlboros from his gym bag. Then he stood next to Henkel smoking and watching the other times come in.

If he didn't win, he complained, first angrily, and finally in a childish pout: people were always trying to take him down; they cheated. (Once it was true: I skipped ten feet on a suicide and beat him to the base-line. No one else noticed.) In spite of all this, Milo charmed me. I hadn't known anyone like him since junior high: a real operator, a bull-shitter, a rope-puller, a brown-noser, a tough guy.

He ended up in Germany after his Zagreb youth team toured Bavaria, and one of the club coaches offered him an apartment, a car and a first-string job. His grandfather, I believe, was German; at least, he had a German passport. I think it suited him, too, moving out of home, making his way as a stranger. His charms are of the kind that run their course – people grow tired of Milo.

I remember the first real conversation I had with him. He was rating various European countries, most of them former Soviet satellites, according to the prettiness of their women and the brutality of their police. Bulgaria had the best and worst of both. A typical underhand boast: about his virility, his sexual experience, his rebelliousness, his knowledge of the world. I once stood three lines away from him at our local bank and overheard something of his conversation with the teller. There was a problem with his checkbook. He was trying to explain to the woman behind the glass partition that he had changed his legal name a few years ago. Just his last name, Moritz; I couldn't hear from *what*. It seemed an odd, unhappy sort of thing for a young man to do and made me distrust everything else I knew about him.

Except for what I had learned first hand: how much he wanted to win, how much it mattered to him. When I saw him in the bathroom stall, *davening* with the music loud in his ears, I supposed that it was some kind of focusing technique. That he knew what he was doing. But he came out to play all hopped up.

His first shot, from the top of the key, hit the back of the rim hard and bounced over the board. He twitched his head strangely against his neck, as if someone had slapped him. Jurkovich figured him out soon enough. Milo had at least ten years on him, five inches, and a good half step; he was too quick, in fact, and tried to chase his man around every pick. Nürnberg liked to run high screens for Jurkovich with their four and five spots. The first time down, he curled very hard off the shoulder and pulled up suddenly to shoot. Milo ploughed into him from behind, the ball dropped in, and Jurkovich hit the foul-shot, too.

But Milo wouldn't learn: it was a point of pride with him, to fight through screens. The next time down, Jurkovich followed the curl into the lane and put up a little lefty floater that dropped through the net like a tired sigh. Milo pulled Plotzke aside and began to berate him in front of the visiting bench – the season was hardly a minute old.

'Step out, step out,' he said, 'you fucking lump.' And then, a curious phrase: 'I won't take that on myself.' He meant, that second basket.

Plotzke said what he always said, 'OK, OK,' and turned his high shoulders, lowered his head, and ran down court. Like a man in a three-legged race, trying to pull his son along.

'Calm down,' Henkel shouted from the sidelines, and

Milo swung suddenly around to find his voice. 'Look at me. Look at me,' Henkel said. But it was no good; Milo stared, but could take nothing in. I thought it strangely sad that his great desire to win was not helpful to him, that it was getting in his way.

Karl also seemed to feel the strain of an opening night. Nürnberg had decided to play him big, with a thirty-something beer-bellied forward named Hans Muller – an American, as it happens, a Berkeley grad, who had let himself go but knew what to do with his weight. Whenever Karl cut inside, he ran into Hans's belly, which seemed to have a life of its own. Once, trying to establish position on the block, Karl ended up at the three-point line with his hands in the air and an expression of righteous bewilderment on his face.

After a while he gave up pushing and stuck to his jumpshot. Hans had a tangle of blond hair, probably dyed, that fell to his shoulders. He shook it out sometimes like a dog coming out of water, especially when Karl was shooting. I don't know if it put him off or not. His motion, so classic and simple, never strayed from the true, but he couldn't find the range. He missed long, he missed short, and picked up two fouls trying to climb over Hans's back for the rebounds. There was a new drug in his system he had to calculate for. The buzz of the real thing.

Hadnot, meanwhile, kept up in a steady undertone, 'Now's the time, coach, put me in. Put me in.' But the minutes passed.

Henkel had the air, both worried and detached, of a man conducting an experiment. Or he was just too proud to admit his mistake. Olaf, at least, managed to clean up a few of the rebounds, and Charlie switched on to Jurkovich. The first time Torsten tried to set a high screen, Charlie pretended not to see him and caught him in the balls with a knee. After that, the spaces opened up a little. At the other end, Hans had pushed Karl so far out of the key that the lane was clear, and Charlie squeezed through for a couple lay-ups and short feeds. If it weren't for him, Nürnberg might have buried us by halftime.

As it was, we struggled to stay within ten, and every time Milo missed a shot my palms began to sweat, and I thought, this is it. Me next. The crowd had begun to stomp their feet in a slow swelling rhythm. Hadnot puffed on his hands to keep them warm and clapped flat-fingered in between, as if to say, let's go. And then Henkel gave me a tap on the head, gentle as a benediction, and sent the two of us in.

Milo and Karl came off. I called over to Milo, 'Who you got? Who you got?' But he didn't answer, and by the time I made it down court, Torsten had snuck along the baseline and knocked down an eighteen-footer. I turned to sprint the other way. Charlie pushed the ball hard and pulled up in the lane for a roller that touched the front of the rim, the back of the rim, the backboard glass, and the little isthmus of iron between, before dropping. I turned and ran again. At the other end, Torsten set a pick for Jurkovich and I switched out and chased him baseline past three more screens, before he cut back and took a pass at the top of the key. I was screaming at him with my arms raised as he released. Jurkovich missed long for once, and the ball came out to Hadnot at the elbow who whipped a pass to me going the other way – I was almost at half court.

Torsten was the only one back, but I could hardly see by this point. A dark edge, like a frame or a curtain, had begun to encroach on my vision, and I could feel the blood in my ear beating the drum in waves. Three long dribbles took me to the foul line, while Torsten gave ground before me. When he stopped, I shot. It was the only thing I could think of, and I felt a surge of relief as the ball touched rim before caroming strangely and out of bounds. Close enough. Henkel sent Karl in to replace me, and I sat down again and tried to breathe.

'Calm down,' coach said to me, and I remember thinking he had told Milo the same thing.

It seemed strange that the fluid haphazard passage of events had frozen so quickly into something unchangeable; that the ball would always bounce against the inside of the rim, away and out of bounds, at that peculiar angle. That it would never go in.

My head slowly cleared, and from the vantage of the bench the rest of the game emerged into focus. Ten men, moving in spurts, in groups of two and three, and dividing a ball amongst themselves.

I decided to follow Hadnot with my eye. He was puffing already. Once, after Charlie lost the ball on the break, I saw him lower his shoulders briefly and dig in before turning the other way and sprinting back. A boyish hesitation: the moment of regret a boy feels, at the effort necessary, before he wills himself to make it. He moved in general both suddenly and sparingly. Setting up on the block, he waited for Olaf to come all the way down to him, before sprinting hard to the wing. Then he stood there a few seconds doing nothing, while Charlie swung the ball around the arc; his hands were down, he might have been waiting for a bus. Olaf drifted up to the elbow and Hadnot cut in to meet him with his forearms crossed. The big man curled off him, and Jurkovich stepped out to slow him down. Bo turned, too, but on the outside pivot, and Jurkovich got stuck on his shoulder. Karl bounced the pass in and Hadnot used the lift of the bounce to send him into his motion. The Russian stood helplessly by as he rose in the air and dropped a soft shot in from fifteen feet.

I said to Milo, to spill off a little of my admiration, 'He just needs two inches – of space.' I wanted to prove to him that I had noticed, to boast that I had noticed. But Milo had his head bent under a folded towel and didn't answer.

At halftime, we were down by nine. Henkel led us quietly into the locker room; we could smell the showers, rich with cold steam, in the air. 'I think you are ashamed of yourselves,' he said.

Nobody answered him. Russell stood in the corner, resting his hand on a box of Gatorades, but he didn't offer them to anyone, and we didn't dare ask him. Even he seemed to have acquired a kind of authority over us: he had a right to his disappointment. After a minute, Henkel brought out a piece of paper from the front pocket of his shirt and unfolded it. '300 a month, no apartment. A car. 500 a month, no apartment or car. 800, with accommodation.' He looked at us. 'I think you know how much *you* get paid,' he said. 'Should I read that out, too?'

Our silence, as he no doubt intended, seemed an acknowledgment of guilt. So he went on. 'Nürnberg have two full-timers. Ok, they make a little money. Shall I tell you what Jurkovich gets paid?' He brought out another piece of paper and unfolded it. 'How many points he make? Twenty-two. How many threes he make?' etc. There was more of this sort of talk. Henkel, in his indignation, tended to rely on his bluntest ironies, his simplest idioms. 'I think they think they get good money's worth.' He wasn't a foolish man, and at other times managed a few gentle pokes at the expense of his profession, but bad play and the prospect of losing always brought out in him the soapbox moralist.

In response, I hung my head and let the appearance of shame cover up what I felt. A little embarrassment. A little anger. Public solemnity, like terrible weather, also provokes in me a quiet good humor. I hang my head to avoid catching someone's eye – Olaf's, Hadnot's. There's an ugly small smile my face sometimes breaks out in, which I don't like myself and which is partly shaped by the attempt to suppress it. Tight in the cheeks; thin in the lips. Henkel's locker-room speeches often brought it out.

Then I heard him again because he mentioned my name. 'I don't know where Ben thinks he is – what he do out there. Maybe I ask him. Back at home, I think, in his daddy's big driveway, playing games.'

Hadnot said, 'If you want to stop dicking around, why don't you put me in.'

Henkel stared at him.

'If you want to stop playing games, sit Milo on the fucking bench and put me in?'

Hadnot spent the first five minutes of the second half beside me on the bench, and then Henkel did what he was told. He pulled Milo and put Hadnot in.

The truth is, Milo had been playing better. He broke up a long pass, even if he knocked it out of bounds; drove and fed Karl for a baseline jumper; hauled in a rebound over Hans Muller's shoulder. But his eye was still off. He tried a straight-up three and sent it long. When Charlie set him up with a little fifteen-footer on the break, he thought about it long enough for Jurkovich to make his way back to him. Then he head-faked and started to drive, got nowhere and pulled it back out again, pounding the ball hard flat-handed and shouting 'Ruhe, Ruhe,' to no one in particular. Calm, calm. When he picked up his dribble, Charlie had to fight his way round the arc for a dump off. Milo just stood there; he couldn't find his place in the offense, until Olaf called down to him from the block, 'Motion, motion!'

Even so, he was angry when coach took him out and kicked at something underneath the bench, which turned out to be a water bottle. It leaked and spread slowly under our sneakers until Milo told Darmstadt to clean it up. A sign that he was feeling better.

I couldn't understand why Henkel had started him. There was no question: Hadnot belonged altogether to a different class. Sometimes coaches like to keep a sharp-shooter back, they like to bring him on in the middle of the game, to change the flow. Mostly young guys, still trying to prove themselves, or veterans, without the legs for forty minutes. Maybe that's it: Henkel was trying to let Hadnot play his way back into shape. But a good coach has that conversation with his player. Henkel was a good coach, but Bo didn't act like a man who'd been talked to. To see Jurkovich running the show at the other end must have been painful. Hadnot had a good five years on him and would have considered himself a more complete player. A better shooter, too; Jurkovich ran hot and cold. There was a kink in his motion that wanted a certain amount of management: he pushed his elbow outside-in on the release. Hadnot was pure. Coach must have had some other reason for benching him, and as I sat there watching I wondered what it could be.

Charlie had complained that Hadnot was selfish. It's also true that the younger players deferred to him. Karl began to drift. Muller had been pushing him off the block all day, and when Hadnot came on, he gave up the baseline, too: it's where Bo liked to work. It turned out that Karl had the makings of a point man in him – he was a wonderful feeder of the post. Muller was too short to block his view of the lane and too slow to pressure him on the ball. Hadnot and Olaf exploited the foul line and that opened up Plotzke on the block, when the help came out. Charlie took over on the wing. He was never a very reliable shooter, but it stopped him from pounding the ball, and with the burden of the offense lifted from him, he could penetrate at will.

Karl ran the offense, but Hadnot put everyone in his place. We ran him through so many screens that the defense began to cluster off the ball. Even Olaf found room for a little drive and dish. Without Charlie running the show, the whole game slowed down, which suited Hadnot, too – he was beginning to tug at his shorts. The only guy who didn't score was Karl.

With six minutes left, coach gave Hadnot a breather, and I didn't have time to break out in sweat when he sent me in. Muller was on the line and we were down by three. He hit one of two, then Charlie pushed the ball on the break and set up Karl for a running one-hander crossing into the lane. First points he scored all half. Muller and Olaf traded baskets inside, then Torsten stepped back for a ten-footer from the baseline and I just got a finger to it. It went in anyway. Charlie brought the ball up slowly and raised a right fist as he crossed half-court. The play called for the wings to come hard off the block for the pass, but Torsten was cheating on my outside hand and I couldn't get free. Twice we had to reset.

'Be there! Be there!' I heard someone shout.

The third time, I cut backdoor and Charlie found me with the bounce pass. Muller came slow on the rotation and in a sudden fever of blood I rose among the crowding arms and muscled the ball in: my palm slapped glass on the way down. A horn sounded and we made our way back to the bench. I couldn't hear a thing, and after the time-out Milo had to pull at my jersey to keep me from wandering on court again. Hadnot had replaced me. There were three minutes left and we were down by two.

By this stage the hundred-odd people in the stands were all standing up. It wasn't a big place, nothing like a real stadium, and the warmth of their bodies had begun to make itself felt in the atmosphere. Sounds thickened in it; lights glared. Jurkovich felt the heat, too. The last few shots he made came flat off the palm. They scooped out the net on their way down, and you figured, once he missed, he might keep missing. Muller scored on a putback, then Charlie drove hard with a low shoulder, spun off it and laid the ball left-handed in. Karl blocked Torsten on a switch, and the ball fell to Charlie who streaked the other way with Hadnot and Olaf behind him. Only Torsten was back and Charlie charged him, then dumped the ball back to Hadnot at twenty feet. It was like watching a man pick his shirt off a washing-line: there didn't seem any question he could miss.

With a minute to go we had our first lead of the game. Muller put down his head at the other end and kept pounding the ball till a path cleared. On the way up, he caught Olaf with an elbow in the eye, which spent the next week going from black to purple to brown, but nobody was going to call it at that stage in the game and nobody did. The shot hit the rim twice, going up and down, first on the outside and then on the inside, and we were trailing by one with thirty-two seconds to play.

Then everything stopped. Henkel called the boys over and we stood around them, feeling their heat in the smell of them, while coach got down on his knees and drew up a mess of lines on the green floor. I was grateful that none of it applied to me.

He said, 'I want you to take the shot, Karl.'

Karl nodded. The features of his face seemed too large for expression, except when he squinted against a run of sweat. He might have been indifferent or terrified. We were going to run the play for Hadnot in the corner. Karl would set the screen for him, then peel off baseline and come off Olaf's backpick hard at the rim. Charlie would show towards Hadnot then float a pass to Karl at the basket, who was supposed to climb up and get it and 'do whatever you call it what you do.' And that's more or less what happened, except that Charlie *made* the pass to Hadnot in the corner, and Hadnot rushed it just enough to beat the stretched arm of Hans Muller roaring at him, and rattle the shot home. 'No no no no no good,' Henkel said, and slapped his hand against his clipboard.

Nürnberg still had time to run a play, and Jurkovich, as soon as the shot went in, fired a quick inbounds to Torsten, who was just as surprised as the rest of us and let it bounce off his fingers. Charlie tracked down the loose ball and after that all they could do was foul. Torsten wrapped him up in two arms.

We couldn't hear ourselves shout and Henkel hid a little smile under his moustache. He was very relieved and couldn't stand still anymore, but paced up and down in front of our bench, so that I didn't see Charlie miss his first free throw. There were two seconds left. Then Charlie missed the next one, too, and Muller pulled it in and sent a long pass football-style down court to Jurkovich, who was standing just outside the center circle, about thirty-five feet from the basket. He caught it and turned and shot, in one motion, and the horn sounded loudly just as the ball went in.

After that the silence was sudden and almost meteor-ological. Something irretrievable had happened, and even though it didn't matter terribly to most of the people there – who would go home talking about it, then prepare for another Saturday night – the sadness of that fact made itself felt. What was done couldn't be undone now. We had lost, quite against the grain, and for a minute nobody knew what to say.

Then Olaf picked up a chair at the scorer's table and threw it against the wall.

In the locker room afterwards, a low sullen anger prevailed. I wondered at Olaf – caring too much was never his public style. But he made a great noise about everything he did, flinging his bag down, kicking off his shoes, etc. until he hit the showers, which he turned on very hard. Charlie sat with his back against the wall and sucking on his lip. He looked puzzled, with an air of concentration: he looked like a man who might have left his oven on. Hadnot, as he passed by him, rested his large-fingered hand on Charlie's bald head. Thomas Arnold and Darmstadt hadn't played and were uncomfortably dry and restless; they chattered to relieve their pent-up energies. Darmstadt wouldn't shut up about Jurkovich, and then, with a sudden contrition almost comically transparent, began to apologize to Charlie, who ignored him.

There was something unpleasant about the whole scene – I mean, more than unhappy, though it was that, too. And I wondered if top-flight players, in their air-conditioned locker rooms, dressing after a game for a night on the town, would take losing so hard. Maybe not. The truth was, most of these guys weren't where they wanted to be, and every loss reminded them of the fact that they belonged where they were.

Outside, through one of the high windows built into the bathroom stalls, we could hear the Nürnbergers climbing onto their bus. They weren't singing, or anything like that. I guess they were tired enough, with a two-hour bus ride ahead of them. But I could hear in their voices the sweetness of the summer evening. Some of them might have picked up a few beers from the canteen on the way out – that's what they sounded like. Like people who had heard some good news. The contrast must have struck Charlie, too, for he shook his head and rubbed his thumb against what might have been a smile. Quiet but very public demonstrations: it was important for him to look the part. Rueful, surprised. In control.

Russell came in dragging a couple of laundry sacks. He began to pick up wet uniforms from the floor. This took him no more than a minute, and he stood in the doorway waiting for the rest of us to undress. Obediently, feeling a little childish, I stripped off jersey and shorts and stood up in bare feet. Eventually he said, 'Die Schwarzen können eh' nicht gerade aus schiessen.'

Olaf was still in the shower or he wouldn't have said it. Charlie looked up at him and suddenly my vague sense of unpleasantness had sharpened to a point. 'What'd he say?' Charlie asked. 'What'd that fat fuck say?'

He looked at me, and I guess my eyes got wide and I shook my head, because he tilted his own, as if to wait me out. 'He said,' it was Karl who broke the silence, in English, in an accent deeper than his native tone, but perfectly clear, 'the blacks never could shoot straight.' Then, by way of apology, 'That's what he said.'

Charlie raised his right hand, in a gesture of disgust, but Russell was on his knees again, pulling shorts off the floor. Then Henkel walked in, glancing over his notes. He looked set for one of his speeches, so Charlie picked himself up and headed for the showers. It occurred to me for the first time that there might be something wrong with our team, something unhappy about us. But maybe that's what everybody thinks, after losing.

13

I met Hadnot around noon the next day, outside the McDonald's on the High Street. He came out, a few minutes late, carrying on his hip a small girl, who had her hands around a paper packet of fries. 'We were early so I got her some lunch,' he said. 'I don't have a kiddy-seat, whatever you call it.' I must have stared at him, because he continued, 'I thought you wanted to go for a bike ride.'

'We can do that, or we can do something else.'

'Well, I guess we can drive.'

He had come by foot into town, so I followed him back out again, off the High Street and into the hills. The girl wanted to walk some of the way, so he set her down, but she stopped and picked things up from the ground and turned back as much as she went forward. Patiently, he lifted her in his arms again, over her protests, which were mild, and we managed to progress a block or two, before he relented and the whole business started from scratch. Her name was Frankie; at least, that's what Hadnot called her. Franziska, I guess.

She had the skinniness of small girls, very touching, which is reproduced in some women after motherhood in middle age. Stringy little legs, a long neck. Someone else had dressed her, I supposed: she was wearing quiet yellow stockings and a blue summer frock. Only her face was plump, with the blurred, rounded look of something not quite awake yet or softened by sunshine. Eventually I had the bright idea of setting her on my bike, which I was pushing beside me. She let me pick her up, and we went along much better.

Not since I was a kid myself had I spent much time with kids. My mother, rather late in life, gave birth to twin girls. As the youngest son, I spent a lot of time looking after them. There's a photograph of me on my mother's desk: I'm wearing shorts, a red raincoat and a fireman's helmet, with a girl on each brown bony knee. I thought of it suddenly, pushing Frankie up the hill. You spend your whole life living inside of a family and then you get to college and have to get used to living outside of one. Then you get used to that, and after a while you get married and have kids and have to get used to the other thing again.

After a short walk we arrived at his car, one of the blue two-door Fiats most of the team drove. It was parked outside a large apartment house with the kind of new glazed windows that look like they've never been opened. Grey smooth walls. A large grey concrete drive in front. A flowerbed beside it containing some ever-green municipal bush. Hadnot didn't bother going in. I chained the bike to a lamp post and he strapped Frankie in her car seat, leaning over with the seat-back down. She seemed very docile; maybe she was just shy of me.

'I usually bike these roads,' I said. 'There isn't really anywhere to get to. Just a few farms.'

'I don't mind driving, day after. Most of me hurts a little.' After a pause: 'Maybe she'll fall asleep.' As if his highest ambition was just to pass the time with her.

He pulled out and steered us under the tracks again and up the crest of my hill. Reaching the top, we left the city behind us, and thick corn, standing tall as a basketball team, stretched away on either side. The earth it grew out of dry and broken into large clumps. It seemed to me strange, to be sitting beside him, with his daughter in the back seat. My teammates rarely confessed to a private life, unless it involved women. I wasn't sure what he wanted me along for, unless he really meant, for translation. The few times I had spoken to Frankie, in English, she looked at me with light grey intelligent eyes and said nothing.

We had come through the fields, and I told him to cross over the highway ahead of us and keep going. The farm road followed the curve of the hill down and away. A stand of pines rose up in sharp contrast to the tilled earth and printed a heel of dark brown shade against it. In late afternoon, when I rode there, the shadow stretched over the road, and I felt the double cool of shadow and wind as I coasted down. But now all was grey and dusty in the heat of day.

'I always get homesick in this kind of weather,' I told him. 'You know, in Texas, when it's really too hot to play, and you shoot for a bit then come inside and cool down, till you get a headache in the air conditioning, then you go out again and shoot a bit more.'

'I worked on my shot before school,' Hadnot said. 'My old man spotted me, over the Caddy in the driveway. That's why I don't miss short. If I bounced one off the Caddy it was time for school. Hot days mom made us come in for a shower before heading to class, which was about every day after March one.'

He went to the same high school in Jackson where his father taught and was later promoted to vice principal. But they lived about a half-hour drive out of town. His mother, he said, was a gardener; his father, a tinkerer, and collected old cars which he left on the grass of the front yard and occasionally 'messed around with.' Every day they drove in together, and during basketball season, when he stayed after class for practice, they came home together, too. In the spring he played baseball, but the baseball field was a bus ride away in the wrong direction, and afterwards the school bus dropped everybody off, including the kids who lived in the middle of nothing, like he did. But even in spring they got up early and worked on his shot for an hour before breakfast.

'Did the neighbors complain?'

'Is she asleep back there yet?' he said, so I turned around and looked at Frankie, who looked back so solemnly I almost blushed.

'No, she's still looking.'

After a minute he went on. 'Not about the mornings.

Sometimes at night after watching a game, I'd go out there. If my team lost, just to work it off. The guy who moved in over the road had a baby. One night he got out his gun and shot off the garage light.' Hadnot turned on me then with a happy smile; his buckteeth, as they sometimes did, caught briefly on his lip. 'I guess I'd just about do the same.'

We had come to a junction at the bottom of the valley. Farm roads either side in the middle of cabbage fields, cool and powdery in the light; the next hill rose ahead of us.

'Doesn't much matter where you go now,' I said. 'Might as well keep straight. You must have wanted to step out into the driveway last night.'

'Oh, I don't mind losing so much anymore.'

We followed the road till it leveled out, and below us on the right the landscape briefly appeared: a series of dips and rises, greens and browns, that darkened sometimes almost to purple. I thought I saw in the distance the flat light over a river – the Isar probably, running south to Munich. But then the hedges swelled again on either side of us, and all we could see was the tangled suggestive glimpses of rural summer: between leaves, down lanes. In the next valley, the road passed by a tin-sided barn and then curved sharply with a dirt drive running off the bend.

'Is this one of those farms you talked about? If she's not sleeping we might as well have a look.'

A few weekends before I had bought a chicken from

the farmer's wife, whom I vaguely remembered: a short, small-waisted woman with pins in her hair. 'I came here on a Saturday last time. There's weddings around here all over the countryside in summer. I must have biked past two or three.'

'I don't buy into all that now,' he said. 'Making faces when you lose. All that Milo bullshit. I went six for eight and scored fifteen points. In about fifteen minutes. I did fine.'

He stopped and swung the car round and drove slowly over the ridged, gritty surface. Then parked at an angle beside a heap of something pungent covered in tarp and tires. We got out, and I was affected almost physically by memories of my sisters when they were two or three years old, as I helped him lift Frankie from the car. She raised her arms over her head, as children do when they want to be set down, and I felt the narrow cage of her ribs under her armpits. Hadnot tapped me on the shoulder and pointed to the opened doors of a barn by the side of the house. There was hay tumbled down inside it, which is what I looked at first; then I spotted over the doorway a cheap plastic backboard nailed in with a bent rim hanging off it.

'My kind of court,' he said.

Frankie followed me to the farmhouse, a few paces behind. When I turned back to check if Hadnot was coming I saw her standing like a dancer with her feet together and looking up at me. She rang the bell – I had to lift her just a half foot off the ground. When the door opened it wasn't the farmer's wife: this woman was younger and taller and altogether smoother and rounder. Her breasts sloped outwards to either side under a loose-knit jumper, and I wondered if she was nursing. She looked inquiringly up.

'I bought a chicken here a few weeks ago. Maybe from your mother. It was very good. *Ich möchte noch eins kaufen.*'

German is my mother-tongue, my first language, but I speak it childishly. Short simple sentiments and sentences. This has an effect on me, on the way I think. I begin to consider the world through the adjectives at my disposal for describing it: warm, cool. Pleasant, uncomfortable. Good, bad.

'Yes, probably from my mother. We're all just finishing lunch.' She looked at me a moment. 'You know, it's a Sunday.'

But then Frankie said to me, also in German, 'I need to go to the bathroom.'

'Does she want to go to the bathroom?' Hadnot called. He had found a rubber basketball in the yard, gone soft, and was holding it in his hands. The woman in the doorway stared at us.

'I want to go with *you*,' Frankie said to me, but in the end the farmer's daughter took her by the hand. Hadnot by this time had joined me on the porch. The front door opened onto a narrow hall, made narrower by the coats piled up on hooks and the boots on the floor. We caught a glimpse of a kitchen behind it, with a marbled linoleum floor and bright wallpaper. Flies settled and unsettled in the hallway.

'She's very confident,' I said, remembering a phrase I had heard women use of other women's children.

He said, 'Let's play H-O-R-S-E.'

Hadnot was wearing a collared cotton shirt, tucked into his jeans, and he untucked the hems of it as we walked over to the barn door. His first shot, from about fifteen feet, hit the back of the iron and came out over the bent front rim. He looked at the hoop as I chased down the ball.

'It's low,' he said. 'About two inches low.'

I jumped up and dunked the ball, which was very easily palmed, one-handed.

'Big man, big man,' he said.

Then I passed it out to him and watched him shoot, standing under the basket to catch the made shots and feed them back. He knocked down about ten in a row this way, unmoving, while we waited for the woman to bring his daughter out. It was hot enough in the sunlight that I could feel the sweat gathering and staining the neck of my t-shirt, which then grew cool and clung to the skin of my chest. The sense of strangeness returned. After meeting Anke on the train to Munich, I told my mother over the phone about the pretty girl who had introduced herself to me with the line 'I have been trying to catch your eye since Gündkofen.' My mother laughed and said something like, 'I never thought Gündkofen was written into your stars at birth.' I had that feeling strongly now: that this scene was not written into my stars at birth. That I had come a long way from home to get here, waiting for a girl to come out of the bathroom while I passed a ball back to her father in a barnyard outside of Obergolding.

'How much English does she understand?' I said at last.

'I don't know. She won't tell me.'

After a minute the woman emerged with Frankie, who was still holding her hand. From my position under the basket, I could see them pause in the doorway. Hadnot had his back to them and continued to shoot. It was almost like a habit with him – he might have been drumming on the table. He caught the ball, lowered it to his right hip, then lifted his elbow and unbent it, following through with his wrist; and the shots dropped in.

'Wait here,' the woman suddenly called, and after another minute reappeared with a boy under her hand, as fair as herself, with the kind of pale yellow hair that sheds a soft light on the face beneath it. He looked about ten years old. He stared moodily at Hadnot, who must by this point have known he was being watched. 'Will you show me how you do that?' he said at last.

'There's a kid behind you who wants to know how to shoot a basketball,' I repeated.

Hadnot looked around and saw his daughter still standing in the doorway with them. 'Tell him to come out here and I'll teach him,' he said.

* * *

Afterwards, they invited us in for tea and cake. The boy was named Henrik; he lived with his mother in Landshut, but they came out together every Sunday for lunch at her parents' farm. His mother introduced herself to us as Liza. There were no babies inside, to bawl or suck at her, and the heaviness I had noticed struck me in a different light.

Henrik's father had been a handball player in his twenties, and Henrik still hoped to grow as tall as him, almost two meters, though he hadn't shown any sign of it yet. I got the sense that his parents were divorced or separated. There was something about Liza's excitement at meeting us that suggested the enthusiasm a single mother might feel about the chance to participate in one of her son's passions.

'Look who I introduce you to,' she said, when Hadnot took her boy by the elbow and taught him how to hold a ball, on the upturned palm of his hand, how to follow through. 'You didn't expect that when you woke up this morning? For all your complaining.'

We sat in the kitchen, which was rather a dark room – what light there was came in through a window in the backdoor – and even at three in the afternoon, on a summer's day, the hanging lamp over the table had been switched on. The cake was very good. Frau Taler, the tidy hair-pinned woman I had met before, had baked an apple tart made up of overlapping slices of apple; there was fresh cream from the farm, too. Hadnot and I had several pieces each. I made an excuse of the fact that I had to give so much of my cake away to Frankie, who asked for it, like a bird, with her mouth open, and a little cry of *nochmal, nochmal*.

It was my job to translate for everyone. Only Liza spoke *ein bißchen Englisch*. She once asked Hadnot if his daughter drank tea, if she might like a cup with lots of milk in it, and I thought I saw Frankie nodding her head. But when Hadnot put the question to her, she looked at him and didn't answer, and so she didn't get any.

There were dozens of flies. They perched on the wax tablecloth and on the plums and lemons in a bowl of fruit; they cleaned their long legs against each other. Frau Taler kept apologizing for them. 'It is what you get used to,' she said, 'when you live on a farm.'

I can't imagine what these people made of Hadnot; he seemed opaque enough even to me. Was there a local equivalent of the southern man? Probably, and the question at least suggested to me the way he might appear to them. Handsome enough, in spite of his thick features and bad teeth. A little unloved. The t-shirt underneath his dress-shirt, which was still unbuttoned, had been washed too often among darker clothes: it had faded from white into a color between pink and grey. Quiet spoken and courteous to women. The kind of guy who turns up reliably to work but is less reliable in other aspects of his life.

'How long have you lived in Germany?' Herr Taler wanted to know. He had taken his boots off and rested his large feet on a child's rocking chair, which he pushed up and down. Liza had gotten her bulk from him.

'About five years,' Hadnot said.

'And what do you think of Landshut?'

'I guess I'd live just about anywhere they paid me to play basketball.'

I didn't translate at once. It struck me as selfish, and I wanted him to make nice – to thank our hosts for the cake and the coffee (Hadnot didn't drink tea) with a few generous sentiments. I had no idea what he expected from the afternoon, but this didn't seem too bad. We were getting a brief look at real life. 'But what do you think of the place?' I asked him. He stared at me, genuinely puzzled. 'I mean, the architecture, the food, the people.'

'I married one of them, didn't I?' he said.

'So you must have fallen in love with the place, a little?'

'I fell in love with *her*. What do you want me to say? I'm stuck here. Did I plan to spend my life here? No. Maybe if I was a better basketball player I'd have ended up somewhere I like more.' Finally he added, shrewdly enough, 'Tell them what you want me to say. The people are friendly.' So that's what I did.

Liza put on another pot of tea and Frau Taler pushed to the center of the table the bowl of plums, which were from the tree in the garden. 'What do you mean, you're stuck here?' I asked. We ate and spat the pits onto our cake plates, among the leftovers.

134

'What do you think I mean?'

'You mean, you're not good enough to get a job anywhere else?'

'No, that's not what I mean.'

Henrik wanted to know what the most points Hadnot ever scored in a game was. 'Fifty,' he said, 'when I was in high school. I missed seven shots all game, and I can still tell you where I missed them from.'

But by this stage his daughter had grown restless. She was sitting between me and Liza, on her own chair with cushions piled on it; from time to time she climbed on my knees to reach the table. The Talers kept a house dog, a terrier, and Frankie tried to feed him the crumbs from my cake. He wasn't allowed any cake, Frau Taler said to her. He would only be sick later and she would have to clean it up; he had a delicate stomach. Frankie threw another bit of cake on the floor next to him. Frau Taler asked her not to, and she giggled, looking at me for approval, and did it again.

I felt sorry for Hadnot – to see the way the rest of us had taken over the management of his child. Maybe he doesn't mind, I thought. But then Hadnot said to Frankie, 'If you do it once more, young lady, we're taking you home.'

She said, *Ich will nach Hause* – I want to go home, and reached for my plate, so he came around the table, picked her up like a sack and carried her sideways around his waist. He was probably ready to leave anyway. She didn't scream, which surprised me, but she didn't help out her father either by clinging on, and he had to let go of her outside the doorway. I found myself apologizing for her as I said goodbye.

'She is really very pretty,' Liza said. 'She must look like her mother.'

'I don't know. I haven't met her mother.'

I remembered to buy a chicken, and Frau Taler went back to fetch one from the ice box. Hadnot was strapping Frankie into her car seat. She was wriggling unhelpfully, and it seemed only decent to give him a little space.

'How old is she, do you know?' Liza asked.

Henrik had gone out to the barn and was pushing the ball against the rim. He was trying to shoot as Hadnot had taught him to, one-handed, with a roll of the wrist, but wasn't strong enough – the ball kept brushing against the bottom of the net. I saw the tension playing out in him, between the desire to please, to do right, and the simple boyish urge to throw things. Eventually he gave into that urge and wrapped his arms around the ball and sort of jumped with it, letting go as late as he could. Mostly it flew behind him over his head.

'Three years, I think.' And then: 'Should she be talking more? They have separated, and she lives with her mother mostly.'

'I think she understands very well what her father says.'

On the way home, whatever had loosened in him closed up again. He drove with a sort of quiet concentration, as if he didn't want it broken. Maybe he was embarrassed by Frankie's behavior, his inability to control her or communicate with her. God knows what he usually did on his weekends alone with her. I could hardly imagine how they passed the time. She sat in back with her eyes open and looked, in her new silence, very much like her father. Patient, not particularly happy. Then she fell asleep, and I saw that what seemed sullen or stubborn in her was only the beginnings of sleep.

I wanted to say again how confident she seemed with strangers. To reassure him, partly, but also because I wanted him to tell me something like, No, it was you, she was very comfortable with you. But Hadnot didn't strike me as the kind of man to play those conversational games.

He said at last, 'What are you looking at?' which made me blush.

I had been staring at him and thinking that his is the face she will look for in a lover, when she grows up. After that I watched the countryside go by. The wind had blown away the haze of the day, but a few darker clouds came in on its tail, and these produced, when the sun went through them, an atmosphere of light that looked almost thick enough for you to breathe it in.

To break the silence (I have never been very good at silences), I asked him if he had heard what Karl said to Charlie after the game. I could still feel the blush in my cheeks, as hot as anger. He shook his head. 'I mean,' I went on, 'Karl just repeated what Russell said, but in

English. Russell said to him something like, Blacks never could shoot straight. And Karl translated it for him.'

'For Charlie?'

'Yes, for Charlie.'

'And what did Charlie do?' But he didn't wait for me to answer. 'Karl shouldn't have done that.'

'Why should you keep something like that quiet? If he's a racist.'

'Because he's a dumb fuck thirty-year-old baby, who lives with his mother. Charlie don't need to know what he thinks, and Karl don't need to tell him.'

'You just don't like Karl,' I said. 'Or Charlie.'

'Me? I got nothing against them.'

'You've been picking on Karl since you came back.'

'I wouldn't have come back if it wasn't for Karl. And Charlie's OK. I'm just waiting till the scouts start showing up, that's what I'm waiting for. If he's good enough.'

'So why are you standing up for Russell?'

But he let it go at that. He only said, 'Anyway, his name isn't Russell,' leaning out at the crossroads to check both ways, then gunning us up the slope. We drove through the field of high corn at the top of the hill outside Landshut. I could see the spire of the church now, rising far above the low-roofed townscape; and then the horse-farm outside my apartment. Hadnot offered to drop me off there, but I had to collect my bike from the High Street and volunteered anyway to help him get Frankie out of the car. But she was still asleep; he planned on

138

driving around until she woke up. It was just as good as sitting parked somewhere and waiting.

I said, 'I'll drive around with you then, I've got nothing else to do.' And then: 'I forgot how nice it is to have people around you small enough to carry. I have two younger sisters, much younger, and used to carry them everywhere.'

He didn't answer at first, so I went on. 'It's funny, you spend the first eighteen years of your life learning how to live in a family. Then you go to college and have to learn to live without one again. Once you get used to that . . .' It struck me that this was not the best thing to say to a man in the process of getting a divorce, but Hadnot didn't seem to be listening. The asphalt had given way to cobblestones, and he was driving as carefully as he could to keep down the noise. You could feel them through your seat and against the soles of your shoes – they sounded like rain on a tin roof.

The High Street was never very busy on the weekends. Not much was open and there weren't many people about, just the usual gang of teenagers outside McDonald's, smoking, standing on the public benches, or balancing briefly, jerkily, on their bicycles.

'The first year's hardest,' he said, pulling up. 'Don't beat yourself up.'

I couldn't see my bike then remembered I had walked it as far as his house and locked it there. So he drove off again, slowly over the cobbles, and up the hill into the more suburban neighborhoods where we both lived. I guess he changed his mind, because he parked in his own drive and, since Frankie was still asleep, stayed in the car. That's how I left him, without a newspaper or anything, waiting for his daughter to wake up.

When I got home there was a message on my answering machine. I had a voicemail account and the first thing I always did coming through the door was pick up the phone. Usually the first sound that greeted me was a dial tone. The phone jack was beside my bed, which is where the phone was, so I tended to lie down at an angle with my shoes on. Then a minute or two would pass before I could will myself up again. But this time the line of the tone was broken up into urgent segments, and I had the brief satisfaction of something to wait for as I dialed into the service.

My father had called. He had accepted an invitation to a conference in Salzburg, which was in three weeks' time. Salzburg, he said, couldn't be more than two or three hours by train from Landshut; he had looked on the map. Depending on my schedule, I could either visit him there and we could make a weekend of it or he was happy to come up on the train himself to visit me. He suspected there was probably more to do in Salzburg, but he didn't mind.

I had reached the age when every cryptic communication from my parents suggested to my anxieties the careful, portentous announcement of some problem, either medical or marital. But there was only the one message, from my father, and I suspected that if the news were very bad, a flurry of calls would have passed between my brother and sisters, and I would have caught at least some of the family crossfire. Unless it was the kind of news that could only be communicated in person or the source of anxiety was me.

14

A few times a week, before bed, I added to my journal, some of which had started out as a long letter home. I wrote at my kitchen table on the boxy laptop computer I had carried with me from college. That was always the plan: that basketball would give me time to write. And something to write about. I was also working on a piece of fiction left over from my student days, about a man named Syme, who believed he could prove the earth was hollow. I'd heard about him in astronomy class and had the bright idea of enlisting some friends to contribute a series of essays about his life and times. Mine, unsurprisingly, was the only one that got written, and I hoped to expand it into a novel – during the long afternoons between morning practice and evening practice.

The two files had a way of bleeding into each other. The novel was full of young men with nothing much to do, playing games together and traveling through the countryside; and the journal described the same thing.

A week or so later, I ran into Frankie in the grassy court-yard behind my apartment block. Or rather, she ran up to me. I had a sack of kitchen trash in hand, which I was taking to the bins lined up by one of the ground floor garages. She offered me the sticky wrapper of an ice-cream cone, which she was still eating. At first I thought she wanted me to throw it away, but she shouted so loudly when I put it in the bag that I had to dig it out again. I stood there stupidly holding the wrapper while her mother walked up to apologize.

Her mother was Anke. She seemed very pleased to see me, in the most natural way, and I must have given her rather a puzzled reception, until it occurred to me that she had no reason to be surprised.

It turned out that she was fully aware of our other connection. Bo had mentioned that we spent the afternoon together, which she was glad to hear, and also somewhat relieved, since Franziska had spoken again and again about daddy's tall friend. She asked me what I was doing now. By this point I had deposited the garbage and was standing there empty-handed.

'Nothing,' I said, so she said, 'Why don't you come shopping with us, then? It's such a pretty day, and I could use the help, if you don't mind.'

So that's what I did. I went inside to wash my hands then followed them down hill to the Spar. Franziska refused to be carried or pushed in her stroller, a flimsy pink fold-up, which I ended up dragging most of the way. From time to time, Anke and I took her small hands and swung the child along, crying (as my mother used to cry to me), *Eins zwei drei, hopsala!* as we lifted her in the air.

Her apartment, Anke explained, also belonged to the club. It was their version of 'married accommodation,'

143

and Bo and she had lived there, uncomfortably enough, for several years before their separation. Really, it wasn't large enough for a child. Franziska slept in a storeroom without windows, which meant at least that she slept very late most mornings, especially in summer. The club, however, had proved surprisingly understanding afterwards about the whole . . . they gave him his own place just far enough away for convenience.

'Was that why he came back to play this year?' I asked. 'They were covering two rents?'

'What do you mean? Bo always plays.'

There was something touching in the way she spoke his name, rounding her lips over the syllable, and giving it a clear strange musical intonation. Bo – it was a sound you might make to a child, pretending to frighten him. How did you meet, I asked; it seemed a gentler question than the other one.

Inside the supermarket, Anke let her daughter roam more freely, and she often stopped to work something through in her head, before carrying on. But the story really began before Hadnot came on the scene. He was, she said, only a part of the story, and if I wanted to hear the whole thing, she would have to start earlier, then she put a hand on my elbow and added, 'You look worried, even so, it isn't much, I mean, not very much has happened to me yet.' She looked at me, and she looked at Franziska, who was sitting on the cold tiled floor with her skirts hiding her legs, and trying to hide more things underneath them. Mostly tin cans.

I thought, you have a lot of days to get through, and a lot of hours in the day. Otherwise, you wouldn't waste them explaining things to me. I asked her how old she was.

'Twenty-five,' she said.

'It seems to me many things have happened to you.'

'You mean Franziska? No, when you have a baby, you will understand. Many things have happened to her – but to me, not much. That was always the problem, but it doesn't matter, I am still young.'

'What do you mean, the problem?'

'I tell you a secret,' Anke said, lowering her voice and speaking in English for the first time. 'I wanted very much to get out of this fucking place.'

On the way home, Franziska accepted the stroller, and we hung as much of the shopping as we could around the handles. Then I pushed her up the hill. By the time we reached the door to their stairwell, she had fallen asleep – her neck bent against one of the bars, and her lips fat with sleep.

'Stay a little,' Anke said quietly, so I stopped pushing.

There was nowhere to sit, except the brick wall that supported the raised grass in the middle of the court-yard, so I hitched myself up on that. Anke wheeled her daughter a few yards further along, into the shade of that wall, then reached her hand to me and I pulled her up. She was very light; her dress might have been filled with rope. Franziska slept for two hours, until the shade of the wall was swallowed by the shadow of the building opposite, and her mother spent most of them talking about herself. But we continued to meet after that day, sometimes unarranged but usually by appointment, on most dry afternoons, and I can't say for sure when she told me what. I asked her questions and Anke wasn't shy about answering them – her life was a topic we both found absorbing enough.

15

Her father was an engineer for the local Hitachi firm. They were one of the sponsors of our basketball team, and it's possible she first met Hadnot at a company function. Every summer there was a team picnic on the grounds, which are just outside Landshut, into the hills. She would have been a schoolgirl still; in any case, she didn't remember.

Eight years ago her father had come down with a mysterious illness. He felt tired most of the time; his head hurt him, not like a headache but like he'd been struck, and he suffered a lot in his bowels. When she was younger she didn't like to hear about his symptoms, but now, after childbirth and motherhood, she didn't mind. He ate less and less and slept more and more. His doctor thought that the problem was his diet and tried him on various foods. They were never a family that thought very much about what was in the kitchen, but suddenly they had all sorts of strange packets in the cupboard, and cartons of soya milk, etc. in the fridge.

None of it helped, or only temporarily. He saw a number of specialists, and eventually one of them gave his condition a name. But the name didn't help either. He retired from the firm several years early, with disability benefits, and for a while her mother nursed him at home, but this turned out to be very bad for their relations, and he shouted at her, and she cried around the house whenever she thought she had a minute to herself, though really she wanted Anke to see her cry.

Eventually they decided to hire a nurse, which meant her mother had to go out to work again. She hadn't had a job in thirty years. The only thing she was fit for was looking after children. One of the younger management types at Hitachi had two small girls, and his wife commuted every day to Munich, where she worked in a law firm, so Anke's mother looked after their girls. This was embarrassing for her father, but on the whole it was better for everyone. Except that Anke hated the nurse.

It's not that she was pretty or young and had supplanted her mother or anything like that. She was middle-aged, with thick legs and thin hair, which she dyed a strange vegetable-like color of purple. Frau Sawalloch; Anke said the name as if it meant 'bad smell.' She was just one of those women, one of those typically German middle-aged mothers, who thought it her business to tell every child on the street what to do. Anke was seventeen at this point, with enough troubles of her own, at school and with boys, besides the unhappiness at home. It wasn't her sense of it (Anke's own phrase) to take Frau Sawalloch's constant corrections lying down.

Anyway, the pressure of all this came out in a few silly incidents at school. Around this time she was also caught cheating on one of her exams. Now this was especially stupid. Everybody cheats at exams in Germany, and everybody knows it. In fact, she was only caught helping out a few of her classmates, for a little money – it wasn't as if she had cheated 'for herself.' Anke never needed to, that's just how she was: things came easily to her. But on top of those other incidents, the authorities decided to suspend her for the rest of the year, and just to show them how stupid they were, Anke decided never to go back.

Stupid, I learned, was a very important word for Anke. (She liked the sound of the English.) The world was full of stupid people: ugly men who made passes at her, doctors who pretended to know what was wrong with her father, parents who told her how to raise her child. Sometimes she was even stupid herself, and this, she admitted, was one of those times. But she wanted to move out of the unhappiness at home, which had become very boring to her. She wanted to move to Munich and find a job. Instead, she stayed at home and worked part-time at the local TV station, as a secretary.

This turned out to be OK. They were desperately short-handed and even the secretaries got to do a number of interesting things: researching stories, sometimes 'on location,' and helping out in the studio, with lights and booms. Meeting guests: mostly farmers and civil servants. Well, she was the only secretary. The older brother of an ex-boyfriend of hers had taken her on, out of kindness and because he wanted to go to bed with her.

For about three years she was flattered, and tempted – he had been to university and lived in Munich, and he had only come back home to start a career in television.

Three years seems like a long time for this sort of thing to stretch on, but you'd be amazed (she said to me), how it makes life interesting at work, and how people can keep something like that going, even when they're no longer attracted to each other, which was the case in her situation. At least, she was no longer attracted to him. Who knows, if nothing had happened, she might have given in anyway, and now they would be married still, with his child, and she wouldn't be working there anymore.

She added, 'I guess we could still end up like that.'

'What do you mean?'

We were watching Franziska try to stand up on a swing and turn around to face the other way, towards where we were sitting, in the corner of a public play-ground about five minutes' walk from our apartments. Anke hated going along to anything that resembled a mothers' klatch, but she tolerated the playground, even if she made a point of sitting on the loneliest bench and pulling a floppy sunhat low across her brow.

'Well, he's still my boss,' she said, 'even if he is engaged.'

That last part was intended to shock, so I ignored it. 'I mean, what happened the first time?'

'What do you think? I met Bo.'

* * *

Hadnot moved to Landshut about five years ago, and the coach at the time (it wasn't Henkel) picked him to represent the team for a short preseason puff on local TV. He had come from a French club somewhere, which had just gone bankrupt. Landshut offered him a lot of money: he was a first division player signing up to a second division club. Lower league teams making a push for the top flight tend to overpay for star talent; then they get stuck with big contracts if they fail to go up. But it's a risk for the talent, too. Hadnot needed a larger showcase than the Zweite Bundesliga Süd if he ever hoped to make it back to the States, or even to the high-paying Serie A in Italy. If Landshut failed to reach the first division, he'd be stuck playing small town ball during the crucial back half of his twenties, which is what ended up happening.

Anke didn't understand much of this then or later. She was twenty years old and saw an American who had just come from France and was passing through on his way to bigger and better things. Since Hadnot didn't speak a word of German, her boss at the studio needed to find an interpreter. This was the kind of role Anke had begun to take on, and if she hadn't married Hadnot and had a kid, she might have made for herself a career that satisfied her sense of ambition. There was still time, of course. She was pretty and looked it on camera, and her speaking voice, though childish and a little sweet, was very clear. In person it came across as flirty and ironic, and she could have learned to project these qualities for TV. The *Hochdeutsch,* or high German, of her class and –

education, in her case, isn't the right word; aspirations comes nearer – had been inflected by a decent local broadening. She seemed, in short, the sort of nice girl a mother would want to listen to, and her son might want to take out.

Hadnot almost asked her out on TV. The pedant in me, by which I mean my father, wanted to know how you could almost ask someone out.

'Well,' she said, 'he asked me, and then they edited the question out afterwards. I said yes, it was very funny, I blushed bright red and said yes, in English, and if you look closely at the rest of the interview, you can see how red I am.'

He was physically very restless and had no interest at all in sticking around once he had his answer. But he sat there dutifully and said yes and no as required. She thought at the time, how forward he was, and gallant, and such things, but he wasn't at all. He just didn't care about being on TV. Most people, even very confident people who think they are above it, care a little, but he didn't care one bit. OK, it was only a small station, in Bavaria, watched by farmers after they milked their cows, God knows, but she had seen it happen a thousand times, if you put a camera on, people change. She wished later that he had been playing up to it a little. He wasn't even flirting; he just wanted to know the answer to a question.

'What was his question?' I said, and she shifted her face around to express his manner: 'Do you want to get something to eat afterwards?'

There was always a point in these conversations when I was forced to expose my interest in her. I mean, Franziska would wake up or fall asleep. We would reach their front door, and I'd set down the shopping or fold up the stroller, because Anke's hands were full with Franziska, and rest it against the closet inside. She would read her daughter a book or make her something to eat. Anke had much more to do, on those empty afternoons, than I did – she had many more calls on her attention. While she was busy I waited, quietly, feeling the pressure to leave rising in me, if only for the sake of my dignity, though I had nothing to go home for. I felt that Anke would respect me more for going, that I suffered some-what in her estimation for having the patience of women.

Bo had somehow decided that he wanted a wife and a child, and he had somehow decided that the wife he wanted was her. It seems too ridiculous, even to repeat it, but he said to her more than once that when his father was his age, his mother had *him*; and she sometimes thought he married her just because of that. 'For someone like Bo,' she said, 'who is really very old-fashioned, living up to your father means more than it should.'

Once, before they were married, he took her out to meet his parents in Mississippi. She was twenty-two years old. She had never crossed an ocean before. She was so excited she could hardly sit still, but she had to sit, of course; it was a long flight. She ate everything they gave her to eat on the plane and then threw it up after they landed. Then his mother meets them at the gate, and she smells of vomit and can hardly put two steps together. And she looks so pale: it was like he brought home an invalid or a ghost. And she thought, this is what they think Germans are, these big Americans.

'You have no idea what kind of a place that is,' she added.

'You forget, I'm from Texas.'

No, you are from nowhere like that, she insisted.

'Like what? He told me a story about a neighbor and a shotgun.'

'Neighbors, there are no neighbors. There is another house and then there are fields and telephone poles. His parents don't have flowers in the garden, they have dead cars. And it is so hot in the summer no humans can survive. At least, not white women, that's what his mother told me once, and she was right.'

I didn't know what to say to this, so I said nothing.

The worst of it was, what Bo turned into when he got home. A fifteen-year-old boy. She thought of him as confident and forceful, even if silent. Very much his own man. But around his father, he hardly said a word. What passed between them as communication was more than anyone else could understand, including his mother.

In the mornings, while it was cool enough, they went out into the driveway and took it in turns to shoot that silly ball. Anke was expected to pass the day with Mrs.

154

Hadnot. They talked about baking and children and what babies men were, that kind of thing. All day, between clearing the breakfast and getting the lunch ready, then clearing the lunch up and going shopping for dinner.

'I was twenty-two years old,' she said. 'I had no opinions about any of these things.'

In the evenings Bo took her sometimes into Jackson, and they had a drink together in front of a TV at a bar. Once, he took her dancing, and she got so excited she cried on the way home. She had spent her whole life wanting to get out of Landshut and the first place she came to was Mississippi.

'Why did you marry him then, if it was so bad?'

She sat demurely with her hands between her legs and her head bent, a pose of sorts, to express the fact that she was still defending herself against these blows of memory.

'You don't understand,' she said. 'I was never more in love with anyone in my life. If he left the room, even for a minute, I felt it here, in the ribs. Like I feel it now when Franziska cries in the night: you have to hold me by the feet and hands to keep me away. It was so hot all the time, all I could think of was sex. Of course, I couldn't sleep in his room, but every night I crept into bed with him, with my heart pounding, into his single bed, which he had when he was a dirty boy, and I lay there with him, like I was his sister almost. I know that sounds crazy, but I mean, like I grew up there, too, with him, in that house.

Like I was fifteen years old. We had to be quiet anyway, so it didn't matter he doesn't talk much. But he made me go back every morning, around one or two, so we didn't fall asleep and forget, and I lay in my own bed till it was light, thinking of him down the hall. When he asked me to marry him, the night before I left, what could I say? He was staying behind another month or so, and I thought, if I say no, I will never see him again.'

All that talk of feeling it in the ribs, and holding her down, etc., left me cold. She liked to see herself as the victim of irresistible forces. I said, 'You don't marry your boyfriend to make sure he comes back home with you.'

'But you see, I liked his father very much. The high school teacher. In fact, that's what I wanted him to be: my history teacher. He wasn't a bit like Bo. At least, he talked easily and asked questions and listened. Not that Bo doesn't listen, but Mr. Hadnot was much more of a gentleman. That's not what I mean, either. Bo opens doors for you and waits to sit down, and all that he learned from his father. But Mr. Hadnot had a way of talking, like a politician, as if he wanted especially to know you and also might need you for something later. That was very flattering. Old men always flirt with me, but some do it only because it seems to them respectful, and he was like that. I thought, if Bo grows up like his father, it will be OK. You see how I was thinking: if Bo grows up . . .'

I had met her for lunch that day, just the two of us.

Twice a week, her mother looked after Franziska, along with the children she cared for: they had come to an arrangement with the family. And Anke went to work at the TV station.

We sat outside on one of the car park benches that overlooked the river. There was an Italian who sold pizza squares from the back of his van, and we ate first one of his slices, then a second. It was really too cold for sitting outside and the food kept us warm. October clouds moved quickly overhead and left the rest of the sky very blue. It seemed a shame, on our first date, to be talking about Hadnot, but I was used to it by then.

'Boris,' she said, 'that's what his father called him. And for a while I called him that, too. Boris Hadnot. Did you know he was a Jew, like you?' Germans can never say the word without sounding daring. For them, it is almost like saying 'sex.' 'At least, his father is,' she said.

The family name used to be Hadnovic. Ellis Island simplified it. Mr Hadnot grew up in Albany but got through college on the GI Bill and spent two years stationed in Jackson; he was in the Air Force. He liked the South and fell in love with a Southerner. When he finished his service, he moved back.

'And do you ever go to—,' she once started to ask him.

'Every year I pay my membership fee to the Southern Jewish Historical Society. That's what I do,' he said. It seemed strange to him that his son had settled in Germany – not bad, but strange.

'I haven't met many Jews, but I like them,' she told him.

'And what did he say to that?'

She had understood me. 'He didn't mind.'

All this puts me in mind of a funny story – about Hadnot's Jewishness. A few weeks after this conversation, we played a day game in Munich on a Friday afternoon. Some kind of national holiday, I can't remember. Once we were showered and changed, most of the guys wanted to hit the town, and the driver of our coach service agreed, for a little extra money, to stick around till one; the last train left at eleven. No later than one, Henkel said. He wanted us to make use of the free weekend to catch up on sleep.

We arranged to meet up somewhere in Schwabing for dinner, and I persuaded Hadnot on our way out to join me for the *shabbas* service at my synagogue. He really felt almost no religious identification, but said fine, why not. I think he associated Jews with nerdiness and physical timidity. Maybe he was just being polite, or maybe he felt sufficiently adrift and far from home that even the comfort of a community he had inherited against his will seemed appealing to him. Anyway, he got very excited at the sight of the gunman outside the door – a sleek, fat young man, confident-looking, who rested his machine gun on a strap against his belly. 'These are my kind of mother-fucking Jews,' he said. But once we were inside, and it was only a handful of old men *davening*, he got bored and excused himself after fifteen minutes.

Certainly, for their wedding, he didn't insist on a rabbi or make any objection to the priest Anke had chosen. They were married at the end of summer in the church at Untergolding. From Mississippi, only his parents came. Anke thought it strange; she thought, he has really cut himself loose, and in a selfish way, took comfort from the fact. Anyway, she didn't expect to stay in Landshut long.

Bo hoped to make it to Italy within two years – he was very specific about the time frame. A player like him, he said, who relies on skill, on what he has learned to do and not what he was born with, can easily stretch out a career into his mid-thirties. But it was very hard to move *up* after you turned thirty. So they had to move now. At the end of two years, Franziska was twenty months old, and they were still in Landshut, though the management had transferred them to the apartment where she now lived, with a storeroom big enough to put a cot in. Something political, which she never understood properly, had happened at the club. The old coach had left, for one of their rivals, and taken two of their best players with him, and not Bo. Perhaps Bo could have gone, too – that is what she didn't understand. By this point, she was twenty-four years old and very unhappy.

16

I wanted to know what these confidences suggested – about her intentions towards me, to use an old-fashioned word. I sometimes joked about being her confessor. Because of basketball practice, in the morning and evening, all of these conversations took place in the innocence of afternoon.

'No, you are not like my confessor,' she once said. 'You are like my' – and she stopped and thought about the next word for a moment. 'Like my little brother. I want to tell you what the world is like, so you don't make the same mistakes I did.'

'I don't understand,' I said, digging in. 'What mistakes did you make? You married a man you loved and had a child by him.'

Sometimes Franziska napped in the afternoons and sometimes she didn't. I felt most awkward when she fell asleep at home, in her cot, because then Anke and I were confined to her apartment. We spoke in low tones, and I had to decide how close to her to sit. It was embarrassing for me to waste the day with her, though I had nothing else to do; I felt it more sharply indoors.

Anke was one of those women whose interest in style, in order, was directed mostly at her clothes and person.

She dressed neatly, in bright and unexpected combinations, and applied a modest, careful layer of make-up to her face. Her apartment, though, was a mess. She never cleared up Franziska's toys, which suggested the aftermath of a terrible plastic war. There were pretty things around, some of which she had picked up off the street, some of which she had spent too much money on. A Nolde print on the wall; a plain wooden sort of Shakerish reading chair. But the place usually stank of wet clothes, which she hadn't had time to hang up; and most of the dry ones were left hanging on the chairs, the dining table, the television set, until they grew stiff.

She was clean, she said, but messy, and I watched her myself take a frantic mop to the kitchen floors. Then I would gather armfuls of washing from the sitting room and drop them in a heap at the foot of her dressing table, which I had seen through my bathroom window. I had entered the rooms I was used to staring at – something imagined had become real, and the thought of that also made me uncomfortable. But Anke liked being at home. She made us tea, and we sat at the kitchen table and talked.

'What do you mean, mistakes? Did you have an affair?'

She gave me a pitying look.

'Did he?'

'There are other kinds of mistakes beside affairs.'

'I think so, too, but I want to know what they are. Was he a bad father?'

At first, she said, he was a very good father – when

Franziska was born. The labor was long and difficult, and after thirty hours of it, the doctors decided on a C-section. (*Kaiserschnitt* is the German word: Caesar's Cut. It sounds much more ancient and visceral.) That laid her up for six weeks afterwards. She wasn't allowed to lift her daughter, and her milk didn't come, which made her feel very anxious. Eventually they put her on a bottle, and Bo did everything: changing diapers, feeding her.

Anke felt terrified by the failure of love. It came out of her as painfully, as meanly, as the milk. The two, in fact, became associated in her mind, and she continued to try to feed Franziska from the breast, even after the baby had a clear preference for the bottle. They fought each other like that, nakedly; she was often in tears, and Bo was extremely patient with her, too. He said to her once, probably more than once, that doing things over and over was what he was good at. And she hated him for that remark: she could see him as he tended Franziska or her, telling himself, this is the kind of thing I am good at. Being patient. Even when she shouted at him, and she shouted a lot, because she was twenty-three years old, and this wasn't the life she had wanted.

Later, she said, 'Maybe you are right. Maybe they weren't mistakes. Maybe I just fell out of love with him.'

I hated such talk, sentimental, self-important. It occurred to me that Hadnot might have walked out on her. But that's not how she told it. As Franziska grew older, Bo's patience turned out to be less useful. She had a will of her own, and you had to get down to her level, sometimes, to amuse her; whereas Bo just wanted her to play catch, and when she didn't want to, or when she refused to eat, or anything else, he simply let her cry. The crying made him angry, though, silently angry. She watched him sometimes, kissing her extra gently when she was misbehaving, because he wanted to hit her. And she thought, that's how he kisses me, too.

Maybe I should say a word here about the kind of mother Anke was. Franziska was not yet three years old, but whenever they went out, they spent a few minutes together in front of the mirror deciding what to wear. Franziska also had strong opinions on this subject. She stood by herself on a sidetable and they considered each other's reflections. A tender scene, but uncomfortable-making, especially since I couldn't work out how much the mother was preening for me. Their relations were sisterly more than anything else. They shared fries together when they ate at a café, smearing the ketchup all over the plate with an air of dissipated friendship, on a morning after. I never saw Anke read to her daughter, but they looked at magazines together, happily, by the hour. All of which says something for Franziska's somber good nature and presentability, but less for her mother's maturity.

One of the things that might have happened in Anke's marriage is that she realized, after the first bout of misery, that she had an ally in her baby now and could do without its father.

My attraction to Anke contained a large dose of

annoyance. She often made me 'uncomfortable' for one reason or another, many of them silly; and I wondered if annoyance would always make up a share of my attraction to women. Like Anke, I was in danger of becoming someone for whom *stupid* was a very important word. Maybe it's one of the things we had in common. Sometimes these conversations brought her to tears, and I sat very still where I was, on the sofa or at the kitchen table, and watched her.

'There's something childish about you,' she said once, 'that you don't respond to these signals.'

Her tears had dried up, and I felt instantly on my palms a fine slick surface.

'What do you mean?'

'You look me in the eye . . . but don't come over to me. It's like you are scared of being where you really are. Like you are waiting for someone to tell you it's OK, or to take you home again.'

This was the kind of talk that always angered me, but I stood up and tried to kiss her anyway.

'No, no, you don't understand,' she said, turning her cheek. One always forgets, beforehand, how soft cheeks are – even freckled ones. 'It is very difficult. I am very grateful to you, and I like you.'

I was perched awkwardly at the edge of the table. It was as if I had offered my seat to an old woman, who had refused it, and I had to choose between the rudeness of staying where I was or the embarrassment of retreating to my chair. I sat down.

'Don't make a face like that,' she went on. 'I know grateful isn't a nice word. But my daughter is asleep just there. I can't take up with anyone I please, even if I want to. And I don't think you will be here very long. Say something.'

'You just wanted me to tell you how much I like you.'

'I don't know what I want. It could be. Is that so mean?' And then, when I didn't answer: 'I am not even divorced yet.'

But I don't want to suggest that all we talked about was her, and afterwards, Anke made a special effort to ask questions about me. Are you a very good basketball player, she said, as good as Bo? I am not anything like as good as Bo. *But you are taller than Bo.* It isn't only that. I am an amateur; he is a professional. Then what are you doing here, she wanted to know. And maybe because I was still embarrassed by what had happened, and hoped to assert myself, to show off; maybe because writing things down was associated in my mind with a kind of revenge, I began to tell her. I plan to be a writer, I said, and I need experience. ('Am I experience?' she asked.) After college, I wanted a job that left me time to write, and basketball doesn't take much time. Also, I like playing basketball, I loved it when I was a kid, and there is something childish about me.

From that moment I began to go up in her estimation. This was a girl, after all, who sometimes thought of becoming an actress. Thought about it, as one of the things she might possibly do, when she grew up.

She dreamed about being 'discovered.' She wanted desperately to get out of Landshut. Writing and books belonged to the world she aspired to, where she would be recognized as interesting and original. But it might be enough to have an affair with an author; he could do the recognizing for her.

'What do you write about? Do you write about me?'

'Sometimes.'

'When do you write, if you spend all day with me?'

'I write a little every night before going to bed.'

'What else do you write about?'

I hesitated a moment, then said: 'Some of the players. Hadnot.'

But she wasn't offended. 'Why do you always call him Hadnot? It makes him sound strange. His name is Bo. And he isn't very interesting. All he does is play basketball and think about basketball.'

'I don't think I've ever seen anybody better at what he does, than Hadnot.'

'But if he is so good, why is he stuck here?'

'I don't know. That's what I want to think about.'

This sort of talk is just as embarrassing in its way as my failed kiss, but there is worse. Books are mostly about things happening to people, I said, but nothing ever seems to happen to me. So I want to write books about that.

'That doesn't sound very interesting,' she said. 'Anyway, lots of things happen to you. You came here, and you met me on a train, and it turns out I live around the corner. And you are falling in love with me, and I don't let you kiss me. Isn't that enough?'

'It's enough for me,' I said, but she didn't like that answer, either.

Also, sometimes, when Franziska was asleep, she did let me kiss her. We sat demurely and rather breathlessly side by side, on her sofa at home or the curbs of deserted streets, and every once in a while she pushed me away again with tears in her eyes.

'It is very difficult for me,' she repeated.

Then I usually made a show of leaving, quite casually, and explaining, in a normal tone of voice, that I didn't mind and could completely understand her position but there wasn't much point in my sticking around if that's how it was, until she drew me by the hands back to her again.

'You are unfair to me,' she said. 'It is much harder for me than for you. You will go away again.'

'But you want me to go away,' I said.

We both became addicted to the intensity of these relations. We stared at each other a lot, and I found it difficult to be around Franziska afterwards. I like to think that she shamed me into a sense of my childishness, but really, Anke used her to ease the pressure of those physical affections building up in each of us. She buried her face in her daughter's belly until Franziska wriggled herself free again, and I had a sudden view of the three of us, in a photograph perhaps, dated by the passage of time: the woman with a wet face hiding it against the little girl; the man standing somewhat apart and trying to say something. And in that photograph we looked much older and more assured than I thought we were, and the whole thing seemed more serious.

Once I said to her, during one of my literary 'confessions,' that I wanted to write stories about people who don't have any major flaws, who don't do anything stupid or wrong, and don't suffer from any unusual bad luck.

We had been kissing and Anke felt gentle and encouraging towards me. 'I think they will be very happy stories.'

But I shook my head, and she pushed herself away.

'What is going to happen to these people?'

'The usual things.'

'And what are those?'

'The truth is, I don't know yet.'

We still talked about Hadnot, though Anke knew I might write down later whatever struck me as interesting. To her credit, she didn't seem to mind. She may have been vain, but at least she had the courage of her vanity. In fact, she became more open than before, because of our new relationship or because it seemed to her more important to be truthful. Of course, I don't really know how truthful she was. I wanted to go to bed with her, but it was difficult to arrange. Once Franziska was asleep, I had practice. By the time I got home, by the time I had showered and forced down some food, it was almost midnight, and Anke was unwilling to let me in at that hour. It seemed too desperate, too secretive to her, too much like an affair.

She said to me once, 'It may surprise you to know, but Bo wasn't all that interested in sex.' Maybe she thought I was jealous of him.

'What do you mean?'

'Not just after Franziska was born, but before as well. He was such a . . . strong American man, I expected . . . I don't know what I expected. But it never mattered very much to him, all that. And having a baby didn't help. For the first few months, of course, sex was the last thing on my mind. But after a while, I began to think about it again. I thought, I am twenty-three years old, and *this* is my life. I had worked very hard to lose the weight. I thought, pay attention. I said to him once, you are like a man on an airplane. All you do is eat, sleep, watch TV and go to the bathroom.'

'And what did he say to that?'

She admitted, 'Maybe I didn't say it. Maybe I only thought it.'

The idea worked its way into the novel I was writing at the time. The hero was a great man whose greatness never found its true expression, and part of the problem was summed up by his sex drive. People turned out to be unfaithful to him, because they accepted the pleasures and relations he considered beneath him. I have no way of knowing whether Hadnot himself suffered, if suffer is the word, from a want of sexual appetite. Anke's account of their break-up was the only one I had. Hadnot never mentioned her to me. Maybe he just lost his appetite for her; maybe he had a dozen affairs on the side.

A few months later something happened that suggested a different side to the story. The league we were playing in covered a lot of ground. Sometimes we had to travel six hours by bus to a game, which also meant, since the club was too cheap to pay for accommodation, another six-hour ride home afterwards. Most of the buses had TVs screwed into a corner of the roof up front, with a VCR installed, and the players took it in turns to bring videos along for the journey back.

Mid-December; snow piled up to the side of the highway, melting and yellow under the lamps. Under the moon, the wide forested distances of Bavaria. We had lost a tough game in Freiburg, which turned out to be Hadnot's last game for us, but if he was on the way out, he was the only one who knew it. I can't remember the name of the movie, some kind of romantic thriller. The roar of the coach was too loud for most of us to hear the words, but we sat there, sleepless, uncomfortable, in the sadness that is sometimes deeper than the disappointment which occasions it, watching the images shift on the small screen.

There was a scene in the movie of a couple on a date: the man had cooked a nice meal for the woman at his place. Candles and folded napkins, etc. Dinner was followed by a little music and a little dancing around the coffee table with its magazines laid out. The music was the only part I could really hear. Eventually they went upstairs and got into bed together, though even that was drawn out and involved a number of artfully angled hesitations. Hadnot started talking as soon as they stood up from dinner, a kind of rumble like the play-by-play of a race announcer. I couldn't make sense of what he was saying, it sounded like so many numbers, and then I realized he was listing a series of odds. From the man's point of view – he was calculating how likely he thought it was that he'd get laid.

This isn't my kind of joke, and it's certainly not the kind of joke I'm good at telling. Besides, you more or less had to watch the movie at the same time, and see the woman accept a cigarette, or blow out the candle, or say something, naked in bed, like 'talk to me.' But Hadnot had most of the guys in stitches by the end. Five to one, he said, in his soft southern accent, both gentleman-like and rough. Three to one. Seven to two. On and on as the highway miles went by.

It struck me only afterwards how unhappy the whole thing seemed, and I gave the incident a sort of caption in my head, like a *New Yorker* cartoon: The Statistics of Love. On the other hand, it wasn't the joke of a man who never thought about sex.

17

While all this went on we played basketball, twice a day and a game on the weekends. Sundays off, and Sundays seemed, for the contrast, to belong to a different world, in which other things mattered again. Unemployment, weather, foreign wars. There was a kiosk in town that sold the weekend *Herald Tribune*, and on Sundays I bought it and sat with a pot of tea over it, looking out the glass door to my balcony and on to the fields across the road.

We won our second game on the road against Augsburg. Hadnot, who had found his legs by this stage, scored sixteen points off ten shots. Milo played well too, under control, and managed to tease and harass their top scorer, a kid fresh from Michigan State, into throwing punches at him; he got sent off. But I was glad to see some of the punches land.

Afterwards, Milo was so happy that he smuggled a girl onto the team bus, who had to be kept hidden from Henkel. She claimed to be at vocational college, training to be a floor manager, but looked no older than seventeen. This seemed very funny for about twenty minutes, until it became clear to her that she would simply have a late ride home again, and Milo and she spent the rest of the journey negotiating how to get her back. In the end, he drove her; it was only an hour and a half. I felt for the moment a part of the whole stupid set-up, laughing at Milo and trying at the same time to keep the girl hidden; maybe I felt this because we had won. I scored three points.

There were ten teams in our league, and everybody played each other twice. At the end of the season, the second place club traveled to the first place club for a playoff that determined promotion to the first division. That was the prize: one game, winner takes all. The first division meant more money, more travel, the European league. National television exposure. Magazine interviews. A different life.

It's hard to describe what matters in sports without resorting to the banality of numbers – which is all that you'd see reported, the day after a game, in the Munich newspaper:

Samstag, 5 Oktober.

TG HITACHI Landshut – TV AXA DIREKT Langen: 83: 85 (49: 41).

A wet thundery night at home; the crowds stank of heat and dampness. Karl played especially poorly and for the first time vented his anger on court. Still, we were up at the break, thanks to the big men, Olaf and Plotzke, who played dirty under the boards and got their way. In the second half, Karl more or less refused to pass. Whenever he got the ball, he launched himself into a shot, until Henkel had to pull him and put me or Milo in. Hadnot played forty minutes. One of those games I'm not sure how we lost. We ran around until our legs gave way and after it was over somehow they had come out on top. Karl continued angry in the shower, and most of us left him alone. I washed back at the apartment, but Olaf stood up to him for once, and they ended up slapping each other and squirting shampoo. Olaf, who was fully dressed, got drenched.

'Young man,' he kept saying, 'this is no laughing matter.'

But Karl had cheered up by that time. We lost the next game by twenty to Koblenz on the road.

Something was wrong, even I could see that. Henkel played around with the line-ups in practice, and for a few days I ran with the starting five. The trouble was, his two best scorers couldn't play together: Karl disappeared whenever Hadnot was on court. That's why he started firing up shots against Langen – a childish bid for attention. Henkel could only get forty good minutes out of the pair of them. I hadn't panned out yet, and Milo was too much of a head-case to be trusted on offense. Which left Charlie taking jumpshots when the first option broke down.

On the long ride back from Koblenz, Henkel walked silently up the aisle distributing stat sheets to all the players. Not just for that game, but for the season. There was something awful about seeing your contributions to the cause so concisely summed up. Markovits: 2.3 ppg 35.1% FG etc. Karl led the team in total points, at just under eighteen a game, but Hadnot shot for a better percentage and scored more per minute. Hadnot was thirty years old, though, and the club was trying to market Karl as a rising star. Henkel wanted the international scouts to make their way to Landshut, but the scouts don't come to watch a div 2 German club that loses three quarters of its games.

As it happens, Henkel was happy with what he called 'my progress.'

'You don't play crazy anymore,' he said.

What he meant was, I had learned my role. It was my job to swing the ball on offense, set hard screens on the block, and take the odd open shot. I played the second line on our press and closed off the corner at half-court. On defense, I pushed the wings baseline, blocked out on the perimeter, and made myself available for the outlet. Then I filled a lane behind Charlie. I did none of these things particularly well, but I did them. Henkel had decided what I was good for and how to put me to use.

Something was happening to me, and it occurred to me, a few months into the season, that all my curiosity and mild general friendliness was a defense against whatever it was. My relationship with Anke had pushed aside everyone else. Olaf and Milo cycled to bars together after practice and checked out girls. Charlie never invited me to lunch again. Darmstadt had his high school friends. Thomas Arnold and Karl began to hang out at his father's big place in the hills. And Hadnot – what I was doing with Anke colored my feelings towards him, too. I was looking after his kid and making out with his wife. The taste of her in those first few weeks, still strange and thick on my tongue, stayed with me all day. Even with the salt of exertion in my mouth. You get used to it, as you get used to your own smell, but sometimes I caught a whiff of that, too.

Hadnot looked out for me more, after our country drive. On Mondays I brought in the weekend *Tribune* and gave it to him after practice: the back pages covered American sports. We sat on the slatted locker room benches and talked box scores.

'I used to play against some of these stiffs,' he said.

Often I left him, holding the wrinkled paper in his hands, damp from the shower steam, still reading out the stat lines.

In the morning, I continued to warm up with Karl, but Bo sometimes asked me to work out in the afternoons, and when I wasn't seeing Anke, I spent an hour inside with her husband in a lightless mirrored room, pushing weights around.

These workouts were almost as intense as my dates with Anke. The sweat of his hands was on my hands; I could feel against my skin the heat of his skin. We both stank. More than these things, the companionableness of shared patience: we had a series of set tasks to get through, and it was dangerous to hurry them. Dumb bells, squats, lat pulls. Before and after, we helped each other stretch out. I pressed back against his lifted leg, while he lay flat; one leg and then the other.

He mentioned to me once that he figured on having another two or three good years. If he kept himself in shape, if he managed to get out of this Podunk league.

'I don't know what I'm sticking around for,' he said. 'My daughter can't talk to me. My wife doesn't want to.'

'How long you been separated?'

'Most of the off-season.' He lay back on the bench press and shrugged his shoulders, adjusting his hands on the bar.

'Can I ask you what went wrong?'

'You can ask me,' he said, and bent himself to the weight.

Afterwards, I went home with a racing heart to see Anke, but she was cool and sweet as ever, and we spent the rest of the afternoon twisting our fingers together under her coat, while Franziska climbed up and down the slide in the children's playground. I didn't tell her about these sessions, or him either about the days I spent with his wife. I used to be secretive as a child, without having much to keep secrets about. I was a good kid. It was a manner, more than anything else; it didn't count for much. But these days I had good reason. So this is what I'm like, I thought.

Anke, whenever we went out, was conscious that Landshut is a small town. We kissed mostly in the kitchen, with Franziska in her cot two rooms away. Or sometimes, on warm days, under the trees on quiet back streets, with the girl asleep in her stroller. But when Franziska was awake, we couldn't help being seen together, and Anke once admitted that the sight of me with her daughter aroused something in her blood, almost a sexual feeling. She felt other less happy and more complicated things at the same time; she didn't mean to frighten me away.

'I'm not frightened,' I said.

Occasionally we treated Franziska to a salty packet of fries from the McDonald's on the High Street. Anke disliked going, she had spent too much time there as a teenager, smoking outside on the benches. And some of the girls she used to go to school with, the ones she despised, still hung around outside, with their babies in buggies, eating chicken nuggets and smoking. But Franziska liked it, so we sometimes went. I liked it, too – the thought of revisiting, a few years too late, the scenes of her teenage rebellion . . .

'It wasn't rebellion,' she said. 'It was just boredom.'

But even her boredom appealed to me.

Once, coming out, I saw Milo making his way along the High Street, hunched two-handed over a Styrofoam box, bending from the heat of the sandwich. I almost called out to him; then thought, maybe it's best he doesn't see me here with them. Then thought: maybe he has seen me already.

Milo had been at the club a few years. I didn't know if he could recognize Anke, though even the sight of me with a girl, a girl with a kid, was enough to make him gossip. But I heard nothing from him at practice that evening, or in the showers afterwards; and nothing the next day. With relief I decided, he probably didn't see us. Even an innocent relation with Hadnot's wife might have been awkward for me, given their public separation and my friendship with Hadnot. We were becoming known as the Americans.

Then, a few days later, I beat Milo for the first time at a suicide shuffle. That was when he complained about my cheating – he had seen me skip one of the repetitions. Out of laziness or tiredness, I don't know; it surprised me as much as anyone when I finished first. Milo always hated losing, but I heard in his protest a little more warmth than usual.

'Ben cheats,' he said to Henkel. The German word is *schummeln*, which sounds to my ears almost Yiddish, and especially hateful and vivid. 'He can't be trusted.' Turning to Olaf: 'Somebody must have seen him.'

'Calm down, it doesn't matter. Who cares about these things, anyway?'

Not exactly the defense I hoped for, though it was true: nobody *did* care. Except Milo and me. But if Milo knew something about Anke, I never heard any more about it.

Once I asked Hadnot what he thought about while going up to shoot. We were feeding each other baseline jumpers, running out at the shooter with stretched arms. 'Screw you,' he said at first, and for a second I thought he meant me, that he knew about Anke. But all he meant was, in a general way, when he played basketball he thought, fuck everybody. You don't succeed at sports unless you have a certain reserve of blind anger. I was building mine up.

18

We traveled to Würzburg on Saturday and the night before the club laid on a special dinner at the gym canteen. Thomas Arnold, Charlie, Henkel all wore jacket and tie; some of the others showed up in sweat pants. One of the administrators, a woman named Angelika, whom I once heard referred to as the Judge's wife, served us – cold meats for starters, and after that, as much pasta as we wanted from large hot tureens. No wine, but a few of the players, when the meal was over, pushed back their chairs and lit cigarettes.

The occasion was a visit from 'our owner,' as she was introduced to me, a widow named Frau Kolwitz. Very small, with colorless straight hair cut like a schoolgirl's. She rarely spoke, and even when I saw her open her mouth, little sound came out. She had the air of a woman who confided only in trusted advisers, clustering at her elbow, and Henkel, in fact, spent much of the evening with his ear lowered to her lips.

Milo, who was sitting opposite, leaned over and told me what she was worth. Eight or ten million, he claimed, though he had a tendency to exaggerate, especially about money. He believed such stories established him as someone with inside knowledge. Herr Kolwitz, he said, had made his fortune by providing processing services for various companies; they outsourced their factory work to him. He had developed a number of buildings for flexible use, in Bavaria. It was all very sophisticated, technologically; these factories brought a great deal of work to the region. When he died, a few years ago, the papers carried his picture on the front pages. His wife used to be his secretary.

She wore rimless glasses, with gold ear-hooks, and instead of her eyes, I saw mostly squares of candleshine. I tried to imagine her as an attractive woman. Russell, I heard, was in some way her responsibility.

The club itself had been her husband's pet project. She wanted particularly for us to beat Würzburg, and I heard again the story of our rivalry. A coach and two of our best players had deserted – Chad Baker, an American, and a big German point man named Henrik Lenz. Hadnot wanted to go, too, Milo said, but the league stepped in. Teams often folded, and there were rules about the number of players that could be absorbed by any one club in a single year. Landshut appealed, and Hadnot got stuck where he was. Even so, Frau Kolwitz had never forgiven him. The episode was connected in her memory with the difficult last years of her husband's life: he had taken these desertions personally. A certain amount of ill-will between the teams was only natural and sporting given the circumstances, but this had a trace of real blood in it.

When dinner was over, Henkel stood up and made a short speech. 'There are a few people here tonight,' he

said, 'who don't know me well, and I want to explain
something important about myself. I am one of five
brothers; all of us played basketball. We used to want to
play football, but my mother got tired. She couldn't
make eleven.' A little pause for laughter. 'But we took
over the local club. I was the youngest and my idea about
the right way and the wrong way to play basketball
comes from that team. A team is family. Maybe you fight
like cats with each other at home, but against everyone
else you fight much worse, like – tigers.'

This was really the way he talked. He had two small
children and doted on them. He had the childishness of
a young parent. Besides, here was a man who had
devoted his life to the game his brothers taught him as a
kid. 'The head of this family,' he said, 'is Frau Kolwitz, to
whom we all owe so much.' And we lifted what was left
in our mugs of coffee and toasted her.

Afterwards, Frau Kolwitz moved slowly around the
table and introduced herself to us one by one. She wasn't
much taller on her feet than we were sitting down, so we
only had to turn our heads. It would have been rude to
stand up. Sometimes she rested her hands briefly on an
arm or a pair of shoulders, and I had the strange sense
that something sexual had occurred, a kind of assessment. You could see the satisfaction she took in us. Look
at all my boys, she might have said; at all this meat. But
she didn't stop at Hadnot's chair, and he didn't look up
to see her pass.

* * *

I heard Karl say in a recent interview that he dates the beginning of his career from his eighteenth birthday, and the game he played in Würzburg the night before it. Some of his high school friends were studying at the university there, and he remembers feeling strange on the long coach ride north, as if he were traveling to visit himself. The person he might have been without basketball. The season had been going badly, and he was disappointed by his own play. Everyone on the club was frustrated; there was a lot of infighting. Perhaps, he thought, I have made the wrong decision, to live this life. Before the Würzburg game, he told himself to have fun, he didn't care. Afterwards, he was going to get drunk with his buddies anyway, so what did it matter. And that's what he did.

But on the coach-ride over he sat in the back with his headphones on. He liked to claim the last row for himself and stretch out; there was a seat in the middle that made it as good as a bed. A six-hour journey spent in the shade of his sweatshirt hood. The rest of us, though, were in good spirits.

Charlie started teasing me about the beard I was trying to grow. 'Cut that thing off,' he said. 'It takes a certain kind of courage to make yourself uglier than you already are. Is somebody paying you to grow it? Whatever they paying isn't enough. I'll pay you twice as much to shave it.'

Even Hadnot joined in. I offered him a sandwich, and he said no, but he wouldn't mind a hand of cards; he'd brought some along. So we played rummy on the tray table over his seat, until Arnold and Plotzke asked to get in the game, and by the end of the journey I had switched places to a window across the aisle, and four or five guys crouched around Hadnot and his cards.

Between deals he was telling them how to beat Würzburg. 'The problem with Chad Baker,' he said, 'is that he's a nice guy.' All you got to do is piss him off, playing mean or dirty, and he loses his head. Lenz is tough, but Lenz is a little slow, too. He has his positions on court, where he likes to get comfortable, and if you double him out of those spots, he tends to pass. They've got a new kid, some black kid called Robert something, out of Alabama, exchanging the point with Lenz. 'Don't know much about him; he'll be Charlie's problem.'

Somebody suggested playing for money, and for the next two hours, they talked nothing but poker. Plotzke cleaned them all out. He had a masters in economics and was getting his MBA, by correspondence, from Berlin.

Hadnot kept saying, 'What you got in those cards, big man?' Friendly but suspicious, too. He seemed genuinely surprised to be losing. He couldn't believe that a guy that stiff on court could beat him at anything.

We arrived in Würzburg as the late autumn sun spread the red of the rooftops over the white walls of the town. My first visit. The highway descended gradually from the hills, with plenty of weekend traffic. I stared out the coach window, taking the sunset in. A very beautiful city, ordered, modest, prosperous, packed squarely around a river. It suggested old German virtues, civic contentment, decent isolation. Then we reached the level of the streets, and these were only ordinary streets, with advertising on the shop fronts and bike racks stapled into the pavement.

The coach parked a few blocks from the sports hall, closing off a narrow medieval road, and we got out quickly bag in hand and watched it drive away. You could feel the river damp. There was always a problem, arriving early enough to eat, and Henkel led us directly to one of a chain of chicken restaurants that we found at the end of the street. We changed an hour before tip off in the visiting locker room, and the pace of life slowed down again; conversation lagged. Already we could hear the crowds arriving, the pressure of their voices in the gym, reaching us through closed doors.

Würzburg had a long basketball history. The club president was one of the founders of the league, and the students came out in numbers to support the team. There wasn't much else to do on a Saturday night, and they filled the *Kneipen* afterwards with pent-up spirits and plenty of drinking energy. Before the game, they put on the usual firework show, and a guy with drums sat behind the home team's basket and banged away between explosions. The refs held up play for three or four minutes while the smoke settled and insisted the drums be removed. There must have been three thousand people in the stands. It didn't get much quieter when the whistle blew.

Coach put Hadnot on from the tip, for once. He worked free for a couple early jumpers; each hit the back iron. Maybe he was rushing, or had too much juice in him. Lenz took him on both ends of the court, and they knew each other well. He had a couple inches and twenty or thirty pounds on Bo. A classic German basketball player: strong in all his limbs, clean-cut, technically good. Not especially quick, and he couldn't jump much, but he held his ground and took up smart positions.

Milo, sitting on the bench beside me, said, 'This man don't get out of bed for less than a hundred thousand a year.' One of his favorite lines. Success for him was always measured in what it would take to get you out of bed.

Lenz played defense like Hadnot did, with muscle rather than speed. He spread his knees and held his arms wide. Wherever you moved, you moved against him, or some part of him, and had to fight your way around his obstructions. Hadnot picked up an early foul trying to push through him, and then another, pettily, reaching in on a drive. Five minutes into the game and Henkel had to sit him down; we were down already by five.

Then Charlie swung the ball to Karl in the corner. Lenz switched over but was too short to bother his shooting hand, and Karl quietly knocked down a three. Baker answered inside against Olaf. A long-haired, leggy American, he moved his head more than was strictly graceful but could hold his pivot through any number of up-and-unders, and score with either hand. Olaf and

Plotzke spent the whole game trying to pin him down. Charlie drove hard at the other end, got stuck inside, and kicked the ball out to Karl, who had drifted to the top of the key. Karl drained another three. Then Lenz finished off a drive by the other American, the kid from Alabama, named Tressell, a short muscular two-guard who played running back in college. He was much too strong for Charlie, but the real problem was that Karl never boxed out. Henkel nagged at him all the way down court, following him up the sideline and past the scorer's table.

'OK, OK,' Karl said.

He called for the ball on the wing, and Lenz pushed up against him. Karl held the ball for a moment one-handed above his head, then strode suddenly past Lenz's shoulder, a single step, and pulled up. Lenz scrambled to make up the ground, and by the time he got his feet back another three had slipped in.

By this stage, a few of Karl's friends in the Würzburg section were standing and shouting at him, mostly good-natured abuse. The score was tied. 'Let me in, coach,' Hadnot said. 'I'm ready to go back in.'

But Henkel never looked at him and only repeated, 'In a minute, in a minute.'

I'd like to paint this as a sea-change in Karl's play, but the truth is, already against Langen he had decided to shoot whenever he got the ball. The difference was, against Würzburg the shots went in. It was like watching the big boy at a birthday picnic take all the cake: he had realized there was no one who could stop him. The next time down, Lenz tried to keep him off the ball, and Karl cut backdoor. Charlie found him with the bounce pass, Baker came late on the rotation, and Karl ended up sitting on his shoulders with his elbows at the rim. Even in Würzburg the crowd responded, with a kind of happiness; people were laughing.

After a while, they didn't care anymore who won, or rather, it's not that they didn't care, but that they wanted Karl to score more than they wanted their club to come back. 'I'm glad they aren't our fans,' Hadnot said, sitting beside me. Karl scored seventeen straight for Landshut in one stretch and finished the half with thirty. By the end most of the people were on their feet – they cheered us on our way to the locker room.

'Well,' Hadnot said, as we sat down among the showers, 'I guess this is what we all been waiting for.' He led a brief round of applause, which maybe came across as ironic.

Karl said something like, 'You are all assholes,' and blushed.

I think he was actually a little embarrassed. We had caught him out in a kind of boast. He had more or less confessed, this is how good I think I am. Of course, he was right, but he looked like a boy who had been discovered kissing the prettiest girl at the party: proud and somehow ashamed at once.

In the second half, Würzburg quit trying; it was impossible to play through the laughter of their own supporters. The only question was whether Karl would get his fifty, which he did, on two free throws, with six or seven minutes left. After that, Henkel sat him down (to a standing ovation) and gave me a chance to work off the nerves I had built up watching him from the bench. Mostly scrubs left by that point. We won by twenty-odd.

Hadnot and Karl stayed in town overnight – Henkel gave them dispensations. I remember seeing Bo, after the game, touch fists with Baker and Lenz, who introduced him to the kid from Alabama. Briefly, I saw him crouch into his defensive stance, with his hands up; I wondered if he was talking about Karl. This is how you defend him. Like this. The rest of us showered and filed out shivering slightly under a sky cold with stars. Happy in victory, but not especially happy. The coach was parked several blocks away, down unlit cobbled medieval streets. Far enough that we were glad of its close, upholstered air as we climbed in. We all felt that something had happened and that it wasn't really to do with us.

19

My father came a few days later. He was catching a cab from the Landshut train station in the early evening. I had offered to pick him up on my bike, but there was no point, he said. He had a suitcase with him, and besides, wasn't sure what train he wanted to catch: there was a lunch in Salzburg he was supposed to show his face at. If it got too late, I told him, he could pick up a key from a friend of mine in the next building. I had to be at practice by eight.

Anke seemed pleased at the prospect of meeting him. Probably just because of that, I explained to her that she might not see much of me in the next week. My family are very close, I said; they expect a lot of attention.

After lunch, I walked into town to buy a camp bed, which I intended to sleep on. I also bought him his favorite German foods: pepper salami and black bread. Two liters of diet coke. The rest of the afternoon I spent rearranging my apartment, pulling dirty towels off the bathroom floor, letting a little air in. Almost no one came to visit me, and the rooms had acquired the stale personal air of a private space. The bell rang around seven o'clock while I was forcing down a sandwich. It sent my heart racing – such was the loneliness I had become accustomed to.

Ever since I was seven or eight years old, my father has worn a full beard, which is sometimes long and untidy, in the summers when he isn't teaching and looks like a rabbi, and sometimes clipped and business-like. But he was beardless when I opened the door. For a moment, I hardly recognized him. He looked like a man I had seen only in photographs: my father in his courting days, with a big head of Jewish curls; and later, in the first few years of parenthood, with a baby over his shoulder in the garden of their house in California.

'Look at you,' I said, as he stood there. Only his hair was thinner on top and not so curly, and his features were perhaps a little finer, narrower.

He goes through great swings in weight. He eats too much for several months, giving in to his fondness for ethnic foods and anything that can be consumed in small repeatable portions, olives, tortilla chips, pastries etc. Then he starves for weeks until he looks like his old self again. I had caught him at the thin end of the cycle.

'I'm a new man,' he answered sarcastically and pulled his suitcase in.

He stood appreciatively in the middle of my bedroom, which was also my sitting room, and looked around him. And I saw myself again, arriving and tearing the curtains from the window.

'What do they pay for this place? I mean, the club,'

he wanted to know. 'Very light. A balcony, even if it overlooks the road. Big kitchen.' He enumerated its advantages. 'Very nice,' he said again.

I had never entertained my father like this before, as a grown man with a place of his own. His shaven face unnerved me. It suggested some kind of mid-life crisis, a sudden revaluation. In fact, as he explained to me, my mother had only cut away too much, giving him a trim, leaving a bare patch, and there was nothing for it but to shave the whole thing off. And the next time I saw him, after the season was over and I had gone home, the beard was in place again. But for that week it contributed to the strangeness of his presence. I imagined him as he might have been once, without ties or obligations to define him. And saw myself through his eyes, too, a young man, becoming less familiar.

I set up the camp bed in the kitchen and told him to eat what he liked. Practice ran till ten, and I should be home shortly after, but if he was tired and wanted to go to bed, of course he should. I insisted he take the double in my bedroom. The cot was very comfortable.

Outside, in the early dark, I felt relieved to be on my own again and walked slowly to the sports hall carrying the gym bag against my hip. A wet warmish night, with the wetness not falling but in the air. This was often my favorite stretch of day: after the idleness of the afternoon, before the business of the evening. I like loneliness with a margin to it and thought of him moving around my apartment, unpacking. Fixing himself some supper. Examining my books. Wondering at the life of his son. Sitting on my bed and calling home, reporting back.

In the morning, I woke early – the kitchen windows had no curtains, and one of them faced south. I ate a bowl of cereal by myself, with the door closed to the bedroom. A bad night: my ankles stretched past the edge of the cot and rested awkwardly on the bar. I kept shifting to relieve them and slept shallowly but full of dreams. Over breakfast, I was reluctant to wake my father, to enter his company. It was enough to know he was there, to feel the slight pressure in my head of his perceptions and opinions.

He joined me on the walk to the gym. 'Not a bad commute,' he said, wearing again the clothes he had arrived in: chinos and leather shoes, a collared shirt, the jacket he liked to teach in. A clear November day with leftover wet darkening pavement and grass. By this point I felt better, and something about the exercise of my own strong tired muscles, the contrast with my father, reassured me. I really was in the best shape of my life, and thought, if I want to look back, years later, on the young man I once was . . .

At the sports hall, I left him to explore and got changed in the locker room. Only Olaf was there, in unlaced hightops, but he had his headphones on and his eyes closed. Another minute to myself. Coming out, I found my dad on court, jacketless, slapping a ball around and warming up his shoulders. 'You want me to feed you some?' he said.

'I usually warm up with another kid. Sure.'

'Until he gets here.'

'Why don't you shoot a couple?'

We passed the ball back and forth, and after a few minutes he pulled out the hems of his shirt. I remembered again what his high school coach once told him. 'Markovits, you may be slow, but you sure are weak.'

Another memory stirred. On the day of his fiftieth birthday, he brought in bagels and cream cheese and made Mexican eggs. A few colleagues came over, and we spent the afternoon outside. March in Texas is sometimes cool enough for picnics, and the mosquitoes hadn't yet arrived. Afterwards, some of the men wandered off to the court with a basketball, and I joined them. I was sixteen years old.

We split up into sides, and my dad said, 'Let me get number-two son.'

For an hour or so, we went at it – a good hard game, not much talk. I realized pretty soon that if I didn't want him to, he couldn't get a shot off over me. For the past dozen years, he'd beaten me at everything he taught me to do.

At the end, however, I relented and with the game on the line let him squeeze out an eighteen-footer, just over my hand. It went in, and I had the strange sense that but for me all of his shots that day would have dropped. On the way back to the food, he rested his forearm on my shoulder and nodded his head to my ear. 'Thanks,' he said. My mother had cut up a watermelon, and I felt very childish with the stickiness of a slice against my face.

I felt childish now, appearing at work with my dad in tow.

'Dick Markovits,' he said, stretching out a hand to Coach Henkel. He was sweating already with an un-tucked shirt. 'Mind if I sit in?' he asked, but he couldn't in fact sit still and stood on the sideline against one of the wall hoops rolling in shots left-handed. When Hadnot arrived, I led him over.

'I want you to meet my old man,' I said.

They stood face to face for a moment; Hadnot wasn't much taller than my dad. Clean-shaven, my father even bore him a slight resemblance. They both had the strong crooked racial nose, though Hadnot's features were generally thicker and rougher. (Afterwards, I said to my father, 'He's Jewish, you know.' My father is always on the look-out for unexpected celebrity Jews and takes secret pride in them, especially in the ballplayers. His response: 'Of course he is.') What he said at the time was, 'I taught this one everything he knows.'

Hadnot answered, 'So it's your fault.'

When Karl walked in, I left them together and hunted out a couple good balls. We warmed up as usual, starting at the baseline and working around the arc. Karl was still in high spirits from the game in Würzburg, but they expressed themselves in a kind of earnestness, in good intentions. He made sure to bend his legs into every shot (Hadnot once said to him, 'Jump like there's someone in your face') and counted out loudly the makes and misses. Eight out of ten he wanted from each spot and wouldn't shift till he got it. I didn't dare to insist on the same standard for myself, which meant in practice that I spent most of the time chasing down balls.

Karl seemed not to notice the discrepancy. 'One for one,' he called out. 'Two for two. Two for three,' and so on.

White light fell through the high stadium windows onto the green gym floor. The hall echoed irregularly. There's a peculiar underwater quality to a basketball court in the morning, especially during the warm-up, before practice begins. A solemn air of self-improvement. Looking over, I saw my father and Hadnot trading jump-shots, too, at one of the side baskets, and felt something like jealousy or embarrassment – as if I had introduced him to a girl I was sweet on.

Years later I wrote a story about a father's visit – to a girl, as it happens, holding down her first job, teaching high school in New York. What I wanted to get right in that story was something of the faint suppression I felt (in which I was complicit and which I partly desired) when my dad came to Landshut. Suppression of what, I ask myself now. The first few shoots of adulthood?

After practice, I took him to lunch at Sahadi's and tried to pay for it. But he insisted, and by the end of the meal had collared the owner, Mr. Sahadi himself, and discussed Turkish market stalls in Berlin.

'Your son don't visit,' Sahadi said as we left. 'Every time he come, I give him *Kirschwasser* on the house. Still, he don't come often.'

'You drink kirsch?' my father asked, when we were out of earshot.

There isn't much to do in Landshut on a Thursday afternoon – or any other afternoon, for that matter, unless you like beer gardens. We looked into the church on the way home, and afterwards my father sat on my bed with his shoes off and made phone calls. In America, the rest of my family, variously scattered, were just waking up. He spoke to my two younger sisters, still in high school, my mother, and then called my brother in Connecticut and spoke to him for an hour. I heard him say again and again, 'A very nice place. There's a balcony, though I haven't gone out on it yet. A big kitchen. He's made it very nice.' And then: 'I met his coach. And a Jew from Mississippi, can you believe it, who doesn't miss.' At the end of each phone call: 'He seems fine. Happy.' Though every time he said it, I suspected him of holding something back, a private judgment. Even over lunch I felt the slight awkwardness produced by a parent's determination not to say the thing foremost in his thoughts.

My brother had investment matters to discuss with him, and after a while I muttered in my dad's free ear, 'I'm just going to step out for a minute to see a friend.

There's someone I'd like to introduce to you.' And I went to find Anke.

She was at home watching TV with Franziska, with the curtains drawn.

'Come in!' she called.

They were huddled coldly together on the couch, lit up by cartoons. I had a brief sense of what I was excluded from, something like happy misery, which they shared, which Anke could draw on when she needed to. But she was also willing to let me open the curtains and take them out of themselves.

'I want you to meet my father,' I said. She looked at me soberly and nodded.

The four of us spent the rest of the day together. Anke could be very proper and charming when she liked and knew how to act, among other parts, the role of the presentable girlfriend. Franziska also gave us something to occupy ourselves with, a purpose. We took her to the park – the day was just bright and dry enough. My father has always liked children, which is one reason he had so many of them. And he likes to teach, regardless of what or who. It's his job, but it suits him, too, and tests his great patience, which I have inherited to a degree, for repetition. Franzisca had found a small plastic ball in the playground, which she wouldn't let go of, even when climbing – she kept nearly falling over wet bars. My father convinced her at last to let him roll the ball up the slide instead of down and crouched at the bottom, propping her on his lap. He threw it against the incline, again and again; they watched it bounce towards them. Franziska tried to catch it by clapping her hands together, but mostly she just clapped. My dad repeated to her in his broken salesman's German, 'Look the ball into the hands' – always shifting, to relieve his back and knees.

Anke said to me, 'I like your father. He is a very good father.'

'He's only trying to impress you.'

Around six o'clock, we went to find something to eat. Franziska was hungry, and unless I ate early, the first half hour of practice gave me a pain in the side. My father, on one of his diets, wanted nothing – he tended to eat only one meal a day. Anke misunderstood him. She thought he meant it was just too soon for supper and suggested the Bäckerei in the stretch of shops by the kiosk: they sold cake and tea and savory pastries, too.

I let the confusion stand. Somehow her presence hadn't loosened my tongue, and I explained my silence by saying, over a piece of *spanakopita*, that the camp bed dug into my ankles. I had hardly slept. My father, of course, offered to change with me, and I refused, until Anke interrupted us both.

'This is nonsense,' she said. (*Quatsch* is the German word she used.) 'You can sleep at mine. There's no point in pretending, is there?'

And that's how I began to spend the nights with her. After tea, we went back to the apartment block and my father helped put Franziska to bed – he offered, and Anke, to my surprise, accepted. I got changed into shoes and shorts still wet from the morning runaround and headed back down the hill.

On Friday, Henkel let us off the evening session (we had a game the next day), so my father and I caught the train to Munich after practice. I expected him to talk about Anke, but we spent the first five minutes of the journey in silence. Outside, a view of fall fields, approaching slowly, departing quickly, according to the strange laws of perspective. The river ran occasionally beside us, and the skies were broken by clouds about as often as the fields themselves were interrupted by trees and hedgerows.

At last I said, 'How did things go with Franziska last night?' I had seen him only briefly for breakfast on my way to the gym.

'She's a very attractive child. Good-natured and attentive. Whenever I spoke, she looked at me and waited – she didn't answer but she looked. I watched her in the bath while Anke hung out laundry. Afterwards, she went down without a sound.'

After another minute, I said, 'And what do you think of Anke?'

'She seems to be a good mother.' Another pause, and then: 'She has a clear pleasant voice. Good features, fine and symmetrical. Excellent posture. I understand why you find her attractive.'

My father has a tendency towards the specific, but even I found his answer odd. I wondered what he was keeping back. He seemed to be grudging me something, and then it struck me, truly for the first time, that as a young man he had also fallen in love with a slim, elegant German girl, a little older than himself. That he might find something painful or suggestive in comparisons.

We were on the local, which stopped at every suburb and farming settlement: Bruckberg, Langenbach, Gündkofen. Another Friday afternoon: the first trickle of weekenders to the city. We watched them get on in groups, mostly boys and girls apart, and probably louder, more openly happy in consequence. Couples tend to huddle quietly.

Eventually my dad said, 'How well do you know this Hadnot guy?'

'Not as well as I'd like to. He doesn't give away much. Maybe there isn't much to give. He's Anke's ex-husband, you know. Franziska is his kid.'

He quietly took this in, so I prompted him. 'And what did *you* make of him?'

'You don't shoot like that if you can do anything else.' He was sitting beside me, next to the window – I could see him doubled by his reflection and behind his reflection the traveling landscape.

'What do you mean?'

He thought it over for a while, pushing his lips inwards and together, a characteristic expression, as if he meant to clean his teeth. Then he said, in the voice he uses for launching into stories, that when he was thirteen or fourteen he started playing a lot of golf.

'I played everything else till then, but around thirteen or fourteen something changed, which I can't account for myself, because I certainly didn't enjoy golf more than the rest of it, baseball, football, basketball, which kept me out at the park most days till dinner. Maybe because golf was solitary, maybe that suited me. Though I liked company when I was a kid, more than you.'

He waited to see if I would take him up on that, before going on.

'I won't say there were clubs I couldn't play in . . . but there were clubs I felt uncomfortable. But why do you think a kid like me, a Jewish kid, at that age, decides to pick up golf? Maybe I wanted to belong, especially in those clubs. What I mean is, this was not happy behavior. When it was light enough, I played every day after school for three or four hours. Saturdays, too, before synagogue, to my grandmother's horror. That doesn't leave much time for the other elements of growing up. By high school graduation, I was scratch. Maybe with a driver I could knock the ball two hundred and forty yards. In those days, with the old clubs, but still. Freshman year, I had my golf scholarship, but I didn't make it past freshman year.'

'Because you realized there were other things in life?'

'No. Because I realized I wasn't long enough. I wanted to win, and I wasn't going to win at golf.'

'How come you don't play any more? Why have I never seen you play?'

'What's the point in getting worse at something?' he said.

By the time we got to Munich I was almost too hungry to stand. Unless I ate every few hours, my hands began to shake.

'The first sight I plan to see is lunch,' I said.

My father wanted to look around the neighborhood his grandparents had lived in, so we marched vaguely north out of the station, towards Schwabing. All the restaurants we passed appeared unappetizing, for various reasons, and the roads we found ourselves taking seemed almost violent with traffic after the calm of the train. The skin of my temples stretched tight towards the eyes; I felt a clenched fist in my ribs. Finally, we picked up two slices of pizza from the back of a van and carried them down a side street to the sandy oasis of a children's playground, where there was an empty bench.

I asked my father if he had ever been to Munich before. He said, no. I asked him if it meant anything to be here now. He said he wasn't sure yet, he couldn't tell.

Something I have inherited from my father is a love of walking around city neighborhoods. Perhaps because we moved so often in my childhood, wherever I go I have the feeling, This could also be my life. We spent a few happy hours exploring the streets my great grandparents had considered home and failed again to locate the apartment they used to live in. Probably it got bombed. At four I told him I needed to sit down somewhere – those days my back and knees ached from everything but sprinting – and we stopped at one of the bakeries that filled out the ground floor of an apartment block.

My father refused to eat or drink himself but was willing to sit with me. I had a cup of black tea heaped up with sugar. We sat on high stools ranged along a counter that spanned the glass front wall. By necessity we looked not at each other but at the traffic in the street; maybe this made it easier for him to talk.

I knew something already about my grandparents' response to his marriage: they were upset, understandably upset, he said, at the thought of his relationship with a Christian woman. They considered it unlikely that his own children would think of themselves as Jews. 'They may have been wrong about that, I don't know, but in the long run undeniably . . .'

What he wanted to talk about, though, was their reaction to the fact that his wife was German. 'It was probably more mixed than you think,' he said.

His mother was a nice suburban kid from Port Jervis. She had Belgian roots but no particular attachment to Europe, or the idea of Europe, and may have picked up a certain amount of anti-German sentiment. But Bill, his father, grew up in a family that still spoke German at home for several years of his remembered childhood, until he was ten or eleven and his own mother died. At that point *his* father, who had involved himself more deeply in the life of the community, on account of his business dealings, had no one to speak German to. Bill himself refused to speak German as soon as he reached school age, and eventually forgot all but a few stock words of what was probably his first language.

Yet it gave him, my father said, a kind of pleasure or pride to hear his own grandchildren speak it. He had retained some feeling for Germany, some memory of it, though he had never been and never would visit – 'even once your mother and I were married.' In the first difficult days of their relationship, my mother and Bill got along personally very well, despite his religious objections and the fact that they had nothing in common but this one thing.

'And would you care if we married Jews or not?' I asked him.

'Maybe I would care a little,' he said. 'It's possible.'

I wondered if he intended some reflection on Anke.

Afterwards, I took him to my synagogue, which was only a few blocks away. I hadn't mentioned to him my habit of going, and he seemed surprised when he recognized our destination – by the guard standing outside with his machine gun. Pleased, too, I thought. He chatted loudly, in his rough German, to the young man who offered us yarmulkes as we walked in.

'Can you guess how my son makes his living?' he said. 'I'll give you a clue: look at him.'

His loudness embarrassed me, though I recognized it as a sign of the fact that he felt more comfortable inside than I could ever hope to. The late afternoon sun moved visibly through the stained glass window above the ark: you could see the paths of different colors in the air. We entered mid-service and groped our way along the first pew by the exit. Below the chanting voices ran the quicker beat of ordinary conversation. I watched my father muttering the prayers. He looked very learned, with his stooped narrow shoulders and sharp narrow face – the latest in a long line of scholars. All I could do was rock back and forth on tired feet and let out from time to time the quiet neutral moan of the occasional Jew. But after a while he stopped praying, and I felt him looking at me, and that embarrassed me, too.

We left before the end of the service – he touched my shoulder and nodded his head. As we came out again, into the twilight, my father said, 'OK, now I'm ready for something to eat.' So we stopped at a Chinese restaurant which had an early-bird special that included the crispy duck.

It was dark already, dark enough for the street lamps to cast their glow, by the time we caught the train home. Just after eight o'clock: a real November night, with the commuters hurrying and withdrawn at once, on their way to the suburbs and the duties of the weekend. Whatever I had felt in the course of the day, awkwardness, love, enthusiasm, had turned a little sourer by this point. I sat across from my father with my eyes closed and my cheek against the window. As we cleared the sprawl of Munich, I could hear the train change speed. The noise of it was oddly comforting and made a compartment of the space around us: the conversations of the other passengers seemed to reach us through a thin wall.

After a while, my dad said, 'Around this time, the jet lag kicks in and I feel wide awake.'

I lifted my head and looked at him. 'I tell you, I slept better last night than the night before.'

He didn't respond for a minute. My father wasn't used to shaving every day, and a smear of stubble had spread across his cheeks and along his neck; he rubbed it with his fingers. 'You seem to have gotten yourself in pretty deep here,' he said at last.

'What are you talking about. She's a nice girl.'

'They're all nice girls. This one has a kid.'

I thought of saying, 'Not my kid,' but it struck me as a little childish; then I said it anyway.

'She is for now.'

Shortly after this I fell asleep. He woke me outside Landshut, by resting his hand on my forehead, and for a moment I felt the strange urge to reach out towards his face. 'Almost there,' he said. I was deeply confused with sleep and stood up suddenly to look for my bag on the overhead rack. It wasn't there, of course, but I had spent most of that summer traveling on trains and carrying what I needed in a gym bag.

We stepped out into a cold night; the station made a tunnel for the wind to push through. My father said, 'If you like, I'll pay for a cab; you're tired enough.' This went against his principles, but there were no taxis, and we ended up walking ourselves warm: along the fields, and through the new developments; into the old town and up the hill to my apartment. I let him in, then picked up a change of clothes and went over to Anke's place.

20

It's one of my father's more surprising virtues that he doesn't repeat advice, and he didn't bring up again my affair with Anke. He even managed *not* to ask me if Hadnot knew about it, probably because the answer seemed obvious enough. Anke pretended she didn't care, which left all the worrying to me. 'Don't tell him,' I said, whenever the subject came up. She would shrug and nod.

My relationship with both of these people involved keeping secret something shameful about myself. I had failed to tell Hadnot that I was going out with his wife, and I had failed to tell Anke that I used to watch her from my bathroom window. What was shameful in both cases seemed the same. There was something detached about me – not so much manipulative as impersonal. I treated people as if I had no effect on them.

This was the judgment, or some version of it, anyway, that I suspected my father of making, of keeping back. The day after our trip to Munich we had a home game against another mid-table team, Breiten-Güßbach. When I arrived with my father at the sports hall, a TV van with a Munich license plate stood in the drive. Two young men unloaded equipment from the back of it.

'I didn't know you guys were on TV,' my father said. I didn't either.

There were three or four rental cars parked beside it; more Munich plates. The crowd itself, when the game began, looked no bigger than before, but I spotted a new element in the stands: middle-aged men in sports jackets, some of them unusually tall.

Hadnot started on the bench beside me, with the kid Darmstadt on my other hand.

'I hope we lose bad tonight,' Darmstadt said. I gave him an odd look, and he turned to point behind him among the spectators. 'Or win bad. I don't care, so long as I get to play. My mother has come tonight for the first time.'

I saw a thin-shouldered woman, slightly stooped, with her son's boyish angular face, holding a program on her lap in two hands. My own father sat a few rows further down and had already struck up a conversation with the guy in the seat next to him: one of the sports-jacket-wearers. I thought, he used to drive a long way to watch me sit down, but he never came this far before.

The TV crew set up at the end of our bench, and I spent much of the first half pretending not to look at them. Hadnot gave Milo a breather, then Milo took Olaf's place, and Karl shifted inside. His jumpshot was off, but nobody could keep him off the boards: he scored most of his points on put-backs. We were down two or three at the break.

Darmstadt spent the halftime shootaround trying to

dunk, just to give his mother something to look at, but the ball kept slipping from his hand. I remembered what my father always told me in high school. 'Warm up your short game,' he said. So that's what I did, working the elbows back and forth until I could feel the slickness of the nylon on my back. 'That's it,' I heard him saying, in my mind, 'That's it.' Back and forth till I was red in the face with anger.

The game stayed close in the second. Darmstadt didn't get in at all – I felt him gradually relax beside me like an old balloon. With five or six minutes left and the score tied, I gave Karl a spell. Charlie came over to me, sweating and palming the sweat out of his eyes.

'Keep the ball moving,' he said. 'Box out.'

His face had the concentrated indifference and sincerity of a performer in the midst of his performance. He meant, don't shoot. The first time down, I curled off Olaf and caught a pass on the wing. For a beat or two, I held onto the ball – for the only time all night, the center of attention. Mostly what I felt was anxiety: the anxiety you get when you're about to do something stupid.

My response to that anxiety has always been, not to. Olaf was being fronted so I swung the ball back to Charlie, who drove and scored. Somebody missed at the other end, and Plotzke picked up the rebound but overshot Milo with the outlet. The pass ran all the way to Henkel, who called time out, and when he sent us back on, Karl had replaced me. He hit a three, Hadnot hit a three, and we pulled away with a minute left. The crowd stood to cheer out the final seconds. Their mood had shifted, and you sensed the subtle elevating effect of the television cameras. Karl raised his hands above his head and applauded in return.

Afterwards, my father met me in the lobby. 'That wasn't so bad,' he said. 'You did what they wanted you to – came in tied, played a minute, and came out ahead.'

The same thought had crossed my mind. My father's son in this, though it struck me now as somehow miserly, the way we counted up our small successes. Maybe he felt it, too; he looked a little embarrassed. 'Anyway,' he went on, 'there's someone I want you to meet.' He turned around, 'Where the hell is he?' and walked back into the gym, against the traffic of people, good-natured, buzzing, stretching their legs into the Saturday night.

Eventually we ran him down outside on the stadium steps, having a smoke. One of the men in sports jackets – narrow and pale in the face, with a lane of baldness running between the hair over his ears. He shifted the cigarette to his other hand. 'Mel Zweigman,' he said, shaking mine. 'Good win. You guys get a decent turnout for a small town.'

'You came out here for this?'

He smiled like a crease in the pants. 'I was telling your father, it's my job. Is there any place to get a sandwich around here at this time? We landed late, and I drove up from Munich this afternoon. When I got here, the canteen was closed; and now after the game, it's closed again. I don't mind buying you guys a drink – call it a tax deduction.'

There wasn't much near the gym but new-build apartment complexes, so we got in his rental and looked around for something by the river. We ended up at an Imbiss outside a place called the Hollywood Disco, which served *Wurst* and fries to sweating teenagers coming out of the club for a breather. There was a low wall running along the waterside, and we carried our paper plates through the kids till it was quiet enough to talk, and leaned against it. Normally, I'm not hungry after a game, but I hadn't played much and ate out of restlessness. About eleven o'clock at night, and the beat of the music had nothing to echo against till it reached the far side of the river and drifted back.

Mel did the talking. He scouted for a number of NBA clubs, he said, Cleveland, Orlando, Toronto, Milwaukee, Phoenix – he had a habit of running quickly through lists, as if he felt uncomfortable giving incomplete information. His work depended on relationships, on both sides of the Atlantic. Sometimes he hooked up kids going the other way, too, guys getting cut from the draft camps. Cleveland was where he was based, where he lived, when he got a chance to go home. I had the sense he was something like a free-lance reporter. He got paid retainers for doing particular jobs, but it was up to him also to find the jobs: the players worth scouting. He worked with agents, too, and took commissions. Every man was his master, which was just another way of saying (he said), 'that I'm an independent.' His speech had a salesman's cadences, quick and repeated. Whatever he said, he tended to say a thousand times, and he recited even his personal history with a sort of stale enthusiasm.

Fresh out of Case Western, where he majored in economics, he got a job at the Cleveland Plain Dealer covering high school sports. He realized early on you could make more money by spotting the talent than reporting the games; it was only a question of who to sell the information to. He built up contacts among college recruiters and put them in touch with high school coaches. Coverage back then wasn't anything like what it is today. A guy like him could still discover a few gems each year in the graduating classes; these days they've got surveillance on the elementary schools.

Ten years ago, he decided to shift to greener pastures and came over here. Europe now was heating up, too, but he had a decade's worth of relationships to trade on and understood how the club system worked. He never played a minute of high school ball himself. Didn't grow up with a driveway hoop. Couldn't make a free throw to save his life. At Case Western, he managed the basketball team and probably spent thirty hours a week on the job – more than most of the players. He developed along the way a few theories about why some people win and some people lose. For the past twenty years, he'd gone to two or three basketball games a week in season. Recently, 'to make it through a hotel evening,' he added them all up: about two thousand games.

Mel continued to smoke and stubbed the cigarettes out on his paper plate, in leftover curry sauce. He smelled like airplanes used to. My father said to him at one point, 'I don't think much of that Milo kid. Everything he does a little too much of. Shoots when he should pass. Passes when he should shoot. Everything a little bit wrong.'

'He's OK,' Mel said. 'He runs around and causes trouble. That's what he's there for. Guys don't like to go up against nuts like him. Am I right?' he added, turning to me.

But my father broke in again. 'Wait till you see my son play. You think you've seen him play, but you haven't seen him play. He has a strong left-handed move, a very unusual move.'

'Dad,' I said. 'Dad.'

But Mel only wanted to talk to me about Karl.

My father and I both wondered if he was some kind of con man – we confessed this to each other after he dropped us home. But I couldn't see any advantage to his taking me in, and my father trusted him for being Jewish. There was also the fact that his presence somehow flattered me. I could imagine already my father telling the story about the NBA scout who flew in to watch me play.

'Not me,' I would say, demurely. 'Not me, really.'

My father left a few days later. On his last night, I slept again on the cot in the kitchen – he had an early flight. I dreamt off and on that I was sleeping badly, and that when I got up at last to wake him, he wasn't in his bed. There was a smell of cigarettes coming into the room, and I followed it out to the balcony, where he was standing in the first sunshine and smoking by himself. Now, my father in life has an abhorrence of smoking, which he considers a very stupid habit. It kills you, he thinks, and why would you spend your time on something that kills you? Never mind that in other ways he is perfectly willing to defeat himself.

Anyway, I was shocked to discover him with a cigarette in hand, and when he turned to look at me, he was again clean-shaven. It was like I didn't know him at all. He was a young man and I didn't know him at all. None of the rules he had lived by were binding to me – this was the message he had refrained from giving. Even over breakfast I found it hard to shake off the impression of this dream, and when I saw him into the taxi a few hours later, I hugged him more out of habit than affection. Only when he was truly gone and my apartment my own again did I feel the powerful new absence in my life.

Zweigman to a certain extent filled the gap my father left behind. Most of the week he spent driving up and down the country, talking to coaches and agents, looking in on scrimmages. Then Fridays he returned to Landshut and stuck around for two nights to watch the game. Friday afternoon he took me out. Karl was his main target and he justified time wasted on me by referring to me as his 'inside man.'

'Consider yourself on retainer,' he said. 'Two bucks a day.'

I have an inherited interest in German cakes and he was willing to trail me across town sampling the possibilities. He ate like my father, too – either not all, or whatever was left, no matter how much.

One of the things I liked most about Zweigman: he was a basketball fan. I realized in his company something I had just about forgotten after four months in the game. All fans are created equal. It's only the players who have to put up with inequalities.

For two hours a week I talked about basketball again as if it was something I loved. We argued about guys like Plotzke and Olaf, followed the NBA through day-old newspapers, remembered past players and games. He shared my passion for statistics and together we bent over sheets of numbers and discussed which numbers mattered the most. Mel knew much more about the game than I did and could break down an offense or defense at a glance, naming them by code: motion 2, triangle with a high post pivot, that kind of thing. These suggested to me a world in which all the apparent variety of play was little more than a few basic patterns dressed up. A depressing idea. I wonder if this is how we appear to psychologists – if we offer the kind of cheap selection you get at a convenience store. But Mel still turned to me for 'inside knowledge.' I could describe for him what it was like to feel Hadnot pin you on his hip, to keep you off his ball hand, before rising and turning to shoot.

On most other aspects of the business, though, he enlightened me. It wasn't just his job to find talent, he also had to assess 'how ripe it was.' Drafting a European, if you could sign him away from his club, gave you three years of rights to him. Maybe in those three years, with a lot of work, he becomes a useful NBA player, just in time for somebody else to snatch him up as a free agent. So, you wanted guys who could step in right away, or you wanted guys who were loyal. Loyal was hard to measure. Sometimes you looked at kids with particular relation-ships to their club coaches. Then you brought the coach in, too, and him you could sign up for as long as he was willing – and often he was very willing. Not that such contracts mattered much in the event; mostly, after three years, the kids get sick of their old coaches anyway. Then you're stuck with them, though these guys don't cost much in the scale of things.

Mel wanted to know what I thought of Karl personally. 'Personally,' I said, 'personally ... he strikes me as somebody who is going to be a famous man.'

'That's not a quality,' Mel said.

'I didn't used to think it was, either.'

The clubs themselves were another part of his problem. Sometimes they got very 'selfish' with their talent, very possessive. Mel also had to work out what approach to make. Most of the small-market teams had money issues, which were easily resolved by the kind of people he reported back to. But sometimes you get a small club with a rich local owner who doesn't see it as a money-making business. He likes wandering around the locker room and putting his arm around the players, that sort of thing. If he finds he's got a 'live one' under contract, he holds on. Mel spent a fair amount of time hanging around the front office, talking to Angie, the judge's wife. The good thing was these small-market operations tended to be careless with their financials. The secretary is a friend of a friend. The accountant went to school with the boss's son. And so on. Angie gave Mel information he probably wasn't meant to see, and Mel passed some of it on to me. This was how I found out what kind of money the guys were on.

Hadnot was the highest paid player on the team. He made three thousand marks a week in season, without taking into account the company car, the family apartment for his daughter and separated wife, and the bachelor studio for himself. Charlie came next, at about two and a half, car included, though he had a special clause in his contract allowing him to pick his own apartment. Olaf had first division experience and took home a grand a week, about twice what I made, with a few incentive clauses thrown in. Then there were a bunch of guys on more or less the same contract: Milo, Plotzke, me. Karl. He had signed up at fourteen for five years and never bothered renegotiating. Money didn't matter to him: he was the son of a millionaire.

Landshut had him under contract for another two seasons. They hoped to ride him into the first division and then establish themselves in the European league, where the real money is. Of course, any NBA team could compensate Frau Kolwitz financially for his loss, but money might not be able to buy the kind of influence Karl could have on the club fortunes. If she wanted to turn Landshut into a serious European player, Karl was her best shot.

In other words, there was no reliable correlation between what we got paid and what we contributed, both measurable quantities. Karl and I made the same money. As Mel ran down the income-list, I started feeling uneasy and said to him, 'Probably I shouldn't hear these things. Money is private.'

But this had nothing to do with my reluctance. I had been assessed at a certain value and had failed to live up to that assessment. It was almost as if I had been caught lying. Mel, with characteristic blindness and bluntness, said, 'No, Henkel only made a mistake. The fault's his. What are you getting so worried about? They have to keep paying you.'

'That's not what I mean. It's just that I'm not worth what I seem to be worth. At first you can't tell, but then it becomes pretty clear.'

'Oh quit being so subtle. Call it a rough start. Think of yourself as an investment, if you want to. A long-term investment.'

Something else turned up in his inquiries. Hadnot was on a three-month contract; it ran out a few weeks into the new year. According to Mel, this was unusual but not unheard of. Clubs, ambitious clubs, sometimes invested more than they had up front at the start of a season, hoping to win a few games early and attract the sponsorship that would see them through. It was a gamble, but small-town outfits had to gamble if they wanted to grow, and such practices explained why so many of them ended up going under. What was unusual, maybe, was just that Hadnot had been around at the club so long. Mostly they signed up new players to these short-term contracts. Guys had an incentive to go along with it only if they were trying to move up a league, or over a league, and wanted to prove themselves against stiffer competition. Athletes are basically delusional human beings. Every one he ever met, worth his salt, figured on winning whenever he stepped on court. They see it as a pay raise and forget they've only cut their salary into fewer slices.

'So what does that make me? You think they'll re-sign him?'

'Would you?'

'Sure.' Then the personal implication struck me.

In fact, I heard shortly after from Anke something that seemed to bear on all this. Bo had asked her whether she might consider, in the new year, taking him in again and giving their relationship a shot. She seemed shocked by his suggestion, though I wondered whether she also had her reasons for telling me about it. 'And you say this comes completely out of the blue?' I said.

'How can you ask me that, when you come here every night?' But it seemed to me some of her anger was worked up in advance.

'I only ask you. And what did you say to him?'

'What do you think I said?' Then she changed tack. 'You take it very easy.'

'How should I take it? A minute ago you accused me of distrusting you.'

This also didn't satisfy her, but I decided to keep from her what I knew, that Hadnot had no guarantee of work after the Christmas break. In this light, his question sounded less strange and abrupt. Maybe he was considering going home and wanted to know his chances before committing himself. I wondered even whether he thought of approaching the club with an offer of economizing: a pay cut, and only one apartment, etc. Getting back together would make his life less expensive.

Anyway, his question had its effect on me. Anke, one afternoon, complained about the prospect of her first Christmas since Franziska was born stuck at home with her parents. They used to go over for dinner on the 24th, but it was only dinner, and this year her mother expected them both to stay the night. By this point in the year it was mostly too wet and cold to go out for any stretch of time, and the three of us made do, as well as we could, with the entertainment possibilities of Anke's sitting room. Cheerless days, and Franziska's fits of temper expressed only what we all felt: cooped up, tied to one another by affection and fear of loneliness.

'What's wrong with Christmas at home?' I asked, partly provoking her.

'I'm not such a daddy's girl as you,' she said.

Later, relenting, she added, 'I thought when she was born my life would change. But nothing has changed, really. Instead of going to school, I look after her. You don't know what it's like to be an only child. Your parents can't be happy without you, so you spend every holiday with a sick old married couple who are not even happy for more than an hour when you *do* come home.'

Franziska had discovered she was tall enough to reach the toaster in the kitchen; I noticed her trying to pull it out of the socket by the cord. Anke moved quickly to lift her away, and the girl slapped her mother's face, not hard but deliberately. Usually, at such displays, Anke sent her to her room, but this time she let herself be slapped, only averting her face from side to side with her eyes closed.

'No,' she said, 'no, my love.' I wondered for a minute if she was trying to goad herself to tears, but Franziska gave up after that minute and the atmosphere remained unrelieved.

We had a two-week break for Christmas, and my mother had been angling for me to come home; she offered to buy the plane ticket. But I asked her instead if the house in Flensburg was empty – the house she grew up in, a few hours north of Hamburg on the Danish border, and to which we returned most summers in my childhood. I had been there in winter only once before. The sun appeared for no more than a few hours each day, but the view of the sea from the terrace was unob-structed by leaves; you could see, across the grey fjord, a stretch of Denmark as wide as your arms. The house itself, built shortly after the war, was plain and comfort-able, and the glass-house in the garden had an old-fashioned space-heater that was rusty but powerful enough. You could spend every mealtime surrounded by trees and water.

My mother, with a catch of envy in her throat, exclaimed how much she loved being there in winter, with nothing else to do all day but shop and cook and walk to the harbor in the morning and the pier in the afternoon. By the end of the conversation, with some reluctance, she agreed to let me spend Christmas there, with my girlfriend and her daughter. And when I invited Anke I was touched and surprised by how pleased she seemed. Bo was spending the two weeks off in

Mississippi, and she could do what she liked with Franziska until new year. For the next few days she kept bothering me about plans: what train should we take and how long should we stay? Was there a cot there? And so on.

I never mentioned our affair to Mel, though sometimes Anke came up when we were talking about Hadnot. I asked him once what would happen to his wife's apartment if the team let him go. 'What do you know about his wife?' he said, but the conversation turned easily enough to other subjects.

Sponsorship money was beginning to come through, though Mel doubted Frau Kolwitz would spend it on her fattest contract. Hadnot had struggled to get court-time since Karl's emergence; meanwhile, we continued to win. By mid-December, our record was seven and three and we sat comfortably third in the league tables: within reach of the playoff. In the last game before the Christmas break, we beat Nürnberg on the road by seventeen, revenge that left Henkel in expansive spirits. Karl had scored thirty for the fourth time in five games, and Bo had put in what was becoming a typical performance: ten points in fifteen minutes, five for eight from the field.

'A super sub,' Henkel called him on the bus-ride home, to placate him. 'What is it they call him? The microwave. Very quick hot . . .'

Hadnot didn't look up. I sat in the aisle opposite, with

my winter coat bunched against the window, and pretending to sleep. From time to time I allowed myself in the dark of the coach to stare at Bo through half-closed lids. He rested a leather jacket on his lap and kept his hands warm inside it. At one point he said, vaguely in my direction, 'Man, I ain't tired enough to sleep.' A two-hour ride back to Landshut.

The next morning Mel found me at home in bed and offered to buy me lunch. He had seen what he needed to see. There was no point coming back in the new year, and he wanted to 'take his leave' of me – sometimes his conversation showed an old-fashioned, bookish turn. He spent a lot of time on the road reading bad novels. I stood in my boxer shorts and invited him in, showered and then dressed in front of him, feeling how strange it was, such familiar proximity with an older, professional man. We walked down the hill and through town, along the High Street as far as the river, until we reached Sahadi's.

It was spitting rain, but we made it in before the heavens emptied and sat just inside the door by the window, in the green shade of a potted plant, watching the water come down. Early lunch, and nobody else was around. Mr. Sahadi himself waited on us, and I was embarrassed by the fact that he mistook Mel for my father.

'I guess all Jews look alike to him,' Mel said quietly to me. This also displeased me.

Over lunch I asked Mel whether Hadnot didn't

deserve more court-time, given his 'efficiency.' It seemed to me just a question of numbers. 'He banks one point two, one point three a shot,' I said. By such talk, technical and brief, I hoped to impress the big-shot scout. 'Very high for any kind of player, especially a guard. Higher than Karl.'

'What does it matter, when you're winning ball games?' Mel said. 'If you ask me, they're easing him out. It's a question of numbers all right, three grand a week. Bo just costs too much. At his age, to take a three-month contract – he should have known better.'

'I've been thinking about that. You know, he held out a couple weeks at the start of the season. I think he wanted to quit – he got fat over the summer and needed a month to play himself into shape. Hadnot told me once he only came back because of Karl. He figured already Karl would attract the attention of guys like you, and it was his last chance to get noticed. Then Henkel benches him.'

'You mean, I guess, what do I think of him professionally?'

He stubbed out a cigarette; the smell of it mixed with the plant smells and food smells.

'I scouted him out of Mississippi ten years ago,' he went on. 'OK, he can shoot, and he knows how to play. But he's three or four inches short for a two guard, and a step slow. On defense, against top-flight talent, all he can do is hack. Don't get me wrong, there's a place for that, too. With the right club, a dominant big man or slasher, he can work himself open off the double-teams and knock down jumpshots. Coaches like shooters like chess players like chess pieces: they can draw up plays around them. But then you look at his character. Some kids can't afford to be selfish, they don't have the talent. Maybe you like the guy personally, I don't know, but there are people who make every situation they're in a little more difficult, and he's one of them. Don't pretend that isn't a part of what's going on here. But let's imagine he isn't a headache; let's imagine he's twenty-two years old. If he counts for a good soldier and some small-market club like Cleveland or San Antonio can claim him for a local boy, maybe they draft him and he spends two or three years at the end of their bench. He's white, after all; at least he's white. Then someone gets injured and he has a chance to prove himself, and takes it. A lot of these guys don't, by the way. They get scared. This way he stretches out some kind of NBA career. But at his age, coming into the league? Ben, I'll be honest. This is delusional, this is unhappy thinking.'

Mel's assurance offended me, as it sometimes did. I felt a little of what Hadnot might feel about him, the righteous anger of the school bully. Listen to this skinny-chested kid talk big! 'You mean,' I said, making a joke of it, 'that if he was taller, faster, sweeter and younger, and didn't come from Mississippi, he might have a shot?'

'Sure, why not?'

'How about the rest of us?'

He tapped his cigarettes against the table and pulled

another one out. Then lit it, collecting his thoughts. His answer, when it came, had the quick cadence of a professional opinion. Olaf was also three or four inches short. Bad hands, too, small and what coaches call 'hard.' Decent ups, a respectable shooting stroke, but no inside moves. His rotational quickness was poor, which is what big men depend on in the pivot. Then he was lazy and didn't care. The rest might be overcome, but sometimes the psychological was harder to fix than the physical. Probably he was the second best talent on the team, but uncoachable. Milo had moderate quickness, moderate ups, moderate hands, but at his position he's competing against athletes like you wouldn't believe. Unless you're a freak you don't get to play, with two exceptions. You're very smart and you don't miss. Milo played dumb and used too much elbow on his follow-through – it might take a good coach two years to correct it, and Henkel showed no inclination. Then he's a head-case, and who needs it? Charlie at least knows what he is. A third-rate talent and a bully. Small European clubs can use a guy like him to lick the rest into shape. He's smart and under control, but two steps slow, a half foot short. Also, he holds the ball too long and drives too deep, shoots corkscrews, and cheats on defense to make up for lack of foot speed. Plotzke isn't worth talking about. This is a guy who doesn't suit up in any other league in Europe, to say nothing of the US.

And what about me, I asked when he was finished.

'My professional opinion?' he said.

'Sure, why not?'

'You're twenty pounds underweight. That's fixable, with a serious regime, though it might take two years.'

Then he did a strange thing. He left his cigarette smoking in the ashtray and took one of my hands in the palm of his own. He had fine-boned fingers, though dirty under the nails; and my skin, at his touch, seemed to me as soft as a woman's.

'Your hands are too small,' he said, and let go of me again. 'You jump off the right foot. As a right-handed player, that leaves you unbalanced in the air. Again, this is fixable, though such instincts die hard. You're one of those guys who's easy to push off the ball. I don't know the reason. High center, low center of gravity, one of the two. Some guys are up-and-down guys: they don't take up much space on the floor, so it's easy to strip them, it's easy to box them out. You're one of those guys.'

He picked up his cigarette again.

'On the plus side,' he went on, 'you've got a quick first step, especially going left, because you plant with your right, and other idiosyncrasies that make you hard to figure out the first time around. That counts for something, but there's always a second time. Your lateral foot-work is terrible, and you end up reaching on defense and catching cheap whistles. Then there's a kink in your shot I haven't seen in twenty years. I don't know where you picked it up, probably the 1950s. Your left thumb pushes on the ball, which makes you unreliable anywhere inside of twenty feet, including the foul line. Another two years

230

to fix. As I say, some of it can't be helped, some of it can. If you put in the sweat, you might turn yourself into a decent second division player in a mid-level European league, a fourth or fifth man. Honestly, though, I don't think you've got the heart for it, the stomach, what you will.'

He looked me in the eyes with a challenging, humorous air. The meal was over, but the rain continued to spread itself thickly against the window. We wouldn't shift ground any time soon. Some conversations, however, also give us the chance to stretch our legs, and I had the feeling, as we sat there, of ranging indiscriminately. Look, I seemed to say, as if pointing out a landmark, that's me, some way below . . . Mr. Sahadi came hovering to remove our plates, but I explained to him that my friend was leaving town shortly and this was our last meal together. The food was so good, I could happily pick at it for hours, if he didn't mind; it seemed to me the kind of meal to be picked at.

'What about Karl?' I asked, when he had hustled off to bring us mint tea. I get cold easily, sitting still, and wanted to warm my hands around something.

'Karl's all right,' Mel said. 'There's nothing wrong with Karl.'

'What do you mean there's nothing wrong with him?'

'What I say. Somebody will pay what it takes to bring him over, and maybe I'll have something to do with it and maybe I won't. Either way, he'll be fine.'

And just at that the muddle of strange feelings acting together (loneliness, friendliness, coldness, wounded pride) produced in me a very simple one, a rush of blood. That a prodigy like Karl, seven feet tall and the best athlete on the team – quick, strong, balanced; technically perfect; clear-headed, confident – should belong to some kind of normal! In the first few weeks of that long summer, which I spent on trains and in corporate hotels, measuring myself from day to day against strangers, I wondered if I was any good at basketball. Suddenly, I had a glimpse of what being good meant.

The memory of this conversation, as I get older, has a somewhat different effect on me. I don't know that I've ever been around a set of people more exceptionally suited, by nature or inclination, to their chosen profession. Charlie, Milo, Hadnot, Olaf. These were the kids crawling at six months, walking at nine. They were first on the playground slide and last off the playing field at dusk. Childhood, for them, was the game you won at. Their whole lives all they practiced was how to get a round ball into a round hoop and stop other people doing the same. And they weren't even close to the big time, not even close. Of course, our failings aren't only professional, and after that year I began to see everything in a cold assessing light. What chance do the rest of us have to give a reasonable account of ourselves, not just at work and play, but in more complicated and difficult contests? How many of us have the talent or skill, or in some cases the opportunity, to lead decent, loving, useful, satisfied lives?

Maybe this climate of assessment affected my feelings for Anke. Once you become used to measuring people, it can be hard to stop. As the season wore on, I retreated deeper and deeper inside my own head.

One more story about my father.

I think he saw what was happening to me and tried in his way to shake me out of it. A few mornings before he left, on the Monday, our first practice session after the weekend's game, he watched me warm up with Karl in the shootaround. Karl, beginning to enjoy his success, was light-hearted and loose, messing around, but still insisted on making eight of ten before moving from each spot. This meant that I spent much of the time chasing down his misses. My father, when he had seen enough, took off his jacket and laid it carefully over the bench.

'Give an old man a shot,' he said, stepping on court. And Karl, who was basically a good kid, passed him the ball. My father short-armed the first and then clapped his hands, calling for the ball again. He said to Karl, 'You know how to play H-O-R-S-E? I'll play you H-O-R-S-E. You want to play H-O-R-S-E?'

'Sure, I know how to play,' Karl said.

'OK, OK.' My father shrugged his shoulders and pulled his shirt out of his belt. 'We'll play. I go first. Age before beauty.'

He bounced the ball a couple times flat-handed and lined up an eighteen-footer from the baseline. Then he thought about it a minute. 'You gonna make me shoot it?' he said at last, with the ball in his hands. 'You don't think I'm gonna miss *this*, do you?'

Karl partly turned to me. 'I don't understand,' he said, in his thick German English, as if he had a mouthful of good cheddar. 'Do you want to play or not?'

'OK, OK,' my father repeated.

He has a characteristic way of cocking the ball at his eye, measuring up and letting go. The act, in his hands, seems carefully considered, never mind that I learned my set-shot from him, with the left thumb guiding. His first shot dropped in. 'Getting warmed up,' he said, making an odd swinging motion with both arms. Meanwhile, I stood stupidly aside, and when Karl's reply bounced off the back rim towards mid-court, I let him run it down.

Until I was seventeen or eighteen, long after he had any right to, my father could beat me routinely at H-O-R-S-E. He never played much, and I spent every afternoon in the back yard working on my shot. Still, he seemed not to feel the pressure of defeating his son, as I felt it the other way around. The fact that he had made and reared me gave him a continued hold.

Some part of that spell seemed to have transferred itself. I could see in Karl's red face, as the game went on, the sullenness of a son. He stopped answering when my father talked and simply waited his turn. My father, for his part, kept up a steady stream of banter. 'You gonna give it to me?' he said, taking position. 'In golf they have something called a gimme. Between friends, when you

can't miss. You don't think I'm gonna miss this, do you?'
And so on.

What I heard, though, and what he meant me to hear, was: You don't have to let these guys push you around. I don't care if they're better than you. Sometimes even when you're wrong you have to stick up for yourself.

I still like to think of the two of them going at it. My father, six one in his prime, but bent a couple inches forward by children and a shuffling habit. Anyway, a good head and neck shorter than the younger man. Hadn't played organized ball since 1956 and spent most of that year on the bench. But growing happy, as he only is in company, garrulous, knocking down eighteen-footers. Karl silent and mechanical in his motions, chasing the ball, back-rimming his shots. Two years later he signed his first American contract, for three years and 25 million dollars. A future all-star; a league MVP.

Another thing my father liked to say. If you got beat to nothing, he called it a perfect *bagel*. The word had a verb-form, too: Karl got bageled.

22

When I was fifteen years old, my family spent a year in Berlin and my brother for the first time brought home, over Thanksgiving, a girlfriend from college. He arrived with a suitcase full of frozen pizza from some campus eatery, and a short, pretty, very nice girl from upstate New York.

Her name was Martha. It wasn't their idea, though, to spend the whole time at my parents' place, and in an act of generosity that was, I now see, as much hers as his, he took his kid brother and three kid sisters away for a long weekend in Flensburg.

It's five hours by slow train from Berlin, and the train we caught had old-fashioned cabins in it. At some point one of us discovered that the two long leather benches against the walls could be folded down to meet in the middle, making an enormous bed. And that's what we lay on, under several duvets, for the rest of the journey – as if my brother's introduction of a sexual life into the bosom of the family were no less innocent than a midnight feast.

On the twelve-hour train-ride from Landshut, a few days before Christmas, I thought of that long weekend. There was no cabin, and Anke and Franziska continually exchanged seats beside me, depending on who needed to sleep or stretch her legs. The day darkened as we made our way north, and the hills gave way to the flatness of Schleswig-Holstein: an endless journey, cramped, sometimes embarrassing, as any journey with a child can be; exhilarating, too. We were playing at families, and I wondered from time to time what my brother would do.

Around nine o'clock the train pulled in, and I paid for a taxi to take us to my mother's house, which is outside of town, about twenty minutes by car. Just long enough, as Anke said, for a small tired girl to fall asleep.

When the tarmac gave way to dirt and stone, I knew we were near. The trees opened up beside us, and we could see the sea – even at night, distinguishable in its darkness from the darkness of everything else. Dirt gave way to gravel on the steep drive down, and gravel to grass, and then there was nothing but trees on one side and water on the other.

Franziska *had* fallen asleep, and Anke lifted her screaming from the warm car-seat, still caught up in dreams.

'Mami, mami,' she cried, slapping her cheeks with small hands.

I stood aside for a moment and breathed in deeply the familiar stony smell, then carried what bags I could up the broken steps to the terrace. Home-coming is always a private experience, and I resisted the strong desire to communicate some part of it to Anke. (Look at the lights of Denmark across the water. Can you hear that boat at anchor?) The taxi reversed loudly up the drive, and then its headlamps shifted on to the road above; it was suddenly dark and quiet. For an awful minute, I thought our neighbor had forgotten to leave the front-door key under the shoe-grate, but then my fingers found cool iron among the grit and pebbles.

Everything was tidy when I pushed my way in, tidy and dusty and cold as a house unlived-in. Dead flowers in a vase on the sitting room table scattered at my touch. Someone had left a note beside them:

Write down the numbers on the telephone meter.

There are two jars of jam in the cellar.

Don't eat them.

It's gooseberries from the garden and I laid them down myself.

A scrawled signature; probably one of my uncles.

In the kitchen, the fridge door was open and the light inside was off. I found a can of soup inside the larder door and began looking for a can-opener. Anke said, 'What are you doing? I have to get her to bed.'

'I'm trying to make us something to eat.'

'I have to get her to bed.' After a moment, 'What are you waiting for? I don't know where her bed is.'

She stood aside for me in the kitchen doorway, and I felt the stiff formality of the gesture. Franziska also turned her shoulder to let me through; she had stopped crying but her lips were thick with sleepiness or unhappiness. I led the way up the narrow stairs into a small room under the eaves. There was a tree outside the window that brushed against the glass all night in windy weather. I opened the window to let some air in and inhaled again, rather self-consciously, deep draughts of nostalgia.

'This is where I used to sleep. She can sleep here.'

'The wallpaper is peeling off over her head.'

'Yes, we all used to pick at it.'

For the next hour, I hunted up sheets and towels, and made beds, and found the hot-water dial, and switched it on, and the central-heating, and turned that on, too. The stairs outside Franziska's bedroom were too steep for a small girl in a strange house, so I stacked two chairs in front of them. Meanwhile, she resumed her screaming, and Anke at last lay down in bed beside her. I went downstairs and made soup, waited for a half hour until it grew cold, then set it on the hob again and ate from the pot as soon as the soup was hot. After that, I began looking through all the cupboards for things I remembered: puzzles, children's games, old maps.

Around eleven o'clock Anke came down again with her daughter in her arms.

'Didn't you hear me?' she said. 'I've been calling for the last ten minutes. The bed is too narrow for two. I'm going to take her in with us.'

'Where should I sleep?'

'Wherever you like; it's your house.'

'There's soup if you want it.'

'Right now I only want you to show me where our bedroom is.'

I led the way upstairs again and along the narrow corridor to the door at the end. Behind it was a wide, carpeted room with two single beds pushed together. The house had been furnished to accommodate various large families and adapt itself to each. Consequently, it had some of the durable, seedy comforts of a seaside hotel: a bedroom sink, rough carpeting. When my grandfather at last grew too old to live in it, he left several pieces of good furniture behind, and these remained, pushed into odd corners of rooms. The result was a kind of shabby gentility of which I now felt ashamed.

Anke sat down and tried to wriggle out of her jeans and blouse. Franziska was by this point perfectly quiet in her mother's arms, but as soon as she let go, the screaming began again. 'Can you help me?' Anke said at last, and I bent down to pull her trousers off. A quiet, intimate act for which I was suddenly grateful. 'When were you coming to bed?' she asked me, lying carefully back with her arms full.

'I was waiting for you to come down.'

'Will you come to bed now?'

Franziska lay in the crack between the two mattresses, against her side, with one hand holding tight to her mother's ear. She was tall and her feet had the boyish roughness and flatness of a child who goes barefoot.

'What's wrong?'

'I've never slept with her in the bed before.'

Anke thought about this. 'I don't think she'll mind.'

* * *

I slept lightly in the unfamiliar bed with the unfamiliar small body under the duvet beside me. There was only one small window in the room, overlooking the garden and drive. None of the vague white noise of city lights reached us there, and the night was properly dark – the sort of dark that is itself a kind of wilderness. Even so, whenever I woke up, my eyes adjusted, and I could make out the shape of Franziska's face and something of her expression: her lips pursed, as if she sucked on a lemon pip. I didn't want to roll over, in case it disturbed them, but I'm a restless sleeper at the best of times and suffered from the sense of restraint. Then there was the mild embarrassment of what happens to a man's body invol-untarily in the course of a night. Around five or six, at the first signs of graying in the curtains, I drifted at last into deeper sleep.

When I woke up, Anke was standing at the small window with Franziska on a chair beside her. 'We're bored,' she said. 'Where is the sea? I promised her the sea.'

'Lean out and look to your left.'

'Oh,' she said, after a minute. And then: 'Get dressed, get dressed. What are you waiting for? It's so still.'

There's a set of routines my family adheres to more or less strictly in Flensburg, and I tried to introduce them then, explaining myself from under the duvet. In the morning, we go into the village and buy rolls, a fifteen-minute walk along the dirt road; then come back and eat them in the glasshouse. At that point, we consider plans – there's a boat that needs a lot of talking about. But

Franziska only wanted to go down to the beach. Anke told her to pull my covers off, which she thought about for a minute, then did. I kissed her mother good morning at the window and felt easy in the girl's presence, since it meant Anke and I didn't have to be alone together.

It was a pale blue watery clear sort of day. Denmark looked about as close as the end of your arm, brown and leafless against the sea. Since the bathroom was unheated, Anke decided not to shower: she would rather be warm than clean. We pulled on yesterday's clothes, then breakfasted on nothing more than mugs of water from the tap and handfuls of stale wheat squares left behind by someone else – cereal for children. Anke filled a plastic bag with some of them, which she took with her, feeding Franziska from time to time as we descended the uneven footpath to the shore.

The sea emerges only at the bottom, once you push through a dark growth of woodland and an alley of sharp rosehip. But once it emerges it is everywhere.

Outside our house there's a patch of beach that used to belong to my family, before the city took over the shoreline, but still we claim over it a kind of seigniory. A spit of weedy rocks jutting out had been built up over time by my uncles and cousins to ease the access for a sailing boat. Franziska helped me to gather loose stones together, which were mostly too heavy for her to lift, and throw them out to sea, where they landed with a great splash and a loud clash. The water itself was much too cold for anything but dipping your hand in. Afterwards, we wandered along the coastal path to the children's playground, an old-fashioned assortment of land-locked boats and wooden slides and wobbly bridges, on which I remembered playing every summer of my childhood.

It occurred to me that I might easily tire Anke's patience for reminiscence. At the same time I felt there was something in my stories she found attractive. Evidence of the fact that I was properly German and at home. Also of something else: that we were 'landed' people.

After the playground, I led us by another route back up the hill and ran into Frau Kohler, the neighbor who had left the key. A short, stiff-backed woman with a good, decisive sort of face. Her husband, who was dead, had known my grandparents well, and Anke sweetly asked her about the family connection.

This involved a few more stories and eventually we were invited in for tea and cake, which Anke accepted, since we hadn't had any breakfast. Frau Kohler gave us toys for Franziska to take down to the house, including an antique rocking horse and a wooden high chair.

On our way home, I apologized to Anke for 'all the family business. My grandfather once did the Kohlers a good turn, and she likes talking about him.'

'Not at all,' Anke said, politely.

She had been on her best behavior; it survived for about half an hour any need for it. In Frau Kohler's presence, she had addressed me with the attractive propriety of a woman being courted. Anke always liked 50s clothes; sometimes she dressed up in 50s manners, too. Her childhood had been a thoroughly prosperous middle-class sort of childhood, until her father's illness, which had the effect of wearing a little thinner the fabric of her family life. Their traditions had more to do with doctors' visits, the routines of convalescence, the allowances made for her mother's late career. When she dropped out of school, she dropped down a rung in the social ladder, too. Occasionally she talked about acting or going to university, but I think what she really wanted were the customs and community of middle-class life.

That afternoon I phoned my mother, just to tell her we had safely arrived. She asked to speak to Anke; they chatted for about five minutes. Afterwards she said to me, 'Your father has been worrying to me about her. I'll tell him, I know just the kind of girl she is.'

She meant by that, a good German girl, someone like me. Nothing worse.

I didn't respond to this, or mention her remark to Anke, but the line stuck with me. Sometimes, when I looked at her, I heard my mother: I know just the kind of girl she is. *It is strange for me, that my son takes a lover, but this is less strange.* In her German youth, my mother looked not unlike Anke, fashionably demure, upright, very slender. Her presence in our relationship seemed particularly strong that week; it cast a shadow on us, but a warm shadow.

23

Later, we went shopping and bought so much food we needed to take a taxi home. Christmas was still three days off, but we couldn't find any fresh goose at the butcher and eventually settled for a frozen one. Some of the food went into the larder, and some down to the cellar. It smells deeply of the earth underneath stones – among the most vivid of my childhood smells. We were always forbidden from climbing the steps alone. I led Franziska by hand down the corkscrew stairway, telling her to breathe deeply in. She sniffed and looked around her and was glad in the end to be carried upstairs again.

Anke said to me, after the food was put away and we had sat down to another round of cake and coffee, 'I think you probably didn't play with dolls' houses when you were a child, but I did, and this is much more fun.'

Franziska was building a tower of blocks on the carpet, and Anke pinched quietly the fingers of my hand. As if her daughter might catch us out. Sometimes, among all the other things we were pretending to be and do, Anke and I pretended to be scared of Franziska.

If I had any illusions left about what it meant to inherit

a family, they didn't last a day. Franziska refused to nap in her crib, which meant in practice that one of us had to wheel her around in the stroller. Usually, both of us. This, in the depth of winter, with a graveled terrace outside and a rough dirt road above us. It was a ten-minute walk from the house to smooth pavement. Luckily, the weather held, and most afternoons cleared up enough for a good walk. When Franziska was safely asleep, we found a bench to sit on, overlooking wood or water, and talked until we got too cold, and then we kissed. We admitted to being sometimes grateful when the girl woke up. It really was bitter, especially in the wind, and Anke, who was long-limbed and restlessly thin, suffered even from drafts. More than once, she ended up blue in the lips and on the edge of those nervous tears that cold itself can bring on.

Franziska also refused to sleep alone at night. I helped Anke bathe her in the shallow basin of the upstairs shower stall, but then there was little more for me to do but wait. And cook; mostly, I cooked and imagined the progress of the delicate operation going on upstairs. Anke put her in our own bed, among her familiar smells, and read to her with only the hall-light on, then kissed her and gently retreated. Closed the door and waited a minute for the small furtive animal noise of a girl getting out of bed. Then the pressure of her daughter against the door. Why Anke locked it, I don't know – stupid desperation. After a moment, screaming, and the whole thing began again.

Eventually, she abandoned any hope of getting her to sleep alone and lay beside Franziska on top of the duvet until she seemed sufficiently *fast* for a quiet escape. But the floorboards were loose, under the carpeting, and the door creaked, and Franziska had an ear cocked and an eye half-peeled for the slightest disturbance, of light or noise. Sometimes, Anke was tired enough that she fell asleep, too, and I had to creep upstairs to wake them both and bring them both down to dinner. Mostly, though, they came down together without me, and Franziska was told to play quietly in a corner if she hoped to stay up with us, which is what she usually did. At nine or ten, she lay down by herself on a comfortable small kelim beside the sofa and fell asleep until we had finished the dishes. Then we all went to bed together.

Anke found her failure to get Franziska 'down' very embarrassing, especially as she went to bed so easily at home. I don't know how much I minded, though I joked once, by way of reproach, 'She's keeping her eye on us, that's all.'

'No, no,' Anke insisted, properly upset by my remark, 'she only wants to be with us, she doesn't want to be left out.'

There was some truth in this. Franziska wasn't entirely a distraction or a burden. We laughed a lot around her, sometimes falsely, but sometimes also with a deep good humor I had almost forgotten. Then there was the appetite for physical tenderness and comfort she brought out in both of us. It was a small triumph for me when Franziska, after falling down the flight of broken steps to the garden, stopped crying in my arms. She weighed about thirty pounds at the time. I said to Anke afterwards, a phrase that tested to the limit my childish German, 'People are much more consolable in small portions.' But you might tell such stories about all children.

My mother once asked me to describe her, over the phone. 'It's like she's always acting in a silent movie,' I said. Her gestures and way of walking suggested struggles and feelings much larger than herself. For example, she often imitated her mother's interactions with me, pulling at my hand, etc. and when Anke tried to do the same, would shout and push her off. She asked to have her picture taken with me and smoothed the hair off her forehead in preparation.

But Franziska *was* a slow talker. Certain phrases came out perfectly formed and clear, May I go down, and so on, but she played around with words very little and didn't trust herself to say what she didn't already know how to say. She wanted to be correct in everything. Occasionally, I insisted on speaking to her in English, out of some curious loyalty to Hadnot, and refused to answer or respond to anything *but* English. No and Thank you was as far as I got, though these words seemed to stir up associations in her, and she offered them to me somberly, as if she understood how gratifying her condescension was. No, thank you, No, thank you – her English accent was just like her mother's.

248

Anke also found it hard to avoid comparisons. The house in Flensburg has a kid's bat and a saggy old softball in one of the cupboard benches. On a cloudy afternoon, a little warmer than the days preceding, I carried bat and ball into the garden and tried to teach Anke to hit, without much success. But she liked pitching to me and watching the ball skitter off in the yellow grass – so much so, that she refused to let me go inside, until Anke came out with a cup of heated milk.

'You are just like Bo,' Anke said to me. 'You don't mind doing something over and over again.'

His name came up occasionally, and more than I wanted it to. But Anke couldn't help herself. Some thoughts need lancing from time to time, otherwise they begin to ache. There was something flattering in the comparisons, which I understood – Hadnot was the guy she married, after all. But I saw the unflattering angle, too. Anke more or less admitted to me that she had 'jumped on' the first foreigner who came her way.

'You mean, I'm the second?'

But I was also German, it wasn't as simple as that. Sometimes she liked to pretend that we were just the same; sometimes she liked to imagine that we were separated by an ocean of differences. Which weren't very hard to find, once you started looking for them, even if you didn't count Franziska. I told her what my mother used to say: that of all the people in the world, she feels most comfortable around American Jews. 'This from a German girl who grew up in the war.'

'But your father,' she said, 'must also have had his reasons for liking German girls who grew up in the war.'

'He liked one of them, but it cost him something. His family tried to have him committed.'

'I don't understand,' she said.

'Because she was German; because she wasn't Jewish.'

'I don't understand,' she repeated.

Again and again, we went over our first meeting on the train to Munich, and I also talked about the synagogue I sometimes attended and the evening I spent with Olaf's family. Anke knew Olaf a little, so I told her a story about him.

Once, coming back from another Friday night in town, I spotted him with a white girl standing outside the second nightclub in Landshut. This appealed to a slightly more hard-core element than the Hollywood. (I knew this, not because I had been inside, but because it called itself The Hard Core and refused to admit anyone under eighteen.) Around midnight – a dripping, dispiriting evening that seemed colder and colder the longer you stayed out in it. Even so, a queue had built up outside the club, with a bouncer at the door, the kind of fat-bellied man who has to lean back to keep his balance.

Olaf and the girl stood outside the cordoned line. She was haranguing him; otherwise I would have stopped to say hello. A bus shelter standing between them and the sidewalk meant I could listen in safely to their conversation. So I listened and pretended to wait for a bus. Olaf had promised he could get her into the club, though she was only seventeen, and she had got all dressed up expecting a night out. Now she was standing out in the fucking cold with nowhere to go. Olaf had nothing much to offer in response but 'I know' and 'I'm sorry.' If he knew and he was sorry, she said, why did he promise he could get her in when he couldn't? He got a girl in before, he explained at last. Why don't you take her, she said, if you like her so much?

'Maybe the other girl was black,' Anke suggested. 'Nobody cares about two black lovers.'

After a minute, I had heard enough to be sick of all three of us and walked on. Even so, I turned around to get a better look at the girl. Olaf, towering over her, had his back towards me. Her eyes were heavily made up, and she wore the type of fashionable clothes that poor people spend a lot of money on. A tweedy miniskirt that showed off her pale long thighs, covered in goose pimples. Bright knee-high socks; a lamé blouse. A tiny handbag written over with gold lettering. 'The kind of girl,' I said to Anke, 'whose main or only expression of ambition is the way she looks.' I had to resort to English for this line, and Anke asked me to repeat it, and afterwards repeated it carefully back to me in German.

She knew just the kind of girl I meant, she said. 'I was that kind of girl, before Franziska. Maybe I still am.'

'No, no,' I said, meaning . . . but I'm not sure what I meant. Anke had real style, even I could see that, and I was beginning to understand this wasn't a quality one should lightly dismiss. With a part-time job and a three-year-old girl, no help at home and unhappy parents, to turn yourself out as she did every day showed more than just an eye for fashion.

24

For Christmas Eve, Anke wanted to put on 'a show' (like many Germans, she larded her speech with the odd English phrase), for my sake as well as Franziska's. I grew up in one of those Jewish households where a tree is lit for Christmas, too, and presents exchanged, but for us the whole business was a celebration of the German side of our family, and we sang German carols and used real wax-candles instead of electric lights. Germans eat dinner on the 24th. She took over the cooking herself and sent me down to the beach with her daughter.

I still found it difficult to pass more than ten or fifteen minutes alone with her; after that, I ran out of games to play and got tired of roaring or hiding or throwing her around. Somberly then, we ventured farther afield, as far as the harbor, where my grandfather used to keep a boat, and wandered among the echoing piers looking at the funny yacht-names and listening to the clanking of loose stays. I told her about the nights my cousins and I slept over in the cabin, with the boat still moored; how the jellyfish glowed in the water. So we looked for jellyfish. There aren't many in winter, but we found a few, breathing slowly with the waves, and I remember saying to one of them, in the deep, hokey voice you use with children, 'You seem to be in pretty deep there.'

Another fifteen minutes gone.

The afternoon was clear and pale and consequently very cold. The sky seemed almost unlit and gave way to darkness by imperceptible degrees. By four, when we turned back again, the coast path was as black as the sea, and we were both so frozen and shrunk inside ourselves that I carried Franziska home just to warm up.

As soon as we reached the terrace, we could see the Christmas lights. The day before we had bought a tree together, from a nearby farm, and dragged it back along the beach. Anke had secretly phoned my mother, who told her where to find candles. The table was laid, and while I admired everything, Anke carried in the food: a pot of potatoes, still steaming when I lifted the lid; a pot of red cabbage. The goose was almost finished in the oven. Anke had set the presents out on each of our plates. Franziska's spilled over on to the table as well, and I spotted among them the shape of the recorder I had brought with me from Landshut to give her. Anke had wrapped it. She seemed as nervous as a performer after the curtain on first night; very pleased with herself, too, wearing my mother's apron, and hurrying back to the kitchen from time to time to check on the bird. The oven had been on all afternoon and the house for the first time that week seemed properly warm. After the goose was carried in, and cooling on its tray, Anke turned off the table lamp and we looked at the tree together, shifting in its own light. Then we turned on the lamp again and one by one blew out the candles before eating.

She was glad my family put up a tree for Christmas, she said, but she wanted to know what else I celebrated, as a Jew. For much of the dinner I found myself rehearsing half-forgotten Sunday school lessons, about Moses and Judah Maccabee. I told the story my father likes to tell, how he once came in to my elementary school to explain Hannukah to the class. Afterwards the teacher thanked him. How nice it is, she said, to learn how other people celebrate Christmas. Then I explained to Anke why my father found this funny. When the meal was over, we unwrapped presents. I gave Anke a necklace, made of alternating silver and green stone, which I had picked up in a farmer's craft shop on one of my bicycle rides.

'Necklaces fit everybody,' I told her. This seemed, as she put it on, not quite the right thing to say.

Afterwards, she led Franziska up to bed and I cleared the table and made a start on the dishes. She promised to be down soon. 'Just once,' she said, 'I want an evening alone with you.'

When the pots were all clean and dripping on the counter, I listened at the bottom of the stairs for a few minutes then put on my overcoat and shoes and headed for the beach. The night was so dark I had to pause at the top of the slope until my eyes adjusted and I could make out the color of stone steps amid the dirt. Dark but not quiet: I heard, opening the garden gate, the deep, insistent beat of some digitized bass line, more vibration than sound.

There are only two walks to take, as my mother said, towards the pier or harbor, and since I had spent the afternoon at the harbor, I made for the pier. It is known for some reason locally as the Big Bridge and extends outwards from the wide stretch of sand at the eastern end of the bay, where the water is too shallow to swim in but good for children. In summer, this beach gets very busy and colorful with towels. A playground abuts it, on the landward side, and the city has set up a couple of poles in the sand for volleyball nets. I noticed as I walked that some teenagers had stretched a line between the poles and hung a disco ball off it, the cheap plastic kind you find in toyshops. They had also pushed a litter-bin under the ball and started a fire inside it.

I sat down on one of the benches lining the footpath and watched them. The kind of scene I was never a part of in my own youth: ten or fifteen kids, all of them with beers in hand or something to smoke. Their voices carried to me, as voices do on a beach, between the beats of the music, though I couldn't make out much of what they were saying. A teacher's name came up from time to time: Herr so and so. Sometimes they danced. Mostly it was the girls dancing, briefly, by themselves, before a boy strode heavily over and pushed them into the sand. After a while one of them spotted me. I saw her pointing me out to someone else and was suddenly flushed by a sense of shame, not unmixed with stupid fears and a dim association of these girls with Anke. Maybe because I first saw Anke from the darkness of my bathroom window.

Two or three of them began waving at me, and calling something – 'Do you want a beer?' – and I had the strong, childish conviction that if I didn't move the trouble would go away. They were making fun of me, for watching them; it was a joke, the idea that I could join in. 'Are you shy?' one of them called, with a smile in her voice. 'Don't be scared.'

After a few minutes, feeling very young, I braved the laughter of the teenage girls and walked home. Of course, no one laughed; they had forgotten me. Anke was waiting in the sitting room, upset if not yet angry.

'I'm sorry I took so long,' she said. 'Where have you been? Well, at least, we can have a few quiet hours together.'

But the color of the evening had somehow changed. We sat on the couch together and kissed, but Anke sensed my reluctance and suggested a game instead. On Christmas Eve, as a girl, she always played games. 'There are games in that cupboard by the dinner table,' I said, pointing, and she spent a few happy minutes looking through them. But there was something settled and heavy in my mood she couldn't shift. What had happened on the beach was too vague and ridiculous for me to mention, but I couldn't think of anything else to talk about. Also, Anke, in my thoughts, was lumped together with those girls.

Eventually she said, 'You are just like Bo. You only talk because you want to.'

'Isn't that what everyone does?'

'No, most people just like talking. They don't have to think about it.'

Shortly afterwards we went to bed.

A few days later we took the long train home again. My slight withdrawal also cleared the way for certain necessary conversations, which we had been putting off. Anke asked me if I intended to play another year. I didn't know; it depended in part on whether the club would resign me. She asked me if I would consider moving in with her, or if I could imagine in the future such a thing happening. My brother had moved in with Martha only after five or six years, and even then they drifted apart afterwards. The problem was they began too young.

'Yes,' she said, 'but you are not your brother.'

He's a little shorter, I joked, and can't go left.

She accused me of playing games with her, so I shot back, 'Who was it talking about dolls' houses earlier on?'

'That's just what I mean,' she said inconsequently. 'You act as if none of this matters very much.'

But we also spoke more calmly and sensibly about other things. Her marriage, for example. On the last night, Franziska went to bed quietly by herself, and Anke and I stayed up late talking, openly, as strangers sometimes do. 'He was very sure of himself, of me,' she said. 'I was quite unhappy before he came, and after he came, too, and found it hard to resist him. At first. When I was shy of him, I was still in love; but when I wasn't shy of him anymore, I don't know how much was left.' She added, after a moment: 'I think I was shy of him for about a year.'

'What happened after that?'

'Franziska was born.'

'Is that really why you got married? Because of Franziska?'

There was a silence, which lasted about a minute, while she took this in. To break it, she said, 'You ask me that as if it would explain everything.'

'It explains a certain amount.'

With a curious and affecting tilt of her head: 'What does it explain?'

'How little you see of each other – and for no good reason I can tell. How easy it seems for you to walk away, even with a child. If it was . . . an accident from the first all of this makes sense.' She said only, in a kind of under-tone, 'I am happy it is easy,' but I was still talking and she waited for me to finish. 'But I don't see why you would be embarrassed about telling me. Isn't this the kind of thing that happens all the time?'

'Yes' – she had got her color back – 'to poor stupid little girls. To the kinds of girls who smoke cigarettes outside McDonald's all their lives. Even with their strollers.'

'Not just to them.'

Somehow this new angle on their relationship comforted me. At least I could assign to the strangeness of their marriage and separation a reasonable cause, and one which played to my suspicions of adult life – that adults weren't particularly good at it. Or not good enough; that's why they ended up the way they did. So I said, 'What I don't understand then is why Bo still cares so much about staying together. If it was an accident in the first place.'

'Does he care so much?' And she went on: 'He is very conventional. If his father has stayed married, he wants to, too. Also, it is like basketball with him. He hates losing. He thinks, all I need to do is practice more. What do you want me to do? I will get better. I tell him, sometimes it is still no good.'

Something about the way Anke held herself then moved me very much. Her small pretty face on its long neck, with her faintly slanted eyes – an elfin effect she liked to exaggerate with make-up. Pretty and brittle she looked; somewhat consciously brave. Look, she seemed to say, how I expose myself for you. There were times I felt that all my reservations about her were really only the hesitations you suffer from in the face of something inevitable, that they would all be resolved as soon as I gave in to it. Maybe, in fact, we had already fallen in love, and this is what it's like. *Tell him*, she had said. I would have preferred her to use the past tense.

Later I discovered how much she was still capable of keeping from me. Anke had known all week that Hadnot's contract would not be renewed, and that the club had asked her to move out of her apartment by the end of January.

25

I spent New Year with a college friend living in Brussels. When I got back, it took me a few hours to adjust again to the facts of my life: the bed in the middle of my room, the view from my window (of horses in a field, across a road); the prospect of the days ahead. Not to mention, the self-assessment that is our constant companion, and which had shifted slightly over the long hours of the journey home. In Brussels, I was a young man drifting out of university, vaguely ambitious and dissatisfied, with an appetite for talking things through. In Landshut, I was a bench player for a minor league basketball club, who was getting paid more than he was worth. Also, something of a cold fish. And it occurred to me that people become who they are after a process they have some control over.

At practice the first day back I couldn't find anyone in the locker room, so I wandered on court in street clothes. Lights off, and the hoops still pinned against the walls; mats left over from aerobics class on the gym floor. No one there either. For a minute or two I nursed the childish hope that I had gotten the day wrong. At reception, Angie, the judge's wife, was talking to Charlie, who seemed to have dressed up for the occasion in a button-up shirt and jacket. He called me over and rested a hand on my shoulder.

'Our turn next,' he said. 'Bo's putting his case to Coach, and then it's our turn.'

Frau Kolwitz had decided not to take up the option on his three-month contract, and Charlie wanted everybody to talk it over. The rest of the guys were waiting in what was called the conference room, a windowless office space with blue carpet and blue-upholstered chairs and sofas scattered around. Charlie and I carried in drinks from reception, bottles of Lucozade from the staff fridge. The room stank of cigarettes and the central heating vents. Milo first complained of the smell and then bummed a cigarette from Angie and lit up.

After ten or fifteen minutes, Henkel and Hadnot came in with a young man I had never met before. He wore a well-cut suit without tie and had the kind of face you see slotted inside store-bought picture frames, handsome without being memorable. Later, I realized this was only a first impression. His curly hairline was receding, and during a brief coffee break, he talked to me about his skiing trip, which he had just come back from, and I noticed on his cheeks the faintly rough, unhealthy reddening of a winter sunburn. His name was Kaspar Schrenkman, and he worked in some vaguely defined capacity for Frau Kolwitz, who was the mother of a friend from school. He didn't speak any English.

This partly accounts for the state Hadnot was in. In their private session, he must have relied on the coach to put his case, but Henkel spoke only a kind of basketball pidgin. Rich in words like 'backdoor' and 'zone,' but not so good for negotiation. I imagine that he more or less ignored whatever he was told to say; that Hadnot retreated into silence. By the time the three of them came in, Bo had built up a head of steam that could be seen in his face. His clothes also seemed to make him uncomfortable. He wore his wedding suit to the meeting; it was his only suit. It surprised me to see him dress up, even for a conference that would decide his future, but athletes learn young at their coaches' hands a faith in formal uniforms, and are often required to don jacket and tie on game days, from high school onwards. Add to this his suspicion of money-men and a natural competitive desire to meet an opponent on equal terms. But the suit only made him look nervous. You took from him generally the impression of a muscular middle-aged man suffering under strong constraints.

'Ben,' he said, as soon as he saw me, 'explain to this cocksucker what I've been trying to tell him. You heard what they trying to do?'

'I heard.'

'Well, tell him.'

'What do you want me to tell him?'

'Whatever I say, that's what you tell him.'

And so on. This is how I came to act as *Dolmetscher*, that ugly German word which describes what it means to be caught in the middle between two languages.

Hadnot was arrogant rather than boastful. He had a

strict if somewhat strange sense of propriety; it didn't suit him at all to blow his own horn. I mean, it really cost him something to plead his case – it upset his pride, as much as anything else. Only dishonest people try to get their way by argument. Throughout my childhood I had a vivid sense of the private, the significant, the unsuccessful side of life, where self-importance breeds. Where we say to ourselves, don't they know who I am? But only to ourselves. Hadnot had been forced to ask the question publicly.

Much of what was said was said in German, and I sat at Hadnot's side, translating, with Charlie listening in. Milo, always confident in his opinions, explained to Herr Schrenkman that it was 'self-evidently' in the interests of the team to keep Hadnot on – adopting the air, which I find oddly charming, of car-mechanics, plumbers, accountants the world over, experts and bringers of bad news. Self-evident, in English, sounds high-falutin', but in German it's a familiar, comfortable sort of word. Hadnot was our second-leading scorer, you had only to look at the team stats; but there were other things Herr Schrenkman would not have the eye to appreciate. For example, that as a shooter alone, he opened up a great deal of space inside.

'What's he saying? What's he saying?' Hadnot muttered in my ear. And I was embarrassed for his sake to translate praise.

Olaf simply looked at Schrenkman, who stood perhaps five feet ten inches tall in his dress shoes, disdainfully. 'What have we to say to this man?' he asked Milo.

For most of the guys this was a kind of tribal occasion, in which we could enjoy righteously our physical superiorities – over the fattening middle managers who determined our incomes, the cars we drove and the apartments we lived in. Righteously, because we never got our way and would not now.

'*Ich verstehe, ich verstehe*,' was Schrenkman's answer. 'I understand.' Nodding his head and smoothing the air with his hands. 'But he had a three-month contract, and we have no money.'

'Don't talk to me about money, I know they got money,' Hadnot said, on the half-beat, after one of my translations. 'The way she lives. Don't talk to me about contracts, either. We had an understanding. You win some ballgames and we'll see you through. Well, we're winning, aren't we?'

Another pause, as I explained all this to Schrenkman. At the end he gave me a look that made me suddenly complicit: it said, *yes, but why are we winning? Not because of him. Even I know enough to see that.* That in this respect someone like Kaspar Schrenkman could see clearer than Hadnot seemed somehow awful to me: what a shameful thing is the personal point of view. I had the impression the others felt the same, and that Hadnot had said the wrong thing. Don't take the credit for winning, that's not what you should take credit for.

Karl, for one, kept quiet the whole way through, and

his quiet was a kind of commentary. 'Don't look at me,' it said. 'None of this matters to me.'

Hadnot must have noticed the look. In any case, something prompted him to say what we all sometimes want to say in our own defense, the private angry boast we learn to keep down and control, like the sex impulse or any other bodily function.

'I'm the best damn player on this team. I'm probably the best damn player in this shitty league. Tell him that, Ben. Tell him that.'

Almost blushing, I repeated: 'He says he is the best . . . and probably the best etc.' Just the act of translation added a kind of irony to his claim, which made me feel disloyal. Afterwards I wondered, on the strength of the evidence, whether a reasonable man could reasonably believe what he said to be true. Yes, he could, just about. So why did Hadnot seem so exposed? By this point embarrassment had driven everyone else to silence, and he had the floor to himself.

'Let me tell you about these people,' he said. 'They don't give a damn about loyalty. All they care about is what they can use you for. Five years in this god damn league. You think you make it up to the first division one of you guys has a contract here? Come on. TV revenue, magazine promotions. They can buy much better talent than you. All you need is a little more money. A little more money always buys someone better than you. That's what this game teaches. You playing to get fired, that's what you playing for. Think about that next time you step on court. Don't worry about me. I'll be fine. Tomorrow morning I'll sign a deal with somebody else. There are people in this league who know how to appreciate Bo Hadnot. You all will see me again.' A nod to Karl. 'I got my eye on this one right here. Then you can make up your own mind how much money I'm worth.'

Charlie put a soft hand on my knee. It meant, you don't have to translate all that. I wish it had ended there, but we had another hour of talking things over before everyone was so angry they really had nothing left to say.

26

A week later, he was gone and more or less everything he promised turned out to be true. Hadnot signed on with Würzburg, rejoining old teammates Chad Baker and Henrik Lenz, and moving by this step from third place in the league to first. Of course, he also moved six hours by car from his estranged wife and his three-year-old daughter.

The most immediate effect on my life was that Anke had to clear out of the club apartment. In the end, she moved home with her parents, about a twenty-minute bike ride away. I helped her clear out, which is how I first came to know her father, one of those retired old men who dresses in a jacket and tie every morning and afterwards does very little else. Most of the furniture belonged to the club, but he packed everything that didn't into the back of a small sedan, a process which took perhaps an hour longer than it needed to. Meanwhile, Anke wept quietly in her empty kitchen. I left her to cry; it didn't seem the kind of unhappiness I could console her for, either because I had caused it myself or because it had nothing to do with me.

Our relationship had changed, that much was clear, though in some ways it only became more conventional.

Living at home, Anke could go out as much as she liked in the evenings, even very late, and she often met me after practice for a late drink and something to eat. Her mother was always around to look after Franziska, and so I saw much less of the girl. I missed her, more than I expected to, but I did not miss the air of fraught, responsible adult life she carried with her. Anke and I began to 'date,' and it struck me at first as something else to be grateful for, in Franziska's absence, that dating was less intimate than whatever it was we had been doing before. The smell I associated with my girlfriend was no longer the smell of warm milk. I made conversation with her; we went to movies. Sometimes, we went to bed together, too, and never worried about waking in the night to deal with the kind of insistent childish fear that makes all other emotions and desires seem temporary and insignificant.

It became clear to me only slowly how unhappy Anke was. What I felt, instead, was that somehow in our relationship I had acquired an advantage. Anke began to depend on me, often sweetly and lovingly, and liked to claim me in little ways all the time – by taking my hand for example, when she met me outside the sports hall, even though I had asked her not to. No one from the club knew about our relationship and we had decided to keep quiet about it. Still, she took my hand. Advantage is an ugly word to use in this context, but I felt it as clearly as you feel, on the basketball court, an edge in quickness or strength. I had freedoms with her that she did not have with me. But they also carried with them a kind of constraint. We were playing a game together, the sort of game you play with kids, when you let them push you to the ground; and I was letting her win.

As the year wore on, she pressed me more and more over various decisions. The season ended in March, and unless the club renewed my contract, I had nowhere to live all summer. Even if they did 'pick up the option,' as it was called, I had nothing to do for five months and no reason to stay in Landshut. Anke wanted to know what my plans were.

'I tend to do things out of laziness or stubbornness,' I said to her once, 'whichever turns out to be stronger.'

'How lazy are you feeling?'

We were sitting in a bar at the bottom of my hill, in a window booth by the front door, which was the only free space. Every time the door opened all the outside February air blew in. It was one of those evenings when nothing turns out quite right, but you stick at it because going home seems worse.

'Well, I'm not feeling stubborn,' I said. *Bockig* is the German word, the kind of word you use to chastise children. 'But a little restless,' I went on. 'Most of the people like me, the people I know, come here to go traveling. They don't stick around a small Bavarian market town all summer.'

'No, I can see that.'

Later, on the wet walk back up hill, she explained that there wasn't much to keep her in Landshut either, until

Franziska went to school in the autumn, and somehow we spent a very happy night together imagining the places we could travel together. I don't know how likely or real it seemed to her, or me.

At one point, I raised the question of conversion. Maybe to put her off. My father, I told her, would prefer his sons to marry Jews.

'But he married a Christian himself!' she said, baffled.

Afterwards, though, she kept returning to it, with a seriousness and persistence that amazed me, and almost the worst part of this whole business was the fact that I let her talk me into consulting a rabbi together about what was required. Henkel sometimes gave us Monday evening off if we had won the Saturday before, which we almost always did. And so, on a bright, windy, late winter afternoon, Anke left her daughter at home and met me at the Landshut train station. It was a journey that could only suggest to us the memory of our first meeting, and for the hour or so it took us to reach Munich, I remember very vividly thinking, Maybe it will be OK. We were in such high, irresponsible spirits that everything seemed ridiculous, and it didn't worry us particularly that the reason for our trip into town seemed especially so.

I hadn't made any appointment, which is one reason I felt so light-hearted. Most likely we would have to come back some other time, giving us a free afternoon in the city to play around with. But as soon as she saw, outside the entrance to the synagogue, the young man with a machine gun propped against his belly, her mood changed. She recognized the seriousness of the occasion. There was no one in the vestibule, and no one in the prayer hall behind it; I could see as much through the front doors. In any case, we had the guard to get past first, and I ended up by asking him what turned out to be a difficult question. Anke had retreated, as she sometimes did, into a still, physical sort of silence, and I had forgotten the German word for conversion. So I said to him: 'She wants to become a Jew. Do you know who she should talk to?'

He stared at me; a bony-shouldered, Israeli-looking young man with a shaved brown head. 'I don't understand what you're asking,' he answered, in a rough East German accent.

'Is there anyone inside we could talk to?'

'I never go inside, except to use the bathroom.' But he gave us a kind of nod and turned away, so we went in.

The afternoon was bright enough that the stained-glass windows over the ark cast a strong, red, living light as we wandered towards it. The rest of the hall was plain and undistinguished. Two stories high but otherwise much like any other kind of institutional waiting-room. Such spaces are always a little oppressive, but the light had the strange effect of making such oppressiveness seem to count for something.

'I think I have to sit down,' Anke said, and so we pushed along one of the pews towards the middle. 'Maybe I'm pregnant, I feel a little funny.' This was one of her persistent worries, and I treated it always the same, with simple contradiction. Then she lifted her hand and pointed. 'What do you call that, that tall cabinet?'

'The ark.'

'And what's inside it?'

'The Torah.'

'And what's the Torah.'

But it didn't seem like a question, and I wasn't quite sure how to answer her anyway. 'The truth is,' I said, after another pause, 'I'm not sure if you're supposed to be here. Only the men sit here. The women look down on us from the gallery upstairs.'

'So I wouldn't be allowed to sit with you?'

'Not here.'

Then, rousing herself: 'OK, let's go.'

I thought for a blessed moment she meant *leave*, but she began walking towards the back of the hall, where a corridor opened on to a set of stairs. I don't know if I can explain why the whole thing struck me as so awful, and why it seemed a real act of cowardice not to put a stop to it. Maybe it's clear enough. Anke had gone ahead, and by the time I caught up to her, she had found the rabbi's office. Next to the stairs, and behind the ark, was a row of doors, and one of them had the name Rabbi Henry Roswald printed on it. Henry isn't a German name, and the voice that answered her knock called 'Come in!' at first. Then he made a mouthful of '*Komm rein.*'

He sat in a windowless room, brightly lit, whose walls

were covered in heavy, legal-style volumes. It hadn't occurred to me before that rabbi was a job for ambitious young men. Beside his desk, in the only clear space of wall, he had hung a number of framed testimonials: several in Hebrew, which I couldn't read, but also a certificate from Harvard, awarding him a masters in economics. He looked about thirty years old, fattening and pale. I hadn't met him before or seen him deliver any of the services. A sparse, uncomfortable-looking beard grew along the line of his cheeks and down his neck.

'I haven't seen you before,' I said to him in English.

'Nor I you.' His voice had the finicky nervous pleasure in it I associate with my father's relatives.

'I don't know if you're the right person to talk to.'

'Don't tell me that. That's what I love to hear. That's what makes me send you along to somebody else.'

I learned later that a younger element in the congregation, many of them American, the children of immigrants, returning to Munich for business reasons, had brought in Roswald to oversee the expansion of the synagogue. He turned out to be a good administrator and fund-raiser; so far, he had taken on few pastoral duties. His German was still very basic, for which he apologized. He apologized also for the fact that there was only one extra chair and gestured for Anke to sit down in it. 'Please,' he said, 'setzen Sie sich.' I stood throughout. This irritated me, too much, although in those days I found it difficult to stand still for any length of time. My back ached and then the ache moved down to my knees. Also, I felt that some part of his response to us was colored by the fact that Anke was a pretty girl.

She left it to me to explain our situation, which, with several hesitations, I did.

'Let me hear it from the young lady herself,' he said. And then, in faltering German, 'If you speak slowly, I'll understand you.'

I found it embarrassing how quickly he could adopt this tone with us – pastoral, superior. He seemed to me the kind of young man I used to meet at my parents' law school parties: a little awkward socially, but also ingratiating. Maybe he even knew my father, who teaches economics as well as law and spent a semester in the early 90s at Harvard. I did not ask him. His figure was womanish and he carried himself, sitting back in his chair, with the delicacy some men show to women. Soon he would look middle-aged and perfectly natural in any position of authority.

Anke said that she wanted to convert. She sat with her hands folded across her lap, as demure as a nun – probably because she considered it an appropriate pose.

'Can I ask you a question? Can I ask you why?'

Her first husband was Jewish, she said, the father of her daughter. It didn't matter very much to him but it mattered to me (pointing). 'I don't know,' she added, feeling herself this fell short of what was necessary, 'it suits me somehow.' *Irgendwie, paßt es* – it was the phrase you might use to explain how you named your cat. After a pause, she continued, responding still to the gentleness of his tone, 'Can I ask *you* a question. Can I ask you how long it takes?'

He hesitated, and I could imagine the different ways he considered answering. Then he said: 'Three years.' Maybe it was only the limits of his vocabulary, but it seemed to me he had decided on the simplest way of putting her off. I disliked him for that, too.

'I didn't know it took so long.' She seemed genuinely surprised but recovered herself. 'I learn very quickly when I put my mind to something. Is it possible some-times to do it quicker?'

'Sometimes it's possible for the whole thing to take a lifetime.' He lapsed into English again. 'Will you explain it to her?' – as if he and I shared a closer understanding. 'If the question is, what does it take to be a Jew, what makes me a Jew, and then, as a Jew, what are my duties and obligations . . .' This was a discussion in which he liked to stretch his legs, and he talked for several minutes along these lines. I'm familiar with this kind of talk, philosophical and practical at once, and often find it appealing. But translating the gist of it for Anke, I found I left out most of what was characteristically Jewish: the delight in these questions for their own sake. She wanted to know only the prayers and ceremonies she was expected to learn. Roswald concluded at last, 'She should understand, it's a lot harder to become a Jew than to be a Jew. She should understand that.'

'No, no, I understand well enough,' she interrupted,

speaking in English herself. Something had set her off. 'You don't want me, that is clear.'

'It isn't a question of what we want.'

'Then I don't understand why you make so much difficulty. I have told you what *I* want.'

He smiled at this, a smile peculiar to teachers of all kinds, enjoying the struggles of a precocious student. 'Maybe it won't take you quite as long as I thought,' he said. Turning to me: 'I'm sorry I don't have a chair for you. All this has been temporarily fixed up. Which means I'll probably be here two years. Are you a member of the synagogue? I'm new here and still don't recognize most of the other kids. Where are you from?'

I told him that my father was born in New York, but that his family came over from Munich before the war.

'Is that why you speak German? Lucky you; it's like learning all over again to eat with a knife and fork. I keep making messes of myself.'

'No, my mother is German.'

'And when did *her* family make it out?'

This is not the kind of thing you can lie about, though I would have liked to at the time, very much. 'They didn't make it out; they stayed put. My mother is Christian.'

After a moment, he said, 'Ah.' And then: 'Are you looking to convert as well? Is that what this is about?'

But Anke broke in. 'I don't understand. Why should he convert? He is already Jewish.'

I could only look away while he answered. 'I don't want to say, some people are more Jewish or less Jewish.

But as far as we're concerned, Jewishness is passed down through the mother. And according to this thinking, your friend is no more Jewish than you are, no matter how Jewish he feels. I should add, this is a common reason people choose to convert.' For the first time I felt the difference between him and the young academics I had met at those law school parties: the religious difference, which allowed him to treat certain subjects without irony, a useful skill. 'Conversion itself can be a rewarding process, which puts you in touch with aspects of your culture you had forgotten or in some cases never known. And it can be especially rewarding for a couple to undertake it together.'

Anke turned to me and made me look at her. I feared she would think that I had intentionally made a fool of her, for reasons it was only too easy to guess; but instead she saw something else. That I was just as adrift as she.

'Tell me again why you want to do this?' the rabbi asked, in a professionally tender voice I found surprisingly moving. Even at that stage in his career, he had seen something of the variety of human troubles; our situation was not unusual.

'I only wanted to make it easier for him. But I think I make it harder.'

She seemed on the edge of tears but unreproachful, and afterwards she told me, over dinner, she felt only very sorry for us both. (Then she added, 'I did not like the way he kept saying Jew, as if it was such a wonderful, strange thing.' She expected this to enlist my sympathies and did not notice that it failed to.) When we came out into the air at last, out of the backroom corridors and stained-glass hall, past the man with the gun, the afternoon had darkened and you could feel the homeward pull in the foot traffic, even in the cars on the street. Then Anke did a sweet thing. She took my arm in her hand and said, 'I feel terrible. Let's go spend some money.'

27

Hadnot's departure had an effect on my professional life, too. I got to play more basketball. Henkel had no one else to turn to on the bench, if Karl tired or Milo lost his head, and consequently I could count on a good ten or fifteen minutes of action each game. This makes a great difference; I stopped looking over my shoulder. Also, it's possible my father's visit had some influence, and it's possible I had learned to play as Hadnot had taught me to play, angry. Meanwhile, we kept winning basketball games. Five out of six after Christmas, and by mid-February we sat comfortably in second place behind Würzburg in the league table.

It turns out that playing for a winning club is kind of wonderful. No matter what else is going on in your personal life, you're always a little bit happy. Not deeply happy, of course, but as happy as you might be in the first few weeks after buying a new convertible. It's enough on a sunny afternoon to be driving around in it with the top down, to be publicly visible.

One small story from this period. On Wednesday evenings, the local American news channel ran a weekly round-up from the NBA that finished as practice began. One night we all showed up late: Michael Jordan had just scored fifty-odd against New York. One of the nights he couldn't be stopped, when a game of ten men became an instrument for his individual fancy. We all came to work slightly drunk on him, talking loudly, saying the same things. Shouting over each other, desperate to persuade, though everyone already agreed. 'It's what I've been telling you,' Milo said, to no one in particular. 'These people, they are not like us, like you and me. And Michael Jordan, he is not like them.'

After practice, Charlie started a dunk competition. Like a high school prom, it had a theme: the moves of Michael Jordan. Milo tried to launch himself from the foul line. He looked like a man losing speed on a surfboard and ended up on his hip. Everyone tried his luck. Plotzke took three steps in from the three-point arc and dunked without leaving the ground. When Karl's turn came he lined himself up carefully at the far end of the court, measuring his strides in reverse. The warm-up Jordan had gone through at the '88 All Star game to stir up the crowd. Then he set off. A few of us beat time during the run-up, increasing speed as he increased his speed. But the ball slipped out of his palm and he had to pull violently down at the rim, empty-handed, to catch his balance. Olaf said to me afterwards, he was almost relieved. 'It wouldn't be right,' he said. 'If even he can do it, what's the point of all this?' I think he meant, this honorable mediocrity.

Most of us followed Hadnot's games in the league

newsletter you could pick up from Angie at reception. Würzburg continued to win, but there were days Bo failed to score a single point. I remember the word Milo used, astonished: *genullt*. It means to zero, or be-nil. Other days he scored thirty. It isn't easy fitting in to a new offense mid-season, and like a lot of bench players, Hadnot rolled with the fortunes of his first few shots. If he missed them, he might easily spend the rest of the half watching the game go by; but some days he didn't miss. I found myself getting caught up in his failures and successes and used to hang around Angie after Thursday's practice till the newsletter arrived. Taking drinks from the office fridge and generally wasting the day. When it came I turned first thing to last week's box scores. Bo had become, at that distance, a character, and I felt for him as simply as you feel for any protagonist.

At the beginning of March, I returned from dinner with Anke to find a message from him on my service. Würzburg had a game in Munich at the end of the week, and he intended to stay on a few days to see his daughter. He wanted to know if he could crash at my place. 'Stick me in the bathtub,' he said. 'I don't care.'

I didn't call back at first and by the time I saw Anke again, they had worked out their own arrangement. He would sleep on her parents' sitting-room couch. This had the advantage of putting him on the scene when Franziska woke up in the morning. He could also help get her to bed. I can't say I liked the arrangement, and I suggested to Anke her daughter would find it confusing to have her father in the house again. But I liked even less the prospect of entertaining him myself. My sense of guilt was stronger than my sexual jealousies. Even so, from Sunday onwards I tried to stay out of my apartment as much as possible. Anke and I had agreed not to see each other while he was in town, but I didn't want to hang around the phone waiting for her call.

On the Tuesday, after lunch, I headed back to the gym to work on my shot and found Hadnot there. No one had turned the lights on, and for a minute I stood in the tall twilight of the sports hall watching him, about twenty feet away. He was working hard; his t-shirt, heavy with sweat, hung loose around his neck and shoulders. Harder than I had seen him work. He moved sharply between the lines and chased down each ball in strong steady strides. It occurred to me he was preparing for the playoff in a few weeks' time. Würzburg had already qualified and they were likely to face us, giving him a shot at revenge. Karl was the reason he came back to play in the fall, and Karl was the reason he got cut. But Karl gave him a shot at other things, too: dozens of scouts would come, from the major European clubs as well as the NBA. Hadnot was thirty years old, with a bum knee and a reputation as a troublemaker. This was probably his last chance of making it into the basketball big leagues.

Of course, whatever he was doing he had done a hundred thousand times before, planting his feet, lining his elbow up and following through. Watching the ball go in or out and starting from scratch. How much would it help him to practice a thousand more? But you do it anyway, just in case, or maybe because you prefer it after all to the real thing. I started to count the makes and misses, then gave up and just counted the misses. There weren't many. He clapped his hands every time a shot rimmed out, but mostly what you heard was just the echo of the ball and the squeak of his shoes, and sometimes, softly between them, his breathing.

There's something about being unobserved that charges the atmosphere. When he noticed me, it seemed to affect him, too. 'How long you been standing there?' he said.

'Not long.'

'Tell you what, since you're here. Why don't you feed me some shots.'

So I did and after a few minutes, he took my place under the net. Some of my childhood friendships consisted of nothing but this: standing around on an empty summer morning, taking turns with a basketball. Not that he would ever have called me friend. Maybe I should have asked about his daughter, but I knew more than I should have and felt shy of pretending ignorance. Eventually I said, 'How's life in Würzburg? I follow you sometimes in the newspaper. In the box scores.'

'Same as it is anywhere else. I get up and go to the gym.'

'You've had some good games,' I said.

'I'm a good basketball player.'

To break the silence that followed, I told him, 'I'm not sure yet what I'll be doing next year.'

We continued to pass the ball back and forth, exchanging shots. For the first time, I felt a little angry towards him. All year long I had shown him nothing but curiosity, but I couldn't think of a single question he had put to me – that any of them had put to me. Hadnot was just as bad as the rest of them, Charlie, Olaf, Henkel, Karl. They gave me advice, they told me what to do, sometimes they even expressed their sympathy. But around them, I was always the one with the questions. I thought, there are worse things than curiosity. Then he said, 'I hear you're writing a book about me,' and my heart began to beat a little quicker.

'Where did you hear that?'

He didn't answer and I wondered if Anke had told him anything else. We had agreed not to mention our relationship, at least till the end of the season – until we had come to a decision about it. But Hadnot was sleeping on her parents' couch, and I hadn't seen Anke or spoken to her in three days. He walked up to me and put the ball in my hands, and I turned slightly away from him. 'How are you gonna write the book,' he said, 'if you don't know a damn thing about basketball?'

'What do you mean?'

'You want me to show you?' he said.

So he did.

There was an old coach at Kansas who opened camp every season with the question, When was the first time somebody really guarded you? Just to make the freshmen scared. Freaks of physical precocity, who had outgrown, in talent as well as height, everyone they knew: parents, brothers, high school teammates. He wanted to remind them: somebody out there is better than you. All year long I'd had the truth of this drummed into me, but Karl was lazy on defense, and guys like Charlie and Milo belonged to the same physical class as I did. What it feels like really to be shut down I had no idea till that afternoon.

We started to play. Hadnot was in better shape than when he left the club. The lazy-footed, strong-arm tactics he used against Karl he had no need of here. I took a hard stride to my right, then cut the ball back between my legs. The same move I used on Charlie at the beginning of the season. Another dribble, and a half-second's hesitation at the top of the bounce. Planting my left foot, I ran straight into Hadnot, who had his chest puffed out like a toy soldier's. Then he brought both hands down hard on the ball and took it away. 'Got to be strong,' he said. 'Got to be strong.'

So it went on. By this stage it was clear he was angry, too, and I had a pretty good idea what he was angry about. Dribbling lightly, advancing, he watched me back off. Just to show there was no point wasting energy, he called out 'headfake, jumpshot' and I bit on the first and watched the second drop softly in. 'Ball up,' he said. 'Winners out.' As soon as I passed it to him, he bent his legs into another shot. 'Got to be quick,' he said, as the ball touched net. 'Got to be quick.'

Everything he did, he told me what he was going to do first, and sometimes he told me what I was going to do as well. If you can win so easily there should be no pleasure in it. And to be fair, he seemed to take little pleasure. 'You gonna write about this, too?' he said. 'You gonna write about this?' After a few minutes I was too tired to talk, but he kept up his end of the banter until I picked up the ball and started to walk away.

'What are you doing?' he called.

'Taking my ball and going home.'

I didn't see him again until the championship game.

28

There was a two-week break after the regular season finished, and most of us went a little crazy waiting for the playoff. Henkel, for the only time all year, insisted that we wear a jacket and tie on the team bus to Würzburg. (They had the better record, which gave them home court advantage.) Several of the players, including Karl and me, didn't own either, and there wasn't a shop in Landshut that could fit us. So a few days before the big match, Henkel organized a coach to take us into Munich for the afternoon, and we went shopping – one of those strange, light-hearted afternoons that seem unconnected to the days surrounding it.

Milo complained much of the way then found an oyster-colored seersucker jacket that reminded him of Don Johnson from *Miami Vice*. Nothing fit Karl. Eventually, he picked out something in unlined linen with a few extra inches on the arms, and the saleswoman recommended a tailor who could lengthen it while we waited. Henkel brought out his credit card at the till and paid for all of us.

'This league is a hobby,' he said to us, 'but the first division is a job. You should dress like it.'

* * *

It's a six-hour bus ride from Landshut to Würzburg. I refused to let Anke see me off, but she spent the night before at my place, and I left her at dawn half-asleep in my bed – an image that stayed with me much of the journey north. We all looked slightly odd waiting at the sports hall for the coach to show up: a dozen oversized men in badly fitting jackets and ties we had chosen ourselves. Somehow impressive, too, and I remember the pride I occasionally felt walking around in a pack. A form of racial pride, itself not very different from the pleasure my mother sometimes admits to taking in the sight of her two tall sons.

Milo was in manic spirits and talked much of the way. I sat one row ahead of him and he kept leaning over to explain things. 'Young man,' he said at one point, 'understand this. In the first division, everyone plays on wooden floors!' And so on. He was convinced that a great deal hinged on this game. That the vague drifting quality of his early career had been brought at last to a sharp point.

Olaf finally interrupted him. 'I played in the 1st division. It is not so different, except that you spend more time on the bench, and when you do play, you have to do exactly what you're told, otherwise everything goes to shit. There is no room for having fun – the other players are too good.'

'Yes, but did you play in the Super Liga?' (It's hard to convey, in cold ink, the childish exuberance of this word in German. It sounds like a jet taking off.) 'Barcelona,

Milan, Athens. Spanish girls, Italian girls, Greek girls. Even if they don't like basketball, girls have a natural respect for TV, for men who are on TV. It is a question of evolution.'

The Super Liga is a knock-out tournament for some of the top European clubs. It runs alongside the regular national leagues, but pays much better, if you win, and attracts more media attention. German basketball players very rarely become household names: if they do, it's because of their performances in the Super Liga.

'I played in the Super Liga,' Olaf said. 'Once.'

'And did you win?'

'Let me explain it to you. It is called the Super Liga because everybody is better than you . . .'

Outside Ingolstadt, the rains set in and followed us through the forests of Altmühltal, covering the windows so thickly with water I could only see the blurred green of trees. But the noise allowed me to retreat into my own silence, and I thought of Anke and tried to sleep. We arrived under a lifting sky in time for lunch, and afterwards Henkel gave us a few hours off to get comfortable in our rooms.

In fact, I ended up staying with him, at the house of Würzburg's club president, a man named Eberhart. Eberhart was famous in the small world of German basketball and one of the founders of the Bundesliga. He used to teach history and fell in love with the sport in the 60s during a sabbatical at Berkeley. Everyone called him Herr Professor. His house had a couple spare bedrooms in the basement, which he offered to Henkel, along with any other player who cared to join him. Henkel picked me, because he considered me the most presentable or the most dispensable, I don't know. My bedroom itself was windowless and institutional, with a rugged beige carpet and cheap furniture. It looked like the kind of room strangers passed through. But the house itself was more attractive, modern and full of gadgets. Glass sliding doors opened from the sitting room onto a narrow deck. Below, the townscape glittered like a beach.

I met Eberhart only briefly as I settled in, a tall, elderly, childish-looking man. He shook me by the hand, a firm grip though slightly wet from something, a fact that contributed to the distaste I always felt for the touch of old people. I wondered when he'd last used the bath-room. Then Henkel claimed me for a late afternoon practice and an early team dinner – just a walk-through and a plate of spaghetti.

Everyone was quiet. Even Milo's high spirits had worn off. Henkel and I shared a cab back together, and I squeezed myself against the window and tried not to look at him. There was something about his decent, assured looks that brought out in me a filial shyness. My father once praised a man for being 'virile, in an attrac-tive way – not in the least a show off.' I was struck by this comment, as evidence of what he admired, and never forgot it. He might have had Henkel in mind.

'When I was younger,' he said, as the car pulled up, 'before all the big games I used to think, this might change my life. They never did.' Getting out, he added, 'But maybe. Maybe.'

Eberhart invited us onto the balcony for a good night drink. He himself always took a glass of mint tea to bed with him, and he offered me the same. Really, it was still too cold to sit outside, even with the door to the sitting room open, but he brought three rugs out and laid them across our laps. He apologized for the smell: his dog used to sleep on them.

For a few minutes we sat looking out at the view, made up now entirely of strings of light. Then Eberhart and Henkel exchanged companionable complaints. Recently, Eberhart had given up jogging; his knees couldn't stand it any more, and even walking up hills caused him pain. 'You probably don't know it,' Eberhart shifted the conversation, 'but twenty years ago Herr Henkel used to play for me. I had a short experiment with coaching; it didn't last long.' After another pause: 'I've never seen anyone who liked winning as much as your coach.'

Henkel said, 'I would like very much to win tomorrow.'

'Tomorrow or next year, it doesn't matter. Some day with that young man you will win.'

'It matters to me. I don't think we can keep him another year if we lose.'

'Is he as good as that?' Then Eberhart turned to me. 'A long time ago, I lived in California, outside San Francisco. Sometimes on a Friday morning I used to drive down to Los Angeles just to watch a basketball game. A full day's journey, then back again the next day.

I had not many friends at first and such trips were an excuse to look around. I bought a second-hand Ford and learned to drive in one day; in Germany, nobody had a car. A very exciting, lonely period in my life. There were wonderful players then: Gail Goodrich, Jerry West. Oscar Robertson. I never thought in my lifetime anyone would come out of Europe who could touch them. But the day is not far off now; it almost saddens me.' He looked at Henkel. 'For a few years, I thought that you might be good enough to play in America, but they had a prejudice then against German players.'

'I was too small. One of my brothers is five inches taller. If I had been born like my brother.'

'And what about this one?' Eberhart asked, pointing at me. 'Is he any good?'

'Yes, a very good *Dolmetscher*,' Henkel said.

29

I've heard that the Spanish have a word for the time wasted before traveling; there should be such a word for the build-up to a big game. Around eleven o'clock the next day, we jogged lightly through the Saturday morning streets of Würzburg, a dozen tall men shaking off sleep. A few photographers followed, when they could, taking pictures of Karl. Pedestrians moved aside and stared at us, recognizing that we were people of some temporary local significance. Some of them wished us luck.

Afterwards, Henkel had arranged for each of us to have a session with a physio at the hotel, but there were only two physios and they called on us in order of significance. That is, I waited two hours. Thomas Arnold discovered an old set of Connect Four among the children's toys in the TV lounge, and Krahm, Arnold, Darmstadt and I played round-robin together. Krahm never lost; he was studying engineering, a stretched-out, skinny, clean-shaven young man with a very small face. All afternoon I took from him the comforting sense that these games mattered as much to him as anything else we expected to win or lose that day. There was money at stake, too. I lost five marks and remembered my father's warning about gambling: 'These aren't the kids you grew up with.'

Milo had begun his long pre-match retreat. He looked like a man coming down with a cold and sat in front of a television watching footage from Würzburg's recent games. Sometimes I joined him on the couch. It was odd seeing Hadnot in another uniform. It was also the first time I had watched him on TV. He looked shorter than in life, more dependent on others to clear out some room for him to work. The fury of his presence somehow failed to come across; also, what was muscular in his precision. He moved in short quick steps, but with an air of neatness and deliberation. You saw the textbook diagram behind each posture or gesture – he gave the impression of somebody who would line up the pencils on his desk.

Olaf spent most of the afternoon on the phone in the lobby, without saying much. He seemed to be trying to apologize or calm someone down. 'Na klar,' he kept repeating, and 'Was denkst du?' *Of course. What do you think?* It upset me, on this, the last working day of our season, that our friendship had come to so little. I wondered if he felt the same.

After an early supper, more pasta and salad and rice, we could finally make our way to the stadium. Already a few fans stood outside the entrance, watching the television crews prepare, but we went around the block and made our way in through a service door. About an hour before tip-off. Olaf, waiting to get taped up, asked me to help him stretch out on one of the gym mats lying on the floor by the trainer's table. Perhaps his own quiet nod to friendship. 'Trouble at home?' I said, lifting his heavy leg and pressing it down against his chest.

'Just my sister.'

Then the other leg. I remember the physical intimacy of athletes – their easy relations with their own bodies and the bodies of others. All this heightened by the steadily increasing pressure of what awaited us outside. Later I said to him something like, It's a funny kind of year that ends in March, and when he didn't respond, I asked him, 'Has it been a good year for you, personally, I mean?'

'Ask me again in a few hours.'

'Is it as simple as that?'

'Of course, it's simple. If you win, you are a winner; if you lose, you are a loser. That's what all of this means.' After a minute, he added, 'Sunday night I have a date with my sister's friend in Munich. I like her; I don't want to be in a bad mood.'

This seemed to me as good a reason as any to want to win. I found the idea that lives and careers might depend, in any significant way, on my performance increasingly awful as the game approached. My own life and my own career as well.

No one in the locker room had much to say for himself. The noise we got dressed to was the sound of Milo's music leaking out of his earphones. He sat on a bench, wearing nothing but his game shorts; his top was draped over his head.

As soon as we emerged on court, other sounds over-whelmed us. The sound of wooden stands on loose wheels filling with people. Disco songs, blasted from tall black loudspeakers at either end of the hall. The echo of basketballs. Then there were the hand-held fog horns, which a few of the fans had snuck past security. Boom boom boom: pure expressionless noise.

Four different television stations had set up their cameras on the baselines. I counted them during the lay-up lines. A local Würzburg station; then a crew from Munich; another one I didn't recognize; and several cameras, on wires and booms, bearing the Eurosport logo. I remembered something Anke once said about Hadnot. That most people change a little, helplessly, in front of cameras, but that they had no effect on him at all, and I wondered if this applied to the way he played basketball, too.

The Würzburg players came in after us and the noise doubled. Tressell, shrugging his head from side to side like a boxer; Chad Baker in long striped socks, pulled up to his knees; Henrik Lenz; Hadnot.

I hadn't seen him since running off stupidly the last time we played basketball together. The sight of him reminded me of something else – one of those dusty corners under the bed that count for little in our lives but which we expose unwillingly. A few days before, while Anke was spending the night, I'd had a vague and in some ways not dissatisfying dream about him. Hadnot and I were alone and had somehow agreed, reluctantly and without attraction, to a kind of expedient sexual exchange. Part of growing up, it seems to me, involves learning to dismiss such dreams more or less lightly. Naturally I didn't mention it to Anke, but the effect of this dream stayed with me and made his presence distasteful.

Henkel, just before tip-off, drew us in a huddle around him and made a speech. I remember his moustache moving over his lips but not a word he said. I don't think I heard him. Performance-deafness had set in. There was nothing in my head but the beat of my pulse and what the Germans call an *Ohrwurm* – an earworm. Sometimes a few lines from a song or a book or a recent conversation would echo around my mind during a game, not so much against my will as indifferent to it. This time the refrain was very simple: *Dolmetscher, Dolmetscher, Dolmetscher, Dolmetscher.*

Of course, I spent the first twenty minutes sitting down. Karl and Chad Baker jumped center together, and Karl knocked the ball to Charlie, who brought it slowly upcourt.

All week, during the build-up to the most important game of his career, Karl had been having a sort of subterranean argument with Henkel, but to the rest of us he presented a very easy face. If he was nervous, he was smilingly nervous. I said to Olaf at the time: he's like a man who has cut himself painlessly, and only realizes later, so he shows you the blood on his finger with a kind of wonder. Look at me, nerves . . . But these had nothing to do with winning or losing. He had invited a prominent American agent to watch him play, a man named Neuwirth Dodds, whom I noticed myself in a front row seat wearing cowboy boots and a skinny tie. Dodds was well-connected, especially among the West Coast teams, and Karl was anxious to impress him.

There's a story I heard about Dodds on the long ride home; I don't know if it's true. That Hadnot had approached him before the game and said something like, 'How about I score more points than your boy, you get me into one training camp next year. I don't care which.'

They were both southerners, and Bo knew him vaguely from his first few years out of college, when he made a real push to reach the big leagues. Dodds said, 'And what do I get from you, when you don't?'

It was a part of the story that he found his own remark very funny. I should add, Milo, Olaf, Plotzke, the rest of them, also found the whole thing funny, and not because they bore Hadnot any ill-will. Athletes just like to see people put down, they like shows of power – it's the business they're in.

What Henkel and Karl were fighting about had something to do with Neuwirth Dodds and the other suits like him lined up along the two front rows. Henkel had decided a few weeks before the game to wrong-foot Würzburg by moving Karl to the point. Karl resisted him, for a few reasons. Partly, because it was likely to cut into his scoring, and he wanted big numbers to impress the Americans. Partly because he didn't think he could play point in the NBA, and he hoped to prepare himself for the transition. Both good reasons from a personal angle, but clubs and players, whatever coaches like to say, have very different interests at heart. Anyway, there was nothing Karl could do. He gave in, but Henkel's insistence might have cost him in the long run, too.

At the time, the guy who suffered most in all this was Charlie. After Karl tapped the ball to him, he crossed half court and motioned everyone into place. Motioned, I say, because there was no use calling out plays. The noise of a big game is most overwhelming right at the beginning, before the crowd has shouted itself out. There's a kind of tradition in some clubs of standing till the first points are scored, which produces, as soon as a shot goes in, a satisfying collapse and collective release of breath. Karl worked himself free at the top of the key, and Charlie swung the ball to him, then cut down to Olaf on the block and curled off. He had become a shooting guard who can't shoot. Karl still had Baker on him from the jump, but there was no way Baker could keep up with him outside the paint. Two hard strides to his right and the rest of the defense converged, leaving both Olaf and Plotzke wide open under the basket. Karl picked Olaf, who lifted himself heavily off the ground and dunked. Two nothing. Everybody in the building sat down again; it was as if the stage curtain had been drawn at last.

Henkel chased Karl along the sidelines, applauding earnestly with his hands just under his chin. 'Auf geht's!' he cried, an almost untranslatable phrase, because it has no real meaning, like a lot of encouraging words: just a kind of vector of meaning. I don't think Karl heard him or cared.

Charlie had a hard time at the other end, too. Tressell was cartoon strong and pushed through him into the lane then jumped full-chested against Olaf's ribs and laid the ball underhanded in. Darmstadt whispered at my side: 'He's bullying the bully.' The teenager had suffered all year long at Charlie's hands; it gave him real pleasure to see the tables turned.

There's a lot of talk in the sporting news about the love of underdogs, but it shouldn't be confused with an attraction to failure. Really what we like to see is people winning and beating others – the bigger the victim, the better. Darmstadt had no chance of getting in this game and knew it. He could look on as coolly detached as anyone else in the crowd. Also, Hadnot had been decent to him; his loyalties were divided. I won't say I felt for Charlie exactly, though it turned out to be his last professional game and one of his worst. (At halftime, sitting by himself on a bench bone-tired, he said not a word – of complaint or anything else.) Most of what I felt was wonder. My first few weeks in Landshut Charlie seemed to me just about the canniest and completest point guard I had ever played against. Now he was getting whipped by a kid I never heard of coming out of college who couldn't land a job in the NBA. What a world it is to strive in.

Karl, on the other end, kept forcing double teams and finding the open man. Würzburg adjusted, but even Lenz, six foot five tall and two hundred thirty pounds lean, was too small and weak to keep him out of the lane. A few minutes in we went up four, five, seven points. Eventually they started cheating inside, leaving Charlie and Milo free at the three-point line. Charlie even tried his hand at a few long bombs. The first one corkscrewed off the front rim and over the backboard; the second landed two feet short. After that, he gave up. He chased Tressell like a dog up and down court, trying to entangle him and draw cheap fouls, but on offense he more or less resigned himself to a bit part.

This shifted the pressure onto Milo, and Milo coped badly with pressure. He knocked down his first three pointer in a red mist and the look on his face had so little pleasure in it and so much relief I almost pitied him. It gave him a kind of license, though, and his next two shots barely drew iron. A minute later, he lowered his head and bulled into Lenz standing his ground at the low post block. When the ref whistled him for charging, he began to shout: obscenities, I suppose, but I heard nothing comprehensible. Then Henkel touched me on the shoulder and the red mist descended on me.

Entering a game is like entering a new atmosphere. The old rules of breathing don't apply; you have to learn new ones. For the first two minutes on court I don't know what happened, then Hadnot came on. He sent his first shot long before I noticed I was meant to be guarding him. I never thought of him as a nervous player, but the last time he wanted to win so much, against Würzburg half a year before, he also rushed his shots. And this time he was on an even shorter rope. His new coach, a nephew of Eberhart's named Oscar, tended to pull him quickly if he missed a few shots. Tall as his uncle, with the large stiff tender knees of an ex-athlete, Eberhart paced gingerly in front of his bench all game like a man trying to put off going to the bathroom.

The next time down, Charlie switched over and Hadnot pushed him into the post. Karl snuck behind them both and knocked his turnaround almost as far as half court. I picked it up on the run, but Tressell was back, so I waited for the help to come. Maybe if the ball had gone out of bounds, Oscar would have taken the chance to pull him. 'There are other people on the court besides you!' I heard him call: the kind of prim, vague, correctional coaching patter Hadnot despised.

'How about passing to Karl?' Neuwirth Dodds suggested, and there was a shout of laughter in the stands that made its way even to my deaf ears.

In general, the presence of the crowd was as powerful as summer heat, pervasive and just about bearable. You felt the fact that you were being watched. You felt it on your skin. Meanwhile, I was dribbling myself into corners – and about to do Hadnot a good turn.

He himself once told me the secret of intercepting

passes. Work out the pecking order on the other team, he said. Most bad passes get thrown *up* the order – guys get bullied into it. When Karl crossed half court, he clapped his hands twice, calling for the ball, and I obliged him. Hadnot jumped the passing lane and made off the other way. *Dolmetscher, Dolmetscher, Dolmetscher,* I thought. There was nobody back but Plotzke, who was too tired to run, but Bo pulled up for a three-pointer regardless, which hardly shifted the net as it dropped in. Returning, he touched my elbow lightly – not in apology or anything like it, but just to make sure I was taking note.

Henkel sent Milo in to replace me, and I spent the rest of the half on the bench, getting colder and watching Hadnot go on one of his streaks. A fifteen-footer from the elbow off a double screen. A runner in the lane; another three. I'm trying to remember what I hoped for when he went up to shoot. I think for the first time I wanted him to miss. Henkel whispered to me, 'Before it is over, I will need you again.' And childishly solemn and grateful to him, I nodded.

Someone had rigged up a large mechanical board in the place of the gym clock, which recorded points, rebounds, minutes played, etc. Instantly, the fluid living unfolding of events was converted into a box score. At halftime, I looked up to check it. Hadnot led all scorers with thirteen points; Olaf had twelve, Karl ten, enough to give us a three-point edge. It occurred to me that Olaf's family might be sitting in the stands. I remembered his father especially, long-limbed, distinguished and balding, with curly hair. This seemed just the kind of experiment, regarding his son's character, he might be curious about, and as I jogged stiffly back to the locker room I scanned the crowd for faces.

Anke was sitting several rows up towards the visitors' end – on her own, in a plain blue dress that showed the brown freckled skin of her neck and chest. Since she wasn't looking at me I couldn't acknowledge her presence in any way, short of shouting. Instead I ducked my head under the doorway, feeling suddenly the flush of some emotion I found very hard to place. She hadn't told me she was coming and I hadn't asked her to. Probably it was only the strange nervous anxieties of the day, but the thought crossed my mind that she hadn't come to watch me.

In the privacy of the locker room, Henkel and Karl continued their argument. Karl, red-faced and restless with unspent energies, shouted at one stage, 'You think it is all coaching. You don't remember what it is like any more.' Russell, looking blank, handed him a towel from a bag of cheap white overwashed towels he dragged around with him across the tiles. Karl folded it over his head like a shawl and strode large-footed back and forth between our legs. 'Out there, nobody cares about the coaches. It's always this way with you. You think too much.' And so on. I could see Henkel reminding himself, like a good father, it is not my job to respond to anger with anger; it is enough that I listen. He may also have felt that such reserve somehow proved Karl's point.

Eventually, he repeated the facts: that we were winning by three in spite of Hadnot's hot hand; that Baker, Lenz and Tressell each had two fouls; that Olaf and Plotzke had twenty points between them, because of Karl's unselfish play.

Karl bent down to him at last, less angrily. 'You must understand. I can do everything I want out there, but for you. No one can stop me.'

Frau Kolwitz, the owner, walked in, wearing a grey mandarin coat buttoned up to her neck. Charlie was the shortest player in the room and he was sitting down; the top of her head came up to his eyes. She stood in the comforting shelter of Henkel's elbow and muttered something at us. Nobody could hear what – words of encouragement, I suppose. But somehow they had their effect. Karl fell quiet and the rest of us took the chance to unwrap and pass around bottles of water from the stack Russell had kicked into the room. At the end I could just make out faintly, Thank you, thank you, bobbing her head, thank you. She really seemed to belong to a different species, and we treated her with the suspicion and tenderness you would show a small animal.

'Give me twenty more minutes,' Henkel said to Karl when she was gone. 'And then you can shout at me as much as you like.'

* * *

When the second half started I found it very difficult not to turn my head and try to catch Anke's eye. There was no reason not to, except that I knew what she would be looking at: her husband. I had a seat on the bench; Hadnot was on stage.

Something else I meant to say about her feelings for me, something that had occurred to me in Flensburg. Anke was a girl who had a natural respect and admiration for good luck in men. I mean the kind of luck inherent in us, something we possess ourselves, like health or looks. Not the other kind, that rolls the dice for us and decides our chances. At my mother's childhood home, a short walk from the beach, among all those family associations and traditions, it was easy for Anke to consider me what my grandmother sometimes called 'a good bet': she meant, a young man worth holding on to. Part of what soured their marriage was the fact that Hadnot seemed to Anke, increasingly, a bad bet. He had a kind of smell to him, the smell of somebody who doesn't get what he wants from life. And Anke, like a good, proper, fastidious girl, wished to avert her nose from it. But no one could sit in that stadium and compare the two of us to my advantage.

I don't know that I ever saw him play better, given the stakes and the intensity of the occasion. I had certainly never seen him in better shape. The summer fat he started the season with had burned itself off; he gave the impression of someone who had sloughed old skin. Most of the crowd, of course, favored Würzburg, and everything Hadnot did was attended by a chorus of general happiness. Milo spent much of the second half chasing him around. Even when the mist descended on him, Milo was an excellent defensive player, aggressive and long-armed. But Hadnot turned his aggression against him. He worked him so hard off screens Milo ended up with a bruise the size of a footprint running up the side of his chest. (He showed it to me in the morning with a kind of pride, hungover, contented, passing time on the coach ride home.) But then Hadnot was just as likely to fade off a screen and drift baseline, clearing out for himself that instant of space which was all he required to catch the ball, dip his legs and shoot.

Maybe what saved us was the fact that everyone else watched him, too. Sometimes a streak shooter can have this effect. Even Tressell, bullish, unflappable, began to pound the ball on the wing, beating time with his hand until Hadnot got open. It was like watching one of those intricate children's toys: you put a marble in the slot and waited for it to come out again somewhere else. Or a mouse in a maze. In and out, around, along the baseline and up, with his quick short steps. Charlie once called Hadnot selfish, and this is what he meant: for him to play well his teammates had to arrange themselves around his performance. Baker and Lenz setting picks; Tressell feeding him. I won't say he didn't care about winning, but winning itself never satisfied him. After a certain amount of disappointment, you need more than a single victory to prove how much of it was undeserved.

Losing might have been preferable in its way. Look, he could say, you see how well I've played and it's happened again. No, not preferable. Eventually you can't help believing you deserve it.

Karl, on the other hand, needed no help from anyone to please himself. He started the second half ignoring Henkel and everyone else and simply launching himself at the basket. Even if he missed, it didn't matter; Karl reached over the heads of Baker and Plotzke with his long arms and tapped the ball in. Then they began double-teaming him as soon as he touched the ball, Tressell and Lenz together confronting him from either side. Sometimes Baker, too, even twenty-five feet out.

'I've never seen anything like it,' Henkel muttered. 'Pass, pass.'

And Karl passed.

Milo had a shocking afternoon. He suffered from a kind of incurable impotence, which, like the sexual kind, was only made more painful by desire. Probably he was the second best shooter on the team, behind Karl, but nothing went in and after a while he stopped trying. You could see on his face a sort of childish resolution: since I can't, I won't. Since I can't, I won't – I imagined the refrain running through his head. Olaf, of all people, began drifting into the open spaces and knocking down jumpshots. In his sullen, indifferent way, he lived up to the occasion.

As for me, I kept waiting for the nod from Henkel. But he decided to go big: Krahm and even Thomas Arnold got in the game. With Karl attracting so much attention, there were plenty of cheap points available under the basket. Nothing came cheap to Hadnot. I don't want to say he never missed, but some things the numbers fail to account for. After a while, everyone knew he was going to shoot, so every shot got harder. Still, he found ways to work himself free, and the way he found them was more remarkable than the simple outcome of a ball going in or not. With three or four minutes left and the score tied, Hadnot pulled up coming off a high screen and Milo fell into him from behind. He had fouled out. So Henkel looked along his bench, once and once more; then he looked at me. I was sitting on my hands to keep them warm.

'Ben,' he said. I stood up, feeling stiff, and walked on.

The middle of a basketball court, like any stage, is brighter than the wings. The lights shine off the wooden floors; you emerge into light. Charlie said to me, resting a wet arm on my shoulder, 'Take Hadnot. It doesn't matter who got him today.' And then: 'If the ball comes to you, shoot it.'

What I remember from the next fifteen minutes of my life, for that's how long it took to play out the game, are mostly impressions. Hadnot's sudden nearness to me, his familiar face. I could hear him breathing through his strong front teeth; he blinked constantly against the sweat running off his crew-cut. All this time Anke was watching us – I wondered who she was rooting for. It occurred to me that this was a test of the affections you could feel in your gut, that you couldn't at all doubt. Hadnot didn't say a word to me, hardly noticed who I was, probably. But it would be fair to say that for the next quarter of an hour I hated him.

The first time down he curled off a screen I didn't see, and by the time I got back on my feet, with an ear ringing, everyone had run the other way. The sequence of events escapes me. They were up by two, and then it was tied, and then we were up by two. And so on. Lenz hit a fifteen-footer; Tressel made two free throws. Once, as Charlie predicted, the ball fell into my hands and before I knew what I was doing, I rose up to shoot. When I first came to Landshut there was a kink in my shot, a touch of left thumb inherited from my father, which I spent the next eight months ironing out. Well, it was ironed at last: the ball dropped in.

You think about the score much more when you're watching a game than when you're playing it. I remember being surprised, glancing up with thirty-odd seconds left, to see that we were down by two. Then Karl waved everybody away. Baker jumped out at him when he crossed mid-court, but he moved around Baker into clear space and knocked down a three-pointer from twenty-five feet. The reason it seemed nothing much had happened was just that everybody in the building went quiet. Three thousand Würzburg fans forgot what they were cheering for. The old-fashioned jury-rigged mechanical scoreboard read: Landshut 81 Würzburg 80 Time: 00:15. I looked to see if the seconds would tick away, but Eberhart had called time out, so we all gathered dutifully around our coaches. I have no idea what Henkel said: we might as well have been under water. Then we drifted on court again and I tried to find Hadnot.

It seemed to me likely they'd run a play through him; I was almost relieved when they did. He held the ball on the wing, comfortably against his belly, while the time ran down. At least, I thought, I don't have to chase him around. Here he is. And then it occurred to me what he was going to do. There's a move he used to practice on the right baseline, sometimes against me. A Russian taught it to him, a very simple move, but the kind of thing Soviet-block players get drilled into them again and again. Hold the ball. Plant your right foot, take two hard dribbles right. Fix the defender against your left shoulder. Plant your left foot, then jump a little backwards with your shoulder still turned and shoot.

If you do it correctly, moving quick and hard, it's almost impossible for anyone to reach your shooting hand. Hadnot alone in the gym expected to make eight out of ten. I watched him do this a hundred times, counting aloud, one for one, two for two, two for three, three for four, and so on. Against a tall defender, who knew what was coming, his chances dropped to five out of ten; he told me this himself. When we were working on the move together, one morning before practice, I asked him again what he thought about while going up to shoot – forgetting I had asked him before. But this time he gave a different answer. 'I always think the same damn thing,' he said. 'Go in.'

The phrase came back to me, in the heat of that moment, as phrases sometimes do – without meaning much. For a few seconds we stood there, amid three thousand people, on one of those strange, sudden islands that emerge from the flow of play. This is how I like to think of him: just as far away as the reach of my arm, with the ball in his hands and everything still undecided.

Epilogue

For several years after leaving Landshut, I had dreams about leaving Landshut. Like school dreams, full of anxiety. Often the train station featured, half buried in snow. In fact, when I did move out in mid-April, it was one of the first warm days of the year, overcast and very still. I look the long train north to Hamburg and stayed with my uncle for a few days, making in reverse the journey that had brought me from college in the first place.

But in these dreams, something always went wrong. The train stalled in the station or I missed it altogether. There were also cars that broke down. Franziska appeared occasionally: we had left her behind and needed to go back for her. Sometimes Anke and I were stuck together, but not always. And other people pushed their way in: Milo, laughing at me; Hadnot with his face in the window; Darmstadt offering very sweetly, if I needed a place to stay, to put me up at his parents' house for the night. Some of the dreams grew out of the violent dreams of my playing days, and I woke from them almost breathless, with a quickening heart.

It took me about two weeks to clear out. A few days after the playoff, once the celebrations were over and the long summer began to stare us in the face, Henkel sat each of us down one by one. Hadnot was right. Only Olaf and Karl survived our promotion to the first division. It's a very different business, Henkel explained to me, and frankly he didn't think I was ready. If I wanted to sit at the end of the bench, year after year, all right, that was one thing. But what I needed was a chance to play, etc.

Sometimes I wonder, if we had lost that game and stayed in the old league, would I have stuck around? Franziska will be fourteen years old this summer. Anke is approaching forty. Laziness and stubbornness, I told her, account for most of my decisions. It really would have taken a fair dose of one or the other to keep me in Landshut without a job. Henkel offered to let me stay on in the apartment till July, but I said to him, 'If I'm going to go, I should just go,' and the way he accepted my answer suggested he knew a little about my personal situation, too.

Anke blamed the club bitterly for its disloyalty. 'If only you had lost,' she said. It was easier for both of us to blame the club, but the truth is, I was ready to leave and I don't think losing would have made much difference. Even for Olaf and Karl and the rest of them.

Nothing, of course, could have kept Karl in Landshut very long, and the first division failed to. One year later he made his way to the NBA, and the rest is not my story to tell. You can watch him a few times a week from October to June on national TV, looking more or less as he looked when I knew him. Although these days his large flat face is partly hidden by a beard. He earns fifteen million dollars a year for doing our old job – we used to make the same money.

Promotion didn't mean much to Olaf, either. Recently, I looked up the names of my former teammates on the internet and was stunned to see how little their lives had changed. Henkel did not follow Karl to a coaching job in the NBA, and Landshut subsequently dropped down a division. He got fired and ended up at Langen, one of the clubs we used to play against. I scrolled down their roster and found a few familiar names: Olaf, Milo, both in their mid-thirties; even Krahm and Darmstadt still play for our old coach. I felt a brief chill, as if the forces preserving them there, so perfectly, in the distant past of my own life, had leaked out of the screen. Maybe Anke was right. Sometimes it's very easy for nothing much to happen.

Charlie proved harder to track down; there are a lot of Charles Golds. But then I remembered he had a sister in Peoria. He got a job coaching high school basketball there, and a few years later his name came up in the *Journal Star*, a local newspaper. One of his players had accused him of making what was referred to as 'improper advances,' and Charlie lost his job. He sued the school on the grounds of discrimination. What he was really fired for, his lawyer claimed, was being a gay, black high school coach with access to a locker room of young men. The boy's story would have been laughed out of any court of law. He had recently been cut for repeated violations of team rules; various students and teachers testified to the fact that he was a problem kid. There was no evidence of any advance. The boy's father had seen a chance to get his own back and played on the anxieties of some of the other parents to put pressure on the school principal. The case settled out of court, and Charlie returned to his job.

Mel Zweigman had dismissed him as a third-rate talent and a bully. 'At least he knows what he is,' Mel said. It struck me that the real test of his personal qualities had nothing to do with the eight months I played beside him.

As for me, I spent the summer at home and then moved in with a high school friend, who was finishing up a PhD., and began a masters in literature. A few years later I married the daughter of one of my father's colleagues, an English girl, and we ended up in London following a stint in New York. My first novel, *The Syme Papers*, came out in 2004, after several draftings and redraftings. Some of the work I did in Landshut survived these.

I never saw Anke again. On the eve of my departure, we fought stupidly. Franziska was ill at home, running a fever, and though we went out for a quick meal, Anke refused to spend the night in my apartment. It wasn't fair, she said, to let her mother do everything. She spent all week taking care of children, at her age, and her father was worse than useless and needed looking after himself. You have done it a hundred times before, I complained.

But she only shook her head, contracting her face, the way Franziska used to when she refused to eat. As if to say, I am all sealed up and self-sufficient. I said, This is very reasonable and mature. You are withdrawing from me already so that I can't withdraw from you. You want to land the first punch. Punch, punch, punch, she repeated angrily, picking up as she sometimes did on one of my English words. But so childishly, that there was nothing I could say to her. And we parted this way, Anke silent and stiff-necked, and me with the air of someone who says, I wash my hands.

In the morning, she came with me to the station, not because we had made up, but because she was going into Munich for one of her haircuts. Franziska was feeling a little better; the fever had passed. We waited on opposite platforms with a train between us, and I stared at that train, bound for Bielefeld, for five hard minutes, hoping it would rumble off. With Anke out of sight I felt very suddenly the fact that she was gone. Something casual had become permanent; her brief absence had taken on a hundred pounds of weight. I told myself, she's still standing there, not twenty feet away. Thinking who knows what thoughts. She is still within reach.

Only she wasn't. When the train between us pulled out the platform behind it was empty. I consoled myself with the fact that we planned to meet up later in the summer, when my family made its annual trip to Flensburg. But then my mother became ill and the trip was postponed. By the time I returned to that trim post-war house on the beach, where we had once spent Christmas, Anke and I had dropped out of touch.

I'm not sure what happened to Hadnot. When his final shot drifted wide, I knew he had missed by the way he turned his head. But I didn't see the shot till later, on the coach-ride home; Henkel had already got a copy of the video. You can watch me at the end of it, carried forward by momentum, falling into Hadnot's shooting arm. For a moment we have to hold each other up. Most of the guys on the bus were still a little drunk from the night before, and as the ball caromed away, off the inside rim and over Karl's head, they shouted again – as if there had been any doubt about the outcome, second time around.

Würzburg stayed put in the second division, and Hadnot probably stayed put with them. Most of his sporting achievements, such as they were, pre-dated the internet, and whatever he's doing now isn't the kind of thing to get a mention online. There's a black kid called Bodie Hadnot who transferred out of Nashville State Community College to Chattanooga in 2006. He averaged 3.7 points a game his junior year. The alumni network for the university is particularly strong and runs a number of fan websites. Even bench players have columns devoted to them. Whenever you type Bo Hadnot into Google, Bodie comes up.

For five months after coming home I didn't touch a basketball. Instead, I learned to drive stick, surging

319

around the shaded streets of my childhood in the old family Subaru, a second car, for the sake of a little independence. By September, I still had no plans. My father said to me, 'You can't sit around the house all day. What are you going to do with yourself?' But he didn't press me. Instead, he kept me busy with small tasks – rarely more than one or two a day. For example, he asked me to pick up my sisters from school, my old high school. While you're at it, he said, why don't you look in on your coach. He'll be pleased to see you.

So I set off early on a late September afternoon. Under a clear sky the heat had dropped to the tolerable levels of high summer anywhere else. Five years after graduation, the route had already become unfamiliar. But I found my way eventually, off the sun-bright strip mall (one of the arteries running through town) into the low curbless suburban neighborhood that surrounds the school. The main campus differs from the rest of the house-plots only by having a wider lawn. There is also a stretch of undeveloped green opposite the car-park, where the school has no jurisdiction, and some of the older kids go to smoke and drink between bells. The present class of drop-outs looked no different from the kids I used to stare at from the portico, waiting for my father to pick me up after basketball practice. Though I had more sympathy for them now. One year out of college I had no idea what to do with the rest of my twenties.

I found my old coach in his office, an old storage closet next to the training room, and near enough to the gym you could hear the echo of basketballs. He was chewing peanuts when I walked in, reaching into his pocket and spitting the shells vaguely in the direction of the gray standard-issue bin. Possibly part of an attempt to get off tobacco, I don't know: among the odd life facts he once explained to us, from the pulpit of his health class, was the right way to pronounce Pall Mall. I was a little worried about what to call him – I had never called him by his name. This turned out not to matter. I called him coach.

Six years makes a great difference in a young man's life, but he looked more or less unchanged. The same muscular bald head and trunk-shaped arms; his light-skinned humorous black face had heavy-lidded eyes. It's often hard, even for a cynical kid, not to attribute to his high school coaches sharp moral vision. They see you every day for what you are: lazy, shirking, selfish, scared. In fact, I was still a little scared of him and remembered again my strong, childish desire *not* to disappoint him.

He was shorter than me – I noticed that when he stood up to take my hand. What I wanted to tell him is that I had made it, in a small way, that I had overcome whatever it was that had held me back before.

'Is that so?' he said, when I gave him my news. 'Is that so?' Pleased; not especially surprised. He didn't often meet my eye. It struck me that now we were equally shy of each other.

Coming home, I nudged my shoes off and switched on the TV set – as I used to, coming home from school.

Then, after a minute, stood up again and went outside looking for a ball. There was often one lying around, under a tree, in the bamboo fence, by the bicycles. Afternoon shadows had just begun to stretch out. The concrete of my father's court was still too hot for bare feet, but I took a couple shots anyway and chased them down quick-footed. Then a couple more, counting out the tally of makes and misses. Feeling the roughness of the paint on my soles. Remembering Hadnot's advice: bend your legs, jump straight in the air, and keep your elbow in. Follow through.

For the next two hours, while the sun descended behind the car park wall next door, and the ground cooled, I worked on my jumpshot. Some of the shots went in and some of them didn't, but I tried to repeat each motion faithfully regardless. When I was a kid on that court I used to imagine some future in which all these shots would matter.